TEQUILA
HANGOVER

Other titles by Elizabeth Maxim

Fiction
Psychic Hangover*
Kerry's Game**
Silicon Valley Hangover*
The Company She Keeps**
Her Sanctuary**

* Hangover Series
** Psi Adventure Series

Non-fiction

Riding the Waves: Diagnosing, Treating and Living with EMF Sensitivity

After Here: The Celestial Plane and What Happens When We Die

Angles & Engineers: Spirits and Angels Among Us

Breaking the Waves: A Primer on Sensitivity to Electromagnetic Frequencies

Flowers That Bloom in the Dark: Surviving Abusive Families and the Communities That Support Them

Amplifying the Waves: The Role of Electromagnetic Pollution in EMF Sensitivity

TEQUILA HANGOVER

ELIZABETH MAXIM

elizabethmaxim.com

JF,

¡Gracias!

TEQUILA

HANGOVER

CHAPTER 1

~~~~~~

Autumn, New York City, 2010

"You should have come to me before I had a family."

"We can do away with them, you know. We can set it up so it looks as if you walked out on them."

"Kyle knows I would never walk out on him."

Without commenting, the man reached across the corner of a mahogany conference table. She could make out the copper threads of his sleeve in the polished surface. He tapped the reddish-brown wood and a screen descended silently from the ceiling.

For several seconds the research scientist stared at the director's diamond cufflinks, not really seeing them. A movement out of the corner of her eye drew her attention.

The people in the images that began rolling across the screen were familiar but the events depicted had never taken place.

Tears blurred her vision and the manufactured images blended together.

There's no choice.

Thirty-four year old Talia Blackmoor drew a shaky breath. "Okay," she said quietly, "just leave my family out of this."

"Of course," he answered smoothly.

"I take it I can go? I can spend one last night with my family?"

"I don't see why not. Do you require a ride?"

"No, I prefer to walk, thank you."

Grateful it was November, Talia shoved her hands in her pockets as she stepped on the elevator. She didn't want the surveillance cameras picking up the fact she was clenching her fists tightly enough to draw blood.

Knowing all too well their ability to detect any emotion, she hummed tonelessly and closed her eyes as the elevator returned to the basement.

Without looking at the woman sitting by the alley door, she set her security pass on a podium and stepped into the breezy late afternoon.

Two right turns and a quick left set her on the road home.

Just seven blocks to go.

The late fall wind slicing at her cheeks, she walked at what she hoped was a pace they would expect. Someone chilled by an early Nor'easter who wouldn't run in high heels but who wouldn't dally a moment longer than necessary.

Five blocks to go.

Never had the vile smell wafting up from the New York City subway grates been so pungent. Never had the sky looked so battleship grey.

Three blocks.

It was time.

You can do this.

She blew on her hands in an attempt to warm them. Reaching back into her pockets, she pressed a button on her smart phone. It was a number she'd hoped she'd never have motive to dial.

She shook herself and began walking, picking up the pace slightly. Damn, it was cold.

Almost home.

Suddenly, a car came careening around the corner.

The last thing Talia Blackmoor saw before her world ended was the familiar face behind the wheel.

CHAPTER 2

American Embassy Santiago, Chile, Spring 2013

Special Agent Tim Brightman stared dejectedly at the pile of nondescript folders stacked high enough they were beginning to lean precariously.

"In the age of technology, why we're still using paper," he groused. Reaching forward, he grabbed a third of the folders, setting them to his left. He grabbed another third and set them to his right.

It wasn't that he was particular about the order in which he sorted through the information. It was that he had to start somewhere. He was about to snatch the top folder from the right when something caught his eye. A yellow something.

His pulse quickened as he stared at the tiny slip sticking out between two folders in the center pile, toward the bottom. He wanted to snatch the folder out of the pile but paused, looked around. He was alone in the small office at the rear of the embassy, but there were plenty of people milling about even at this time of night.

He walked to the door, poked his head out, and after making sure the hallway was clear, shut it.

Returning to the desk, he sat down and slid the folder from the pile. He positioned a small desk lamp so that it illuminated the space immediately in front of him and opened the folder, scanning the contents. Somewhere, a phone started to ring.

Frowning, he closed the manila folder and began sifting through the bottom half of the center pile. There was another file, also part of the cold cases that he needed to see. If he was lucky, whoever had slipped this information into the pile had put it near that other folder.

"Bingo!"

Tim tapped a finger against the yellow tag, mulling the situation over. He could count on one hand the number of people who had clearance for yellow tagged information, and the man at whose desk he was sitting wasn't one of them.

How the hell did it end up on the desk of the Duty Officer?

He could think of only one possibility. Someone knew it was his turn to sort through the cold cases.

Every three months, a different special agent combed through cases where the trail had gone cold. The idea was that a new set of eyes may pick something up that others had missed, or perhaps new information had been gained that might breathe new life into a case. Problem was, Tim hadn't known it was his turn until he showed up at the embassy that morning. No agent knew ahead of time. The number of cases passing into and out of the cold files fluctuated wildly and it was often difficult to know who would be available for the task.

He mentally sifted through the day. Who had been in the duty office? Without reviewing video, he would never know for sure. His office was across the hall but he typically kept his door shut. Obviously, someone had slipped the file in with the cold cases, ensuring someone with the proper clearance would find it. Ensuring *he* would find it.

Somewhere, a phone continued to ring. He cocked his head.

"Hell."

Grabbing several folders, he quickly left, making sure to lock the door behind him. Fumbling for the keys to his office, he worked to bury the yellow tag, making a mental note to rip it out of the folder when he could. He sure as hell wasn't going to do it at the embassy where the cleaning staff may see it in the trash and pass that bit of information on to an all too interested party.

His phone quit ringing when he was two steps from the desk but began ringing again soon after.

Setting the folders down, he yanked up the handset.

"Tim Brightman."

"Is this line secure?"

"Of course," he snapped, his eyes on the yellow tag. "Who is this?"

"There's been an incident with one of your agents."

Tim let out a breath. "I see."

"He is being transported to the hospital as we speak. My colleagues do not wish to involve themselves in any way, so no one will remain to answer questions. We felt you would like to be there to assist with any unforeseen difficulties."

Not to mention heading off a potential nightmare.

"I appreciate your thoughtfulness."

The man's laugh underscored the irony of the situation. Whoever was calling had probably had a hand in the agent's condition.

"Let's just say we have a great deal of respect for this particular agent, though perhaps his bravery borders on the foolish."

Juan.

Tim closed his eyes. "What hospital is he being dropped at?"

Tim flipped through his Rolodex.

"Who can I thank for this generosity?" he asked, dialing the hospital number on his cell phone. "I would like to show my appreciation in some way."

"No need. As I said, we have a great deal of respect for your agent."

The line went dead just as someone at the hospital picked up. Tim spoke briefly with the nurse on duty and hung up.

Squeezing the bridge of his nose, he debated. He had to get to the hospital. He didn't want anyone else involved. The agent had been deep undercover and the fewer people involved, the better. Bad enough the emergency staff would need to be watched. No, it was better he took care of this himself.

Setting his cell on the folders, he grabbed his keys, shoved everything into a backpack, and headed for the back door. Climbing into an embassy car he asked to be let out three blocks beyond the hospital. He would double back on foot. Dressed in jeans and carrying the backpack would attract a lot less attention than a suit and briefcase.

As the driver slowed he frowned, considered. He would have issues with the hospital staff.

"I'm sorry, sir, but no one is allowed in the triage area."

He sighed and reached into a pocket. Withdrawing a document, he hesitated only a moment before handing it across to the administrator. "I'm afraid you don't have the authority to deny me access."

He hated flashing his credentials but it was imperative that he be present when the agent was being treated. Although whoever called him had said no one would remain at the hospital, he couldn't be certain that there weren't spies on the premises.

"Follow me," the woman said tightly and walked at a fast clip toward a row of emergency rooms, her nose in the air. It was clear she didn't appreciate his superseding her authority, but she was too in awe of the seal he'd displayed to argue.

"I promise I won't get in the way."

She glanced over her shoulder. "See that you don't. Not everyone in that room will care about your papers or who signed them."

"Understood."

When he walked into a small space behind the woman, the doctor began to protest, but she drew her aside and whispered frantically.

"Sit over there," the physician snapped, pointing at a plastic chair positioned as close to the door as was possible without being in the hall.

Grateful at being ignored, Tim sat quietly while the staff worked to stabilize the agent and pondered what had been revealed in those files. Maybe Fate was playing a role of sorts. The agent best qualified for what came next lay bleeding on the table across the room.

He pursed his lips and tried to read the doctor's expression. Would the agent live to take the case?

"He needs surgery."

Tim blinked, looked up. The doctor had come to stand next to him.

"Any idea how long he'll be in there?"

"Six hours. That's assuming there are no complications. He seems healthy. Is he?"

"Very."

She pointed at a nurse standing nearby. "Follow Therese. She will show you were to scrub."

"Scrub?"

She gave him a frosty smile. "I've worked on his type before. I know the procedure."

Tim didn't want to speculate on what type the doctor thought his agent was, but he stood, indicated he would follow. In reality, he could have found his own way. A year and a half earlier, he'd been in the same part of the hospital, with the same agent being treated for the same thing.

He followed the nurse to a surgical prep area where she helped him wash up and change into scrubs. It also wasn't the first time he'd walked into an operating room dressed as part of the surgical staff.

Protocol dictated that whenever one of his agents was administered anesthetic, a senior agent, or someone equally qualified be present. The risk wasn't medicated agents mumbling secrets so much as the trustworthiness of the staff. Especially, if they knew the patient was connected to government work. That seemed to be doubly true for foreign nationals. In fact, Tim sometimes wondered if some of the staff at hospitals near embassies weren't spies.

That wasn't such a far-fetched scenario. His agency employed specially trained medical and dental staff at all levels.

"This way."

He followed the nurse through double doors into a brightly lit room.

"Care to watch?" The doctor's tone made it clear she believed he was the type to faint at the sight of blood.

He stepped forward. "Would you mind?"

"As long as you don't get in the way," she snapped.

Tim didn't laugh but he didn't have to. Even if the doctor couldn't see the smirk beneath his mask, she could see his mocking eyes. He watched as she cut.

"He's lucky the shooter's aim went wide."

He nodded. He'd seen enough gunshot wounds to know she spoke the truth. Based on what he knew of his agent's whereabouts, he guessed he'd been caught in a crossfire. What he didn't know, was why.

"He lifts weights, yes?"

"Yes."

"It's difficult to cut the muscle."

The anesthetist adjusted the face mask.

"Was he in the wrong part of the city?"

"What?"

"How did he get shot? He is not part of a gang. Too clean cut. Unless there was a domestic dispute, I would say he was where he shouldn't have been."

"That's the truth."

In Tim's opinion, anyone who ended up shot was where they shouldn't have been; in the line of fire.

Too clean cut.

Another truth. Juan's features meant certain undercover assignments were off limits. Not all of those features were physical. The man had too much confidence to play the role of a subordinate. Sooner or later that confidence, which bordered on arrogance, came out, and when that happened it always spelled trouble.

Tim also had difficulty putting him in positions of power. Unless someone knocked off a man in power, it was difficult to get to the top of an organization. Additionally, such a group was too small and generally too elite to be easily infiltrated. It was possible and one of his own agents had been successful, but it had taken years of careful oversight that had enabled the man to rise up through the ranks within a crime syndicate.

He studied his agent's profile. With a strong jawline, high cheekbones, and a nose that would have been at home on a Roman soldier, Juan excelled at the place in between, which was a good thing, given the assignment Tim had in mind.

"We're closing him up."

"Three hours, nine minutes."

"He was lucky. The bullet did not penetrate deep enough to do any serious damage. He'll be sore but he should have a complete recovery."

"Thank you."

She nodded, tossed her gloves. "I will see him to post-operative care." She went on to dismiss the staff, except for Therese.

There was one other patient in the post-op ward. Tim helped the doctor guide Juan's bed against a wall where she proceeded to connect several tubes and wires. Two machines beeped and a yellowish liquid tainted with red flowed into a bottle.

"Drainage."

"When will he wake up?"

She shook him. "I will let him come out of it naturally once I ensure he is waking up." She flashed a penlight in each of his eyes. He twisted his head and mumbled a complaint. She smiled.

"He's fine. When he wakes up, push that button. If the drainage turns red, push that button. If you see anything unusual -."

"Got it."

"I'll be back to check on him in fifteen minutes."

He slid a stool he suspected was only used by doctors over to the bed, sat down, and pulled out his phone.

"No use el celular aquí!"

He smiled apologetically at the nurse and slid the phone into his backpack. He glanced at his watch. God, his eyes burned with fatigue. An unexpected surprise inspection had resulted in enough violations to keep him busy for a year. He sighed. It was his own fault.

When it came to management style, Tim Brightman was too soft. At least, that was the word from above. He believed, however, to do otherwise, to try to run his small elite group with the same level of discipline that he himself was held to, would render them ineffectual. In point of fact, he would end up with a full out mutiny.

"If it ain't broke," he'd complained to his supervisor, *"don't fix it. We've got a hit rate that's kept us funded longer than any other special interest project."*

"That's the problem, I'm afraid. Funding."

"What?"

"Let me clarify. It isn't a matter of whether or not you should be funded, it's by who, or more precisely, what."

"Jack, don't give me that doubletalk bullshit. What's the problem? Whose nose got bent out of joint?"

"You're funded by the military."

"We're funded by the tax payers."

"Do you know how many umbrellas you have to rise above to find that link?"

"Cut to the chase, Jack. If I have to go tit for tat with you, and I can do that in multiple languages, we'll be here all night and day for a month."

"With all the cuts in military funding, every project is being held under an electron microscope."

"So, this isn't about how many nit-picky violations your white gloved lackey found. Some general's pissed because his pension check is in danger of being reduced."

His boss had stared at him in silence for about ten seconds before he burst out laughing.

"I can't wait to see the President's face when I tell him what you just said."

Tim shifted impatiently. He wasn't amused. Still, he knew when to push back and when to listen. The man sitting across from him was one of a handful who not only got face time with the President of the United States, he had his phone calls accepted by the leader, no matter what the clock read when they came in.

"Are we in danger of losing funding?"

"It would be nice if I could find a way to push the peas around on the plate. It would certainly take the pressure off."

Tim nodded. One of the best parts about working for Jack Porter was that, unlike his peers, politics didn't enter the picture. He had nothing to prove. He didn't backstab his subordinates when the heat turned up. He worked with them.

"How can I help?"

"I need to shore up the case."

It's too bad he couldn't have turned the focus on another group, one that perhaps wasn't performing up to standards, but that wasn't Jack's style. He didn't kick anyone when they were down.

"Do you want a win that will make the military look good or do you want a political win?"

"Good question."

"I ask because if it's a political win it may help you rob Peter to pay Paul, but then you run the risk of loyalties lost if the sponsor moves on. If you keep us within the structure we're in and enable us to continue working directly with the military, they can bring the success to the committees at appropriations time. Not only would that show extra value, it may help motivate someone to funnel money in for support."

Tim hated politics. The heads in Washington were doing their best but with the economic and demographic challenges the world was facing, they didn't have the resources to put toward projects like his. How could they care about a small elite organization when they had bigger problems to consider?

"When do you need this by?"

"Yesterday would have been ideal."

Beep!

Tim jerked his head up. Had he been falling asleep?

"It's only me," the doctor assured.

"Is he -?"

"He's fine. I was just adjusting things." She pointed behind him. "There's a chair over there. You could catch a nap. He's not going to wake up for a bit yet."

Tim rubbed a hand over his face. He needed to get someone over here. To do that, he needed his phone.

"There should be coverage in the stairwell," he mumbled, coming to his feet.

That had to be far enough away from the equipment so as not to cause problems, didn't it?

Juan Hernandez's eyes fluttered and he took a deep breath, letting it out with a groan.

Tim Brightman stood, inhaling sharply as the circulation returned to his legs. He'd fallen asleep in what had to be the hardest chair on earth. He suspected a seat of nails would have been less painful.

"Juan?" he said softly, walking toward the bed, "can you hear me?"

"Tim?" The agent's voice was gravelly.

"Yeah, it's me. How do you feel?"

"Like I've been shot."

He smiled. "That's good then."

The agent opened his eyes and took in his surroundings.

"How long have I been out?"

"You just got out."

"Surgery?"

"To remove the bullet." He pressed a button hanging over the side of the bed. "They told me the anesthesia would wear off and I was to ring for the nurse as soon as it did."

"How did you -?"

"Later," he answered as the door opened. He briefly met the agent's eyes, amused to see him struggling to come out of a sleepy state. "I'm going to get a bite to eat."

"Who's outside?"

Tim walked toward the door, satisfied the effects of the anesthesia were wearing off. "Alvarez."

Juan nodded and let out a sigh of resignation as the doctor stepped up to the bed. Tim sympathized. The physician would poke and prod and leave the agent in more pain than he was in already.

Shaking his head, the supervisor stepped into the hall, pulling the door shut behind him.

Two hours later, Juan had been moved to a private room at the far edge of the nursing station, a good distance from the elevators. Tim chatted briefly with the man posted outside his door before going to take a seat near the window. Juan was sound asleep.

"Good idea," he murmured before leaning back and closing his eyes.

"When do I get out of here?"

Tim blinked and sat up, glancing at his watch. He squeezed his eyes shut, opened them again. Late morning sun was streaming through the window. He swung his gaze to the bed.

It was impossible to tell what was going through Juan's mind. His expression was hidden by tubes and wires hooked to machines beeping in multiple octaves.

"How do you feel?"

"Ready to get out of here."

"I think they're planning to move you out of the intensive unit as soon as possible. They need the bed and you're too healthy to be in here."

He stood, winced at the horrible sound the chair made as it scraped backward. "Sorry."

"Nails down a chalkboard, just what the doctor ordered."

"Listen, I need to get back to the embassy. Alvarez will stay until I return in a few hours."

"It isn't blown, you know."

"I know."

The agent stared at him silently.

"You're too good."

"Fuck."

"Never could take a compliment, could you?" He patted the bed. "Go back to sleep. We need you."

"Put me in coach."

Shaking his head, Tim stepped into the hall to brief the other agent.

CHAPTER 3

~~~~~~

Santiago, Chile, Summer 2013

Tim closed the file containing Juan's medical report, dropped it on his desk, and dragged a hand over his face. God he was tired. His eyes burned from hours of reading reports and he was starting to get a headache.

He glanced at the monitor on his desk, then at the folders waiting to be sorted. So much to do, so little time before his eyes were too blurry to see straight. Blowing out a sigh, he flipped on his monitor.

Twenty minutes later someone knocked on, then opened his door. His secretary carried a steaming mug in his direction. She shook her head.

"Don't you ever go home?"

Without taking his eyes from the monitor, he reached for the coffee. He took a sip and gave her a grateful smile. "I was home three days ago."

"You look like shit. When was the last time you slept?"

"Cat naps," he replied, his fingers tapping keys. One of these days he would take a typing class. His two finger method had improved over the years but was still woefully inadequate. Or better yet, maybe a voice transcriptor kit. He frowned. The software was probably banned for security reasons.

"Do you want me to bring you anything to eat?"

He glanced at the corner of his desk. Just visible behind a growing stack of paperwork, a clock showed him he had a meeting in less than an hour.

"No time, but thanks. I'll grab a bite later."

She sighed, shook her head again, but left, closing the door quietly.

He let out a sigh and swiveled his chair so he could see outside. The small courtyard containing a manicured garden and a small fountain had, throughout the years, provided him a rest, however brief, for his eyes and his mind.

Agent Hernandez had been cleared for duty, and not a moment too soon if the intelligence reports that had crossed his desk that morning were accurate. Still, he hesitated.

It was the fourth time that the agent had taken a bullet. He would have thought someone had a contract on him but for the fact that the injuries were in no way related. One of them had been a freak accident and the others were related to the cases he'd been working. Cases involving different crimes that had occurred in different countries.

He'd even considered the possibility of a vendetta and had asked the department to look into it but that came up negative. He'd asked the agent himself, in a roundabout way.

On his last hospital visit he'd joked that Juan enjoyed getting shot because it meant all the pretty women, including a doctor this time, took care of him. The answer had been a bland stare and an inquiry about his next assignment.

Tim felt sure the answer was in that look. It had been too cavalier, as had his attitude about being wounded in the line of duty.

"It goes with the territory," he'd said with a shrug. "You know that."

As to the agent's inquiry about his next assignment, an envelope had been delivered by courier to his apartment that morning.

Tim swiveled the chair back around and slid the agent's medical report into a drawer. For better or for worse, Juan was the answer to a very complicated situation. Tim might have concerns about how soon he'd been cleared for duty, but the truth was, he needed him back in the field. Knowing he would be hearing from the agent soon, he picked up another folder and began to read.

Less than an hour later, the door to his office slammed open, banging off the wall. Tim glanced up long enough to identify the man responsible and to see the Duty Officer look over in curiosity. He returned to his reading.

"What if I'd had a gun?" Juan snapped from where he stood just inside the doorway.

Without looking away from the computer screen, the supervisor answered. "I suppose if someone wanted me dead, I'd be pushing daisies. Call me crazy but I have faith in those meant to prevent that."

"That's assuming a lot."

He gave up. Closing the lid on the laptop, he nodded. "True, but it kind of goes with the territory, don't you think? Jumpiness isn't a good characteristic for a spy."

He calmly rearranged the folders on his desk as the agent stalked over. Stalking might have been pushing it. Two months out of the hospital, Juan was still recovering from his wounds, only one of which was a gunshot. His gait, deliberate though it may have been, was not without a hitch.

"Good to see you up and about Agent Hernandez."

"Don't give me that crap," he snarled, tossing an envelope. Papers spilled out as it coasted to a stop midway across the desk.

"Something wrong?"

"That," Juan snapped, pointing. "That's a bullshit assignment and you know it."

Across the hall the Duty Officer raised his eyebrows.

Tim worked to hide his amusement. It was true that he and Juan had a friendly relationship, but he was the man's superior. Encouraging such outbursts probably wasn't the best idea.

"Close the door."

He waited until the agent was walking toward him before saying anything further.

"I assure you that the assignment fits in with your particular abilities."

"It's a goddamned babysitting assignment. There are any number of agents who could take care of that duty. Agents in training," he sneered.

Tim grabbed a cup off his desk and sipped. The tea bought him time while he debated. The agent was canny, would see through even the slightest fabrication and would know if any detail had been left out.

Truth it is.

He indicated a chair on the other side of his desk. "Have a seat."

Juan dragged the chair so that it was on the same side and dropped into it, folding his arms over his chest. The message was clear. The agent was in control of his life, not some cog in the bureaucratic wheel of command.

Tim reached down and pulled a manila folder from a backpack at his feet. "I assure you this is a real assignment." He turned the folder slightly but didn't hand it over.

Juan glowered at the file.

"I can tell by your expression you see the yellow tag."

The agent thrust his chin in the general direction of the folder. "All that means is that the person I'm supposed to watch over is important to somebody. It's still a bullshit assignment."

Tim shoved the folder back into the pack and studied the man sitting across from him. "You realize you shouldn't be getting any assignment in the first place?"

"Is that a threat?"

"A statement of fact. You've been out of the hospital less than -"

"I'm ready to go back to work," he argued. "And I've been cleared to return to duty. Without restriction, I might add."

"Juan, I appreciate your dedication but I could do without the theatrics."

"*Theatrics?*"

Tim fought a smile. If there was one thing Agent Hernandez prided himself on, it was never losing his cool. He'd known the agent would be insulted but he had to get him focused. He let out a breath.

"I'm quite serious. This is a legitimate assignment and you're the best one for the job."

Juan's mutinous expression was comical and under other circumstances he would have said as much, but this assignment was too damned important to waste time on platitudes.

"Will you take the assignment or not? I'd hate to have to pull someone out of the field for this."

"Before I answer, tell me who your next choice is."

"He's in the field."

"Humor me."

"Dan."

"*Foster?*"

A knock interrupted any reply Tim might have made. As he went over to answer it, he knew he'd never been so grateful for an interruption. Throwing Agent Dan Foster's name out had been a dirty trick but he was desperate. Juan Hernandez was the best operative to take the case but he had to let it appear as it seemed, a bullshit babysitting assignment.

He opened the door and took a note from his secretary.

Sharing additional details would only put Juan's life in jeopardy.

He scanned the note, nodded, and handed it back, certain it would be torn up. Across the hall the Duty Officer wiggled his brows and smirked. Tim shook his head and shut the door.

I work in a looney bin.

His hand on the door, he let out a sigh.

That would make me the head looney, wouldn't it?

He turned but said nothing further to the man sitting at his desk. He would have to rely on Juan's innate sense of survival to figure out what he needed to know.

"Alright."

Thank god.

He walked over and stood beside Juan's chair. "When can you be ready to fly to Costa Rica?"

"Day after tomorrow."

He stepped back as Juan made his way to the door.

"There's one thing you should know."

"I'm sure there's more than one but I'm listening."

"The subject won't go along without -."

One heartbeat. Two.

"Persuasion?" Juan supplied.

"Right."

The agent nodded and left, shutting the door behind him.

At one point the color had been aqua. Flecks of blue-green paint showed through rust and caked mud. But Juan didn't care about the color of the hood so much as what was beneath it. Would the thing run?

Finishing his inspection, he slammed the hood shut and nodded. "It'll do." He pulled a wad of cash from his wallet and handed it to the young man selling his vehicle. Taking keys and paperwork, he slid behind the wheel. Inserting the key into the ignition, he leaned out the window and asked for directions to Plantation Village.

The kid, who was in his late teens, gave Juan an assessing look. "What do you want to go there for?"

"A job."

He shook his head. "If you're looking for work, you might want to check at the resort instead."

"Could they use someone who works with his hands?"

The kid smirked. "They are always looking for someone to clean the place, sure."

"A different type of maintenance. Painting, perhaps."

"Talk to Susannah."

"Susannah? Is not a Spanish name." He'd purposely used the vernacular to appear uneducated.

"She's American. She and her husband own the resort."

"Do they own the plantation as well?"

The boy shook his head. "They lease the land but they do not get on well with the owner. There is often trouble there. You would do well to look elsewhere for work."

Juan studied the kid a moment longer. He pulled a few dollars from where they'd been stuffed into the front pocket of his jeans and handed them over. "Thanks for the advice. You probably saved me -."

"Time in jail?"

"What?"

"Something tells me you settle disagreements with your fists. You would find much trouble at the plantation." He stepped away from the truck. "Talk to Susannah."

Juan gave the kid a salute before driving toward the village where those who worked on the plantation lived in ramshackle huts clustered together.

The agent sucked in a breath as the truck slammed into a pothole that was more like a crater. The burning sensation in his shoulder from the jolt served as a painful reminder that he'd been shot only two months earlier. Knowing he had at least thirty minutes more on the miserable excuse of a road, he pulled as far to the edge of it as he could in an attempt to avoid the worst of the holes.

Twenty minutes later he decided there must be another way in because other than an occasional pickup truck or tractor, there was no other traffic on the road. He would have expected to see a bus or at least a taxi ferrying guests to the exclusive resort.

Nestled in the rainforest that flourished within the Cerros de Escazu Mountain Range, the resort was located adjacent to a coffee plantation where his *assignment* was employed.

"Intellectual capital," he groused, referring to Tim's explanation of why it was so important for Juan to take the assignment. "As if some goddamned idea is important enough to put your best agent on babysitting detail."

Before he could reflect on it further, he was forced to avoid a black sedan driving down the center of the road. Swerving into the shrubbery, he narrowly escaped a collision.

Where the hell had the car come from? His insides tensed as he considered. Reaching into a backpack on the passenger side floor, he pulled out one of two cell phones he carried.

"Brightman."

"Do you have anyone in the area?"

"No."

Juan ended the call, tossed the phone on the seat, and turned into a driveway he believed the car had come from. It was actually a road.

"Bet you go to Plantation Village," he murmured, bringing up a mental image of the car that had blown by him. He visualized every detail he could recall. Pulling off the road, he jammed the truck into park and hit last number dialed.

"Yeah?" Tim said by way of an answer.

"I got a partial plate. Run it."

"Did you see a driver?"

"You're kidding, right?"

The windows had been tinted heavily enough to make seeing inside an impossibility.

"Okay, I'll see who's in the area."

"I'd rather you focused on the plate. Anyone and everyone could be in the area, half of them on vacation. It's useless information in that context. I'll assume someone else is interested in our quarry until further notice."

"About that further notice -."

He sighed, stared at the dirt road. More potholes meant more pain. *Damn.*

"Juan -."

"I got it. SOP, right?"

"In this case -."

"I know. You're protecting me. The less I know the better. I went to spy school too, Brightman."

The line went dead.

Pulling onto the road, he thought about what else was in his little pack.

"Okay, so someone is willing to kill for this intellectual property. Still doesn't make them any more clandestine than a company looking to steal Kraft's secret for mac-n-cheese."

Twenty minutes later he was driving through Plantation Village, a cluster of nondescript dwellings on both sides of what barely qualified as a road. There was a market at one end. He'd done the right thing in buying the old truck. He could feel eyes watching from shadowy corners. A sedan or even a Jeep would have set up an alarm for sure, and he didn't want to tip off the woman he sought.

Tim had given him very little information about her, which wasn't unusual. The supervisor believed that front loading, or sharing too much information early in a mission, led to poor decisions as a result of bad assumptions. It was a philosophy Juan agreed with.

There had been a point, early on, where he'd believed withholding information needlessly put lives at risk. At this stage of his career, however, he preferred to scope out a situation and draw his own conclusions which could be later checked against whatever assumptions masquerading as facts had been passed to him.

He had to admit, though, he was at a bit of a loss. Nothing of what he saw fit with what he'd expected. He couldn't picture the subject living in Plantation Village. He decided to drive up to the resort.

In the end, he'd had to go to the maintenance gate. The main entrance was restricted to registered guests.

"All others must use the maintenance gate. No exceptions."

The security guard hadn't needed to explain what would happen had Juan pushed the issue. He'd thanked him and asked for directions to the appropriate entrance.

"What's with all that security?" he'd asked. It had been easy to come across as the wide-eyed, intimidated working stiff. He was baffled by the fortress-like quality. In point of fact, his field radar had him wondering if their clientele might not be on the up and up. A retreat for organized crime? He'd seen it before.

"A marketing ploy, amigo," the man at the gate had explained. "The owners put up the appearance of exclusivity and word gets out. Suddenly, people want to see what they might be hiding."

"What are they hiding?"

"Certainly not the best chef," the man replied, laughing. "I have seen a fair number of celebrities recovering from plastic surgery, however. They don't have to worry about paparazzi. What brings you here?"

Juan wasn't fresh from the academy. The man might have been making friendly conversation but there was no doubt he had easy access to a weapon and would use it if he felt there was a threat.

Marketing, my ass. He decided to play it straight.

"I'm looking for a woman."

"You don't look as if it would be a problem finding one to suit your tastes."

"On behalf of her soon-to-be-ex-husband. Messy divorce. She's hiding assets. He needs to prove it."

"European?"

"British."

"Well, there's plenty of them here. Mostly retirees, though. How old is this woman you are seeking?"

"Not old enough to be retired, though God knows, her husband is."

The man studied him for several moments. "Is the man violent? This husband of hers?"

"No, just determined to hold onto his stake in his beloved football team."

"Two possibilities but neither will be easy to get at."

"I don't need to get at anyone. I am simply paid to find her. The rest is up to his solicitors."

He shook his head. "No one here wants trouble."

"Then it would be worthwhile encouraging her to move on, don't you think?"

He nodded. "None of my business."

Juan handed over two hundred Euros.

"With the fate of the Euro in doubt, I don't know if this is such a good deal."

"It's all I've got."

That was far from true but there was no way in hell he was handing over American currency.

He scribbled something on a piece of paper and handed it over, accepting the Euros in exchange. I'm not sure either will lead you to what you seek but there you are."

"I appreciate it."

"You may not want to hang around here much longer. Strangers tend to draw a lot of attention."

He nodded. "Thanks for the advice."

CHAPTER 4

~~~~~~

Talia Blackmoor knew without looking up that something was wrong. She'd spent too many months honing her survival skills to miss the sudden tension in the man standing five feet from her.

She dropped a bright red coffee berry into the bag at her feet and slowly bent down to retrieve a canteen, using the opportunity to glance over at him. His expression confirmed her suspicions.

"Policia?" she whispered, handing the canteen over.

"Gracias." He waited til he was drinking before shaking his head ever so slightly. His eyes were trained on something or someone behind her.

The tension had spread to everyone in her vicinity. A low murmur flowed from plantation worker to plantation worker, their voices filled with speculation, and fear.

"I'm looking for a Senora Blackmoor."

The voice was deep, almost pleasant, and definitely not threatening. But she knew better.

Her companion's eyes were locked on her. "I can -."

"No." She smiled at the man she'd been working alongside for months.

Stick as close to the truth as you can.

She took one step closer to him and lowered her voice. "Carlos, I've done nothing wrong."

A truth.

"I'm not hiding from the law."

Another truth.

She took a long swallow of water. "I'm not hiding from the government either."

Well, sort of.

She patted his arm, gave him what she hoped was a look of confidence, and turned.

"I'm Senora Blackmoor."

"Good day, Senora. My name is Jorge Gonzales."

Behind her Carlos hissed. "He's lying."

She nodded once, acknowledging the message, then studied the man.

"I wonder if I might have a moment of your time?"

The soothing quality of his voice, like his gaze, was hypnotic. She swallowed. Something told her the game had changed, that her life would never be the same. Behind her, Carlos shifted.

Talia pointed to the partially filled bag on the ground in front of her. "This isn't convenient."

He smiled.

Oh, boy.

"I understand. When is your next break?"

And manners. Someone had gone to great lengths to keep her from panicking.

"Depends on how long you think this will take. I could take a very short one now or you can wait until I get off."

"I do not think this will be long."

Acutely aware of the silence that had descended around her, the research scientist assessed the man. A few coffee pickers sent curious gazes her way, though most simply seemed relieved not to be the one he was seeking out.

She could feel Carlos' concern without looking. Years spent reading every nuance radiating from those around her left her able to detect subtle feelings most would never be aware of. She put those talents to work.

The man might be Latin American, but he most certainly didn't fit in. It wasn't just the expensive European suit tailored to perfection that made him stand out among the hot and sweaty laborers. It wasn't even the arrogance he tried to tone down.

Hypnotic eyes.

"Senora?" he said softly, effectively halting her appraisal. She swept her gaze toward the workers standing just behind him. She owed a lot to these people. She didn't want to get them involved. She sighed.

"Alright. Give me a moment."

"Of course. Thank you."

Knowing he wouldn't move until she did, she turned back to her coworker. "Take my bag. Dump the contents in with yours."

They got paid by the weight of the day's work. The more coffee picked the more money. During her first weeks she'd had difficulty filling her quota. More than once, Carlos had shared his yield with her. As money had been tight, a few of those times had been the difference between eating or not. He stiffened.

"But you -."

"I don't think I'll be back to work today."

"Then I will not let you go."

She smiled, put a hand on his arm. "I will call you. It's going to be okay."

"Will you at least tell me what this is about?"

She pursed her lips, considered. To say nothing would be worse than prevaricating. And she owed this man more than any of the others. *Okay. As much truth as possible.*

"Back in the states I worked in research. Although I no longer work for corporate, I have periodically done some freelance consulting. I'm sure he is here about that."

Her friend studied the man waiting ten yards away.

"That is no businessman. He is a government agent. A spy if I'm not mistaken." He looked into her eyes. "What does he want with you?"

"I have no idea."

A truth.

"Do you have to go with him?"

"What do you think?"

"Will I see you again?"

"I hope so."

For several seconds he said nothing. "You are going to run, aren't you?"

She smiled. "The first chance I get."

He sent her a brief look of admiration and reached for her bag. "He is waiting. God go with you, Talia. Call me if you can."

Not when, if.

"I will."

She turned and followed *Senor Gonzales* as he slipped between rows of lush bushes and into the street. Intense heat radiated off the dusty road where piles of clothes were heaped. Picking coffee meant sweating profusely and not just because it was labor intensive.

Starting early, the pickers stripped off everything but what was necessary before wading into the bushes, leaving their clothes in a pile at the edge of the road. Depending on the weather, that sometimes meant wearing only the basics. She'd never seen so many men in skivvies before.

Locating her lightweight blouse, she drew it over her shoulders, covering the sports bra she wore. She didn't bother to button it. The shirt hung past her hips, making it seem as if there was nothing below instead of her Nike running shorts. She looked up and pinned the man with a glare that dared him to look anywhere lower than her eyes.

"I am here on behalf -."

"No."

"I beg your pardon?"

The incredulous look that was wiped from his face almost before she had time to process it made her want to laugh. She guessed he wasn't used to hearing that word too often.

"I said no. I told them no before and my answer is still no."

Carlos was right. The man before her was not who he seemed. A spy? It wouldn't have surprised her and since *need to know* was SOP in the world of espionage, she guessed he'd been told very little about the situation, which meant the cards were hers to play.

"Look, I don't know how they tracked me down but I don't do freelance consulting anymore."

The man folded his arms over his chest and scowled at something over her shoulder. She fought a grin. She didn't have to turn around to know Carlos was standing there, likely glowering right back at him.

So much for Mr. Calm, Cool, and Collected.

She was touched. Her friend had more or less adopted her the day she showed up looking for work. He'd also made no secret of the fact that he would be her lover if she so desired.

"This probably isn't a good place to discuss this," Gonzales said, his tone suggesting he was losing patience.

"I agree."

She had to get out of there.

"My hotel is not far from here."

"You're kidding, right?"

"I think you misunderstand."

Not likely. Judging by the loud snort from behind her, she wasn't the only one supposedly misunderstanding.

"I was simply suggesting we discuss this over a coffee or perhaps a meal."

"Great idea! I know just the place!"

§ ♪ ♫

Juan was impressed. The restaurant, filled with a handful of coffee pickers, was actually a café at the edge of the plantation. Obviously the woman sitting across from him knew how to ensure a home field advantage. It irritated the hell out of him.

"If your bodyguard shows up, we'll have to go elsewhere."

Wanna bet? She smiled.

"He brings his lunch to work. Most of them do. They can't afford to waste time sitting when they could be picking coffee."

"And you could be pulling in six figures if you wanted."

"Is that a commentary on my career decision?"

Juan was going to have a long talk with Tim Brightman. Persuasion didn't begin to describe the prima donna sitting across from him.

"What is it you want, exactly?" she asked, impatiently.

"There's a gentleman in Santiago who would like an hour of your time."

"Then why is it I'm talking to you and not him? Couldn't swoop down out of his Ivory Tower to come himself?"

She could almost hear him counting to ten. The smile he sent her way reminded her of an alligator she'd seen at a conservation farm in the Florida Everglades.

You so need to work on your approach.

"He sent me ahead to make arrangements for a visit."

She laughed. "What in the world makes you think I'm going anywhere with you?"

She gave him credit. Other than a brief change in his irises, he hadn't reacted to the insult.

Juan was going to kill Tim Brightman. What an intellectual snob this woman was. She was the lofty PhD while he was the lowly messenger. Swallowing a reply, he shoveled a forkful of refried beans into his mouth.

Talia debated whether or not to continue acting as if she believed the man sitting across from her was employed in the world of corporate as opposed to something more sinister. It seemed safer to pretend, to go along with the charade. She sensed a lot of passion beneath the surface and didn't want to unleash it. She had a feeling doing so would only come out badly for her. She sighed. Pretend it was.

"Put yourself in my shoes. You show up at my place of employment and ask me first to your hotel and then to fly away to another country to meet someone -."

"It's about Kyle."

Tim had assured him the name would come in handy if his charm failed him.

"Who?"

Oh, she was good. He was definitely going to have a talk with Brightman at his earliest opportunity. *Persuasion my ass.*

"My boss said to tell you it had to do with Kyle."

Talia took a sip of water, grateful her hands didn't shake. She eyed the man over the top of the glass. Could he hear the pounding of her heart? Thank God she'd prepared herself for this day. She only hoped those hours spent in front of a mirror would buy her the time she needed.

"That name means nothing to me. Is it a code name for a new product?"

She suspected he had hadn't been given anything but basic information, ensuring he wouldn't become empathetic to his subject. He might know a name but he had no idea what the name meant.

Juan considered his options. Tim wanted to talk to her, in Chile. For whatever reason, he wasn't willing to come to Costa Rica. He needed her there.

"What would it take to convince you we mean you no harm?"

The sound that carried across the table was too harsh to be called a laugh. It was almost a screech. It dripped with accusation.

Brightman, what haven't you told me?

Talia wrestled with her emotions. It was becoming clear to her that she'd spent too much time among people she trusted. She was having difficulty stuffing her feelings back where they normally resided, away from the world.

If only he had a cruel mouth or hard eyes.

She swallowed. She had to get out of this. She parried.

"No private jets. I'm sick of CEOs trying to impress me."

The man visibly relaxed. "That's good because we don't have a private jet."

Lie number one, she thought sourly.

"And I don't want a babysitter."

Got you!

His reaction told her all she needed to know. Handsome he might be, but there was only one reason he was there and that reason meant her life would be a living hell.

Not if I have anything to say about it.

He was the enemy.

Juan wanted to kick himself. *Babysitter.* The word he'd used with Brightman sent him jerking as if he'd had a tack shoved into his ass. He worked to breathe normally.

"I assure you I'm not a babysitter."

Lie number two.

"Can you put me up in my own room then?"

"Room?"

"I live a bit far from San Jose International Airport, Senor Gonzales."

Talia fought the urge to smile. Either the guy sitting across from her wasn't an agent or he wasn't a very good one. It appeared he hadn't thought things through.

"Tell me where you're staying. I can get my things and meet you there."

Juan fought the urge to swear. How in the hell did she do it? How did she manage to throw him off so completely?

"I'll provide the transportation, of course. Let me drive you to pick up your things."

She'd expected such an offer.

"That won't be necessary. I wouldn't want to put you to any trouble."

"It's no inconvenience. My car is close by."

In order to complete the charade, he'd rented a car right after selling the truck to an old farmer for half of what he'd paid for it.

"You don't understand. I live in Plantation Village."

That surprised him. He'd assumed she lived up at the resort.

Hmm, mingling with the little people. Interesting.

"I really can go by myself. I'll meet you back here in fifteen minutes."

"I would be happy to accompany you."

"I wouldn't want you to get your suit dirty."

"A little dust won't hurt. I could use the exercise."

On the way to the little hut she'd been calling home, Talia mentally replayed the conversation at the café. Jorge, or whatever his name, left her unsettled. It wasn't just that he was handsome, though God knew that was true enough. It was the inconsistencies, small details that just didn't add up.

For one thing, he used contractions. It was clear the man was educated and in her experience, Latin Americans who were educated were more likely to say *will not* instead of won't. And when he'd told her he could use the exercise, she'd gotten the sense he'd been telling the truth, though she couldn't imagine why. It was obvious he worked out and was in impeccable shape. She shook her head.

The man was a puzzle and the fact she had unanswered questions, small details she couldn't put her finger to, meant he was a danger. She had to remember that.

If only he'd been a thug.

Talia stopped five feet from her door.

Someone's been in there.

"Let me."

Well, that seals that. You are a spy. How else would you have figured that out?

She probably should have argued but the truth was, he was more qualified to deal with the situation than she was in this case. In a weird twist, he'd gone from potential danger to protector. At least temporarily.

He moved past her, knocking her aside in the process. His entire body tensed as he slowly approached the door. She glanced over to see a wide-eyed child watching silently. Talia could imagine how it looked. A perfect stranger, wearing a suit that cost more than a year's wage using a well-heeled shoe to edge her door open, then going inside without her.

"Did you see anyone come from there?" she asked, pointing at her home. The child shook her head and ran off. Talia understood.

"They left."

One of the neighbors came to a stand a few feet from her and looked past her shoulder, obviously watching for the agent.

"Carlos called me," he said quietly, still gazing toward her hut. "There were two of them, in a black sedan."

"What did they look like?"

"I only saw them briefly. They weren't Latino. Too big, and stocky, like one who plays rugby or maybe American football. Jet black hair."

"Not European?"

He shook his head. "Wrong skin color."

"Pacific Islander perhaps? Or Asian?"

"If I had to pick, I'd say Islander."

She opened her mouth but quickly shut it when he stiffened suddenly and took a step backward.

"There is no one inside," the agent said from where he now stood beside her, "but you should go in, see if anything is missing."

Talia knew better than to thank her neighbor in front of the agent. In fact, she sought a good excuse for his presence. If it looked as if he knew something about the break in, it could spell trouble for him. He seemed to sense her worry, because he shook his head slightly and smiled.

"I came to see if she needed any assistance." He directed the comment to the agent.

"That was kind."

"We look out for each other. You are not a familiar face and yet you went into her home. I assume you got her permission first?"

Talia smiled. The agent had better think of a damned good response because God knew she wasn't going to help him out by defending his actions.

In the Latino culture, the relationship between men and women was actually quite formal. There were social customs to be observed and families were very protective of females. Women dated in groups and chaperones were common.

"I acted out of instinct," he responded smoothly, "to protect."

"I see," her neighbor replied.   It was clear he didn't approve.

"I would be happy to accompany you inside to see if any of your things are missing?" the agent repeated.

She looked into her neighbor's eyes, saw what was there; concern and question both. Did she want him to go in with her? The decision was an easy one. She shook her head ever so slightly then covered it by tossing her hair. She turned to follow Jorge.

"I don't know what they hoped to find. There isn't much in there; certainly nothing worth stealing."

CHAPTER 5

~~~~~~

When they came out twenty minutes later, the area around her hut was deserted. She had no doubt dozens of eyes watched from the safety of shadowed corners, however. She couldn't blame them. Strangers rarely showed up in Plantation Village and when they did, more often than not, it meant trouble for the laborers.

"I'm glad nothing was taken," Gonzales offered, opening the car door for her. She was surprised by the sincerity in his tone. Either he was a good actor, which in her experience, spies weren't, or he actually gave a damn. That didn't make much sense either. Why the hell would he care whether or not she lost anything? It was obvious she didn't have anything of value or else she would be living in better quarters.

"Will it be a problem to take off work?" He put the key in the ignition.

"No."

In reality, it didn't matter whether or not a picker showed up to work. If they didn't work, they didn't get paid and in any event, there were plenty more people looking for work. Her position would be easily filled.

The ride to the Costa Rican capital was quiet. She was grateful the agent wasn't pressing her for conversation. It gave her a chance to think. She'd always known her time at the plantation was temporary. Still, it had come as a shock to see it end so abruptly. She stared out the window at mountains in the distance and considered what she was leaving behind. More than a sense of security, she would be losing friendships. Many of the families in Plantation Village had more or less adopted the woman who was so obviously lost in life. She smiled sadly, her heart aching.

Of all of them, Carlos would worry the most, but she didn't dare contact him. If they found out she cared for him, albeit as a friend, they wouldn't hesitate to use that to their advantage.

"Are you hungry?" Juan asked, disrupting her daydreams. "I have a cooler in the -."

"No, thank you."

Without further comment, she went back to her ruminating.

"Is it because I'm Latino?" Carlos asked, his voice barely above a whisper.

She'd been taken aback.

"Wh-what?"

"Why you won't take me as a lover."

She shook her head, almost relieved by how easy it would be to give an honest answer.

"Absolutely not, Carlos, though I'm afraid you've put me in an interesting position."

"I do not understand."

"How can I prove I'm telling the truth? If I explain myself, you may wonder if I'm lying to cover any prejudice I may have against Hispanics. If I go ahead and allow you to make love to me, I may have proved my statement but it would be a hollow experience. I love you, Carlos, but as a friend and, truthfully, someone -."

"There is no need to continue this conversation. I am sorry I brought it up."

"No, please, let me explain."

He looked as if he'd protest further. She placed a hand on his forearm and looked directly into his eyes. *"Please? Can I explain?"*

"Go ahead then."

A gentle breeze caressed her, swept her hair against her shoulders. The sun disappearing behind the mountains lent an almost mystical feel. And there was Carlos, his presence making her feel safe, the heat of his body seeping in through her skin. It would be so easy to become his lover. But she knew better than to go that route. She knew the cost. They would use him against her. She turned to him.

"I'm an orphan."

"I see."

"You can imagine the hole inside of me, having grown up without parents."

"Were you adopted?"

She shook her head. *"I was raised -."* She stopped.

"You do not need to disclose anything painful.

She nodded absently, her mind a million miles away. She'd never told anyone anything close to what she was going to tell him, but she'd come to know him as someone she could trust.

"I had counseling. I was warned of the pitfalls of seeking out older men as a way to fill that hole. You know, a father figure?" She spit out the last as if it were poison. She took a deep breath and continued, unwilling to focus on the seductive feel of his fingers as they slid over her shoulder, down her arm, ending at her hand where he drew tiny circles. It was a challenge, one she understood. He would comfort her any way she would allow.

God, it was tempting. To feel strong arms around her, pulling her close. To close her eyes and lose herself in a comforting embrace. She drew a shuddering breath, looked into his eyes.

"As intelligent and resourceful as I may be -." She paused. *"A life alone is a lonely and difficult one. I needed to be extra cautious to avoid being taken advantage of. Men will lay flowery words at*

the feet of someone they want to conquer, so I just learned to tune them out."

He gasped. "You are a virgin then?"

She couldn't help it, she snorted, then laughed, a bitter sound. "No, definitely not."

She'd lost her virginity in the loft of a neighbor's barn. Recently graduated from high school, she would be moving to the east coast for university. Late August, a low pressure system had brought ungodly heat and humidity.

The dog days of summer.

Her neighbor's son, a sophomore at Kansas State, had swept her off her feet, seducing her with sweet words and sweeter kisses. His touch, more than the weather, had set her skin on fire.

"No," she said again, shaking her head, "I'm not a virgin. But I am choosy about who I have sex with. I make it a rule to avoid father figures and would-be protectors. They're too close a second." She patted his hand. *"Sorry, Carlos."*

"I think I understand. As you said, it would be a hollow experience."

"We're here."

Talia let out a ragged breath and pushed herself away from where she'd fallen asleep against the window. What a vivid dream. She could almost smell the soap Carlos used.

"Here?" she asked, trying to orient herself.

The passenger door was opened and a young man in a uniform smiled at her.

"Welcome."

She somehow managed a smile. "Thank you."

Not quite awake yet, she stumbled getting out of the car. The young man was quick to steady her.

"Thank you."

"My pleasure, Senora."

"I was asleep and I'm afraid I'm not quite awake yet."

"I understand."

The sight of Juan standing a short distance away, holding her bag, gave her a burst of energy. She smiled at the young man and followed her would-be captor into the hotel lobby.

She walked over to a restaurant while Jorge secured their rooms. "Do we need a reservation?" she asked, eying the décor. It was obvious they catered to an upscale clientele. She slid her gaze toward the reception desk, back to the hostess. If nothing else, she would eat well while in captivity. A captivity, she reflected, that would be brief if she had any say about it.

"You are a guest at the hotel?"

"Yes. What's available?"

"How many are in your party?"

"Just two of us."

"We have a table at seven thirty, if that would suit?"

"Perfect, thank you."

Juan walked over. "Reservations? Excellent. What time?"

"Seven thirty," the hostess replied, preening beneath his attentions.

"We'll see you then."

He steered her toward a store located in a rear corner of the lobby.

She stopped ten feet away. "What are you doing?"

"I thought perhaps you might want something to wear to dinner."

Juan felt the heat of her stare as it raked him from his polished shoes to his Armani tie. He stared blandly in return. "I thought you might be more comfortable wearing something other than your work attire."

"Embarrassed to be seen with me?" she replied. Damned if her eyes weren't challenging him.

Tim was going to answer dearly for this assignment. Not a babysitter, huh? Hell, he was babysitting one of the most spoiled intellectual brats he'd ever encountered, and that was saying a lot given that his mother had been a professor at the University of California, San Diego.

"Forgive me for my presumption." He glanced at his watch. "Why don't we go upstairs? You can take a shower or a nap or simply relax before dinner."

She swept an arm toward the elevator. "After you."

"A gentleman always allows the lady to lead. After you."

She stared at him silently before turning and walking away. He smiled. Damn if he wasn't starting to enjoy himself.

Game on.

Juan pressed the button and handed her a key that she carefully examined.

"Will you excuse me a moment?"

Before he could say a word, she'd walked over to talk to the receptionist. She was at the desk only minutes.

"I asked her to rekey my room and to put a note that you are to be denied any access to my room. I'm sure you understand."

"Of course," he replied, again pressing the button.

"I told her we are business associates."

Juan swore beneath his breath. The woman was beyond confounding. He didn't need a hotel key to get into her room but it would have been more convenient if he could have used the duplicate he'd asked for to do just that if the need had arisen.

"This way." He guided them toward connecting rooms located halfway between the elevator and the stairwell at the opposite end of the hall. Both were a good distance away from her room, effectively decreasing the likelihood she would be able to slip out without his knowing about it.

"I suggest you take the opportunity to finish your nap."

"What?"

He mentally sighed. She was very jumpy which put him at a disadvantage. He would have a much more difficult time of things if she remained a rabbit ready to run. He smiled.

"You fell asleep in the car. I was simply suggesting that you take the time before dinner to continue your nap."

"I'll take that under advisement." She closed the door in his face.

Stubborn woman. He'd seen how tired she was. Picking coffee beans was hard work. Long hours under a hot sun would leave anyone wanting a nap. He sent a smirk at the closed door. She'd be asleep the minute her head hit the pillow. He'd bet on it.

He let himself into his room, tossed his bag on the second bed, and loosened his tie. He was anxious for a shower but first things first. He pulled out his cell phone and stepped onto the balcony.

He wouldn't bother checking in with Tim. The man knew that unless it was important he wouldn't be hearing from him until the assignment had been completed. He did, however, have a very important phone call to make.

The call was brief. His shadow was already in the hotel. He closed the sliding glass door and walked over to look out the peep hole. Within a few minutes a woman in a maid's uniform came to stand outside his door. He gave a soft knock and she gave him the signal.

Time for that shower.

Juan hissed as hot water hit still tender flesh.

Damned bullet wounds!

While the steam soothed ravaged skin and muscle, the pressure from falling water felt like so many needles punishing scars that were still healing.

The pain wasn't enough to keep him from thinking about the woman in the adjoining room. She had gone along too easily.   He had no doubt that she'd run if given the opportunity, which is why he'd pulled in the shadow agent who was camped outside her door. He'd insisted the agent send him text updates every five minutes, then propped his phone so he could read them from where he stood. The latest update stated his assignment was still in her room, so he closed his eyes and turned his face into the spray.

Juan finished dressing and picked up his messages. There were two, one of them from the agent. Talia had indeed gone shopping but was back in her room, in the shower. That was no surprise. He'd known she wouldn't want to sit down to dinner in sweaty dusty sportswear. He smiled. Knowing he was reading her right boded well for a quick and successful completion of the bullshit assignment.

The second message was from Tim. There were no agents working in the vicinity of the coffee plantation. He frowned. The men in the black sedan had been the ones who broke into her hut and tossed the place. He'd heard enough of the conversation with the neighbor to deduct that tidbit.

They hadn't taken anything but it was clear they'd been looking for something. He thought back to what he knew about Dr. Natalia Blackmoor, neuro-bioethicist.

Whatever the hell that meant.

She'd worked as a research scientist for seven years. Long enough to rise rapidly through the ranks before an abrupt departure in 2010. Tim had managed to secure the notes from her exit interview. She had been fired for misconduct and violation of corporate policy.

At the time he'd read that, Juan hadn't thought much of it. Now he considered. Someone working as an ethicist being fired for misconduct?

He pulled out his laptop and the USB drive Tim had given him just before he left Santiago. It contained additional information on the research assistant. Until it was certain he was taking the assignment, Tim hadn't felt it appropriate to give him the entire file. He pressed his thumb firmly into the biometrics pad until the light turned green, then opened the files and began to read.

His neck stiff from sitting and staring, Juan leaned his head back and shrugged his shoulders. His eyes burned from all the reading. Rubbing his neck he glanced at his watch. Dinner was in an hour. He closed the file and shut the laptop lid, drumming his fingers on top. Was it possible this wasn't a bullshit assignment after all? Tim had gone out of his way to assure him it wasn't, but he'd assumed that was just to push him into taking the job. He'd thought it likely Tim didn't believe he was well enough to return to full duty. Juan figured he'd been offered a soft assignment so he could continue to heal, even as he was working.

Foster.

Tim had thrown the name of another field agent into the mix and like a juvenile schoolboy, he'd fallen straight into the trap. Although he could count on Agent Dan Foster to cover his back in a firefight, he wouldn't exactly call him a friend.

Years ago, he'd worked with the agent on a rescue mission. At the time, Dan had been a member of the Air Force Special Forces. Sean Andrews, a good friend and former teammate of Dan's was being held captive, as was his girlfriend, Kian Ross, and her sister, Kaila. Not to mention, Juan himself, but that was a whole other story.

Watching Dan plan and perfectly execute the rescue and capture of the crime ring leaders had earned Juan's respect. Watching him walk off into the sunset with Kaila Ross not long after had driven a wedge between them that would have affected their ability to work together if the two men hadn't been consummate professionals.

Tim had known what he was doing when he'd dropped that name. Juan had taken the assignment. An assignment he was beginning to suspect was going to be more challenging than he might hope for. He had a passion for what he did and even if the assignment turned out to be babysitting duty, he would give his best to see it through. After all, he was a consummate professional.

Since the shadow was still in the hall, vacuuming, he decided to go down and have a drink and think over what he'd read.

"Would you care for an appetizer while you wait?"

Juan smiled up at the waiter. "No, thank you. The beer is enough." He took a deep drink and thought about his assignment.

Either Talia Blackmoor was a psychopath or the company she'd worked for was covering something up. Prior to her being fired, she had been a rising star. She'd secured several patents in the company's name which led to FDA approval of neurological diagnostic equipment. That had turned into serious bucks for the corporate ledger. Why fire someone who was basically a cash cow?

He thought of her position at the company, a bioethicist. He would think any type of ethicist would have pretty strong values. Values she likely formed as a youth growing up, as she had, on a farm in the Midwest. Had she stumbled on something the company was working on that went against her personal morale code?

If that was the case, why fire her? Why not simply move her to another department or put her on a different assignment? Unless she'd threatened them somehow? Perhaps threatened to go public with some bit of news that would affect the company's ability to secure IPO status?

Under those circumstances, he could understand why they'd want to fire her. On the table, his phone buzzed. Talia was on the elevator, dressed for dinner. The agent had stepped on, vacuum in hand, to ensure she made it at least to the lobby. He could take it from there. He stood and walked to the entrance of the restaurant and stared patiently across the lobby. The elevator doors opened and two women stepped off, one of them carrying a vacuum.

He gulped and worked to keep his mouth from sliding open. The woman walking toward him was definitely not the one who'd shut the door in his face before taking a nap. To say she cleaned up well would be like calling a rain forest a nice garden. She was magnificent.

She'd selected a simple blouse and a peasant skirt in some sort of a tropical pattern. She wore sandals with no heels, which made sense given that she was five foot eight. She had taken her hair down. Dark brown, it fell in waves to her shoulders. The skirt swayed gently as she walked toward him. To his surprise, she was smiling.

Wow. His assignment had just taken on a new, more positive energy.

"We're over here," he said, then led her to the table.

"What time is our flight?"

Juan studied the menu. "Eight fifty-five."

"Don't you find it amusing that flights rarely take off on the hour or half hour?"

He looked up in surprise. She was making polite small talk?

"It's always some odd departure time, like eight oh three, or two thirty-eight."

"Yeah, I guess you're right."

"So, who am I going to see?"

"My boss. His name is Tim."

"Tim?"

"Tim Brightman. American transplant brought down to oversee South American operations."

As much truth as possible. Spy school 101.

CHAPTER 6

So, Talia thought, he was sticking with the corporate story. It actually made her part easier. Her plan would go a lot smoother if he felt she believed his bullshit story. It helped that she'd worked in the corporate space. It meant she'd spent plenty of time wading in that same bullshit, right up to her eyebrows. She took a sip of wine.

"I think he's going to be disappointed. I told you, I don't do consulting gigs anymore."

"Why not?"

"Burn out."

That was true enough. It was amazing how quickly burn out set in after one learned they'd been working for the wrong side.

"We should be at the airport at six."

"I agree. That will give us plenty of time to get through customs."

"Can I offer you dessert?"

Talia smiled up at the waiter. "No, thank you. I'm too full."

Juan shook his head and handed the man a credit card.

She decided it would be better to wait and go back up together. She needed to keep up the appearance she intended to go with him to Santiago.

"Does anyone ever call you Nat?" he asked, stepping off the elevator.

"No one who wants to participate in a conversation with me."

He put his key in the door, then turned. "I'm glad you went with my suggestion."

"Oh, the outfit?"

He nodded, smiled. "You charged it to the room I hope?"

"Yes."

Down the hall a maid stepped off the elevator.

"Shall I call you in the morning?"

"Why not?"

"Until then. Good night."

"And you."

Talia walked over to the balcony and pulled a cell phone from her purse. It was pre-paid, kept for just such an emergency. She'd grabbed it, along with a change of clothes, when she'd gone back to the hut. She began to text.

The reply was brief.

Acknowledged.

As she crawled between the sheets, she thought about what she'd come to realize. She was being hunted, and by more than one party. She was pretty certain that Jorge Gonzales wasn't associated with the thugs who'd tossed her place. He'd been too unsettled by it. She thought about what her neighbor had told her. Pacific Islanders. Filipinos? Samoans? Close enough to enemy territory to be recruited. She was pretty certain the agent had heard at least some of what her neighbor told her. He'd been standing too close, paying too much attention even as he tried to look like a corporate dweeb.

Talia smiled into the dark. The man really should have picked another persona for this assignment, and she was certain she was an assignment, complete with a tail.

How long did it take someone to vacuum a hallway?

Jorge definitely didn't fit the image he was trying to project. Oh, he was charismatic enough, but he had far too much self-confidence, too much power held in check, to pass off as someone else's corporate lackey.

He couldn't exactly present himself as who he was, she supposed, but it suited him better than pretending to be a cog in the corporate wheel. No. From the tips of his designer shoes to his beautiful brown eyes, he was every bit the spy, if a well-dressed one.

He had shrewd eyes that tried to cut to the core but failed because of his flaw. A flaw that would ensure she lost him. He only saw what he wanted to see.

She'd caught his expression when she'd stepped off the elevator. That he was so surprised by her appearance told her he was the type of person who, once they had an image of someone based on a first impression, wouldn't let it go. Like an aging relative who always saw someone as cute little Jane or Bobby, the man would continue to see her as an awkward American, dressed as a jogger, out of sync with her environment.

She supposed that would work to her advantage, though it was irritating. There was so much more to her life but given that she couldn't share those details with the agent, it wasn't worth thinking about. That she found it irritating told her something. Something disturbing. He was getting under her skin.

Throughout dinner she'd had to work not to stare at the handsome agent too long. She told herself she was just studying him as she would any adversary. After all, she would need to be able to recognize him in a crowd. If she was successful in getting away from him, she had a feeling he would come after her. Not because of wounded pride but because it was his job and he took it seriously.

She'd always considered herself a good judge of character but years of studying neurobiology had enabled her to go further, to read people in a more detailed, intimate manner. The slightest change in eye movement meant a significant change in emotion. How someone tilted their head or shrugged their shoulders spoke volumes about their stamina. These observations, plus numerous others, had led to her contributing to improved testing methods in the fields of psychiatry and social sciences. Unfortunately, it had proved to be her undoing.

She had become overconfident in her observations and quit looking for alternate interpretations. She'd come to rely so heavily on her first impressions that she stopped looking deeper. She quickly decided whether someone was in the friend or adversary category and left it at that. And in the black and white world she'd created, smears of grey got in and slowly but surely destroyed it. Destroyed it so completely that she'd been left with no alternative but to run.

In the early weeks she had spent hours thinking back, wondering where it had all started to fall apart. Hours reexamining every event in a series that had brought her to the point where her life was no longer her own. She'd gotten sloppy.

She'd quit using her own abilities. She looked at the surface but no further.

Well, fool me once.

She thought back to dinner with the charismatic agent. He was Latin American and judging by his features, one of European descent. What the locals referred to as Mestizo. Latinos who had intermarried with Europeans, by choice or not, were taller, with facial structures that set them apart in appearance from those who'd descended from the South American indigenous tribes.

High up in the mountains, descendants of those tribes didn't get on with the mixed race peoples and tended to keep to themselves.

She was pretty sure he'd spent a significant amount of time in the United States, though she doubted Southern California. He didn't speak with any accent reflective of the dialects scattered from Los Angeles to the US-Mexico border.

She also didn't think he'd grown up in any of the Hispanic Districts found in cities throughout the US. He didn't carry himself as someone who'd been part of a community that worked to blend in. He was too proud, too willing to stand out, something she found appealing, if not sexy. He looked directly at her as if daring her to walk away. She yanked her thoughts back from that path and worked to unravel the mystery.

If he'd spent time in Canada, she would have detected it in his accent. Langley? In her experience, residents of the Mid-Atlantic States didn't have much of an accent. She considered. It didn't fit.

She knew in her gut that there was much more to the handsome man but the truth was, the only thing she could be certain of was that he was a Latin American male who'd spent time in the states, probably when he was training to be a spy. It was a shame they hadn't crossed paths under different circumstances.

Her eyes burned with fatigue but her mind whirled. Her contact had assured her everything was set for tomorrow morning, not to worry. But she did worry. Her stomach hadn't been so knotted since she'd stood in the customs line at the Costa Rican airport several months earlier, waiting to see if she got a green or red light.

She'd flown from Sydney and it was the first time in a long time she'd used a passport with her real name. She'd never intended to spend the rest of her life living under an alias. After some eighteen months Down Under, her identity hidden by falsified documents, she'd decided it was worth a try.

If she had been stopped and detained, she had an escape plan in the form of a contact who worked for the airport police. Fortunately, that hadn't been necessary, though she'd paid him just the same.

The green light suggested she was that much closer to obscurity but she'd only taken it to mean that the airport security folks working that day didn't think she was trouble. She would be a fool to let down her guard.

This time she would be at a different airport but the contact had assured her it was no problem. He was well connected and had a plan as well as a backup plan. She had to admit, she hadn't cared for his backup plan at all. To be arrested while waiting in the gate area could backfire if the agent decided to use some sort of diplomatic authority to ensure she never made it out of his sight. She rolled over onto her side and stared at a narrow slit between the curtains. It let in just enough light to keep the room from being pitch dark. She sighed. She had to hope the primary plan was successful, though that had its pitfalls as well.

Knowing there was nothing more she could do, she closed her eyes and prayed for sleep.

🌶 🌶 🌶

Something was wrong. Juan knew it in his gut. The woman was being too cooperative. She was up to something. Problem was, until she made her move, he couldn't do anything for fear he'd blow his cover.

He replayed events of the morning. After a quick breakfast they'd gone to the airport where they'd gotten through customs without any difficulty. The flight looked to be fairly full. There was very little seating in the gate area.

"I need to go to the bathroom."

He'd have to have a damned good reason to say no, so he simply smiled. He'd anticipated she might try to use such an excuse in an effort to lose him so he'd made sure he had another shadow ready.

"Of course. I'll wait."

He watched her disappear into the women's room. Two minutes later a service worker rolled a large gray cleaning cart inside. He grunted in satisfaction. All was well.

"Let's see what's going on in California." He brought the news up on his phone.

"Hmm, techies pushing out the locals, eh?"

It certainly wasn't the first time San Francisco had seen real estate controversy. Beginning before the Gold Rush and continuing on to the present day, the City by the Bay had been periodically overrun by opportunists who were more than willing to push out the locals.

He glanced at the bathroom. The agent stood outside the door. He continued reading.

These people thought they had problems? They should read a bit of history, paying particular attention to what happened to the Natives during San Francisco's boom years of the nineteenth century. First terrorized by soldiers fresh out of work after the end of the Mexican American War, then by eager beavers ready to make their fortune in gold, many locals lost their homes, if not their lives, at the hands of New Wave residents.

He looked at his watch. Five more minutes had passed. He looked back at the agent. Something wasn't right.

Her hair!

When she'd pushed the cart into the bathroom her hair had been in a bun. Now it fell to her shoulders. He stood and made his way toward her. If he was wrong and Talia walked out and saw him talking to a maid -. He shrugged. He'd just have to convince her he was flirting.

"Any sign of her?"

"The bathroom is empty."

"What? Why didn't you tell me?"

"You told me to tell you if there was a problem. I've been standing here and she hasn't gone in or come out."

"Of course she went in," he snapped. "She went in ten minutes ago and you went in shortly after!"

"I went in when I first got to my post and I'm telling you, the bathroom was empty." She left the cleaning cart to go in, returning quickly. "No one is in there."

Damn it!" He looked around frantically. People milled about, waiting for planes or waiting for people to get off of planes. Then there were the employees, hundreds of them. It would be pointless to run through the crowded airport searching for her.

"Do you want to talk to the head of airport security?"

He shook his head. That would only lead to questions he preferred to avoid. "She's long gone by now. Besides, she isn't dangerous. That much Brightman would have told me and I would have done this a lot differently. No, better to put a secondary effort in place," he said, referring to tracking the research scientist.

"You think she's on the airport grounds?"

He looked out at the runway. Two planes were in line to taxi. "If she's not in the air."

"We can find out where the planes -."

"Don't worry about it. I'll put the secondary effort in place." He looked at the shadow agent. He'd worked with the woman periodically throughout the years and there was no doubt she was reliable and good at her job. She was meticulous about detail which meant she rarely made mistakes. He could see the uncertainty in her eyes.

"It wasn't your fault."

"I don't know how this happened."

"I take full responsibility. I should have let you know the moment she began walking toward the bathroom. When I saw a woman roll a cleaning cart into the bathroom, I assumed it was you. My mistake."

"Two cleaning carts?"

That was another thing Juan liked about this agent. Like him, she didn't believe in coincidences.

"What else can I do?" she asked.

"Go home. I'll take it from here."

Juan returned to his seat, his mind racing. There was a slight possibility that the timing of the other service cart had been a convenient coincidence. There were enough of them in the area.

He decided to pursue that angle later. For now, he needed to set the tracking protocol in place. Which option should he follow first, the one that says she did slip out of the airport and was making her way to a safe place nearby, or the one in which she flew out of the country? Both would be time consuming but one would give him quicker results. He pulled a laptop out of his briefcase and began typing.

Tim stared up at the screeching bird circling overhead. He frowned. Ravens didn't sound like that.

Over and over the black bird chattered, its caws growing louder the further away it flew. He slapped his hands over his ears and shut his eyes. The noise wouldn't stop.

"Jesus!"

Jerking upright, he reached for his cellphone. He cleared his throat and brought it to his ear.

"Brightman."

"I lost her."

The superior rubbed a hand over his face and tried to focus. He'd fallen asleep at his desk. "Juan?"

"In the fucking airport."

He said nothing while he processed that information, which was taking much longer given he'd been lost in a dream.

"She got on another plane," the agent told him. "To Sydney. Do we have anyone who could be at the airport ready to tail her?"

Come on, Brightman, think. He gulped what was left of the coffee on his desk, winced. It was cold. He stood and walked to the door knowing the movement would help him cast off the fatigue.

"Hello?" Juan asked.

"Yeah, I'm thinking."

"My flight starts boarding in fifteen. I'll assume you'll have someone in place."

The line went dead.

Tim yanked open his office door and called to his secretary. Across the hall, the Duty Officer was conducting an interview. He looked tired and a little impatient. Tim couldn't blame him. Time not spent catching up on paperwork was often considered a painful waste.

"You rang?" his secretary inquired, stepping in and closing the door.

He smirked. She must have been watching reruns of *The Addams Family* in Spanish again.

"Who do we have in Sydney?"

Juan buckled his seatbelt and wondered what was worse, his anger at having been duped, his wounded pride because of it, or the admiration he felt for the resourceful woman. Damn if he wasn't starting to enjoy himself. Knowing there was nothing more to do until he set down in Sydney, he closed his eyes.

CHAPTER 7

Talia propped her feet on the railing, leaned back, and gazed out at the horizon. A stratovolcano rose majestically in the distance. Forming the northwest part of the island of Ometepe, Concepcion was quite active, having last erupted just four years earlier. Maderas, a second volcano on the island was considered dormant.

A sudden gust of wind left her scrambling to keep several papers from being carried into the freshwater lake that surrounded the island. Setting a rock on top of the pile, she sat back and watched a sailboat cross paths with a pleasure craft. Behind her, a sliding glass door opened.

She accepted a glass of orange juice with a grateful smile.

"Would you care to join me, Chloe?" she asked the housekeeper. "Surely, Christoff won't begrudge you a bit of a break?"

"I will be right back." The housekeeper disappeared into the house, returning a short time later with a rolling cart. "Care for some tea?"

"I'd love some, thank you, and thank you for bringing some of your scones. They are incredible."

"It's my pleasure," the housekeeper replied, handing her a cup and saucer.

"This is good. Black currant?"

"I know you like it."

That was one thing Talia had always appreciated about the small woman arranging the mid-morning snack. She went the extra mile to ensure that whoever was in her sphere felt comfortable, if not special. She remembered small details such as a favorite color or food and worked to bring them into the environment whenever possible.

"Where is your brother?"

The older woman poured herself a cup of tea and sat down. "In his lab, of course."

The Andris siblings had come to Nicaragua several years back, in part to retire, and in part to pursue personal interests. Although Chloe worked to make sure her brother's estate ran smoothly, she worked very few hours as a housekeeper. A small staff that reported to her directly did most of the hard labor though she did do most of the cooking herself. She was typically finished early in the day, which left her afternoons free so she could volunteer at an animal sanctuary.

Prior to joining her brother, Chloe had worked with a circus in Eastern Europe. Her ease around exotic animals made her an invaluable addition to the sanctuary staff. Several times the owners had tried to hire her full-time but she refused to accept money to do what she loved. She told them the money would be better spent caring for the animals that often arrived sick and traumatized.

Talia suspected that was only part of the story. She suspected Chloe didn't want to spend too much time away from her brother. A brilliant doctor who was never happier than when in his lab, Christoff Andris would very likely forget to eat or sleep if his sister wasn't there to take care of him.

In their obsessions, the brother and sister were very much alike which made them perfect housemates. Christoff watched over his sister as carefully as she did him. He always had.

Their parents had been killed in a boating accident off of one of the Greek Islands when Chloe was still a minor. Her older brother was applying to medical schools at the time and scrambled to find a way to care for his sister and pursue his dreams of becoming a doctor. The long and winding path their lives took led them to Europe where he pursued his dream and she finished high school. Preferring to work rather than go to university, she put a great portion of her meager salary to ensuring her brother ate while going to school on a shoestring budget. This earned her his loyalty just as having taken her with him had earned him hers.

"Have you looked over the papers?"

"Hello, Christoff. I did a quick overview last night and I was planning to read them more carefully this morning."

The doctor accepted a cup of tea and a scone and sat down between the two women. He looked out at the lake but glanced over periodically.

"Did you get any sleep last night?"

"I slept on the plane," she assured. "Thank you for getting me out of San Jose. It went off perfectly, just as your aide promised. It was a clever plan."

He smiled. "The credit should go to Chloe. It was her idea."

Shortly after going into the airport bathroom, a maid had rolled a cleaning cart inside. A contact hired by Christoff to help her escape, the woman had waited while Talia climbed into the industrial sized garbage container and then piled rags and refuse on top. She'd then taken her on cleaning rounds before transferring her to a service truck that drove her to a part of the airport reserved for private jets. Once inside the nondescript hangar, she was rolled into a janitor closet where the maid helped her climb out before escorting her to a sparse bathroom that was thankfully equipped with a shower.

Used primarily for emergencies such as rinsing spilled chemicals off airport maintenance staff, Talia had ignored the icy water and smelly soap. She was just grateful to be away from the man trying to get her to Santiago.

The maid had supplied clean clothes and a duffel bag filled with toiletries, another change of clothing, a new cell phone, and other essentials necessary for her escape.

After an hour spent hiding in the hangar, she'd been put aboard a private jet where she joined a small group of people flying to Managua, Nicaragua. Chloe had stepped out of a nondescript car, wrapped her in a much needed hug and promised her that everything would work out. Then she'd driven her to her brother's lakeside estate.

"Well, it was brilliant, thank you."

"When I worked for the circus, there was an awful man who was cruel to the animals and crueler to the female employees. There were times when it was better to hide from him than risk a confrontation."

Beside her, Christoff stiffened. She didn't know whether or not he'd heard the story but one thing was certain, he didn't like the idea that his sister had been mistreated.

"We used to hide in the drums that were scattered throughout the circus grounds. Since women who work in a circus are often small in stature, it wasn't too difficult for us to squeeze ourselves into the metal containers, even when they were filled with toys used by the animals."

"That's incredible."

"You do what you have to, yes?"

"Yes," she agreed.

"Whatever happened to him?" her brother asked. He looked over at Talia. "She never told me of this. If she had, trust me, I would have solved that problem."

Chloe put her hand on her brother's arm. "Be at ease, dear Christoff. I didn't tell you about him because for the most part, he left me alone."

"For the most part?"

"He never hurt me," she quickly replied. "Not the way that you mean. Besides, there is justice. The members of the circus take care of their own."

"What happened?" Talia asked.

"He got caught."

"I don't understand."

"He was a cruel man but he was not stupid. He knew the management would never allow him to abuse the women outright so he made sure he never left physical evidence."

"How horrible."

"Well, he might have been smart but he had no control over his temper. He got too rough with one of the girls, hurt her so that she wasn't able to perform for several shows."

"Did the management finally do something?"

"No, they may have spoken out against abuse but in reality, they wouldn't have done anything about it. He knew this and it is part of what made him so bold."

For a few moments she said nothing, just stared out toward the lake.

Talia knew Chloe wasn't seeing the beach that ran behind the house, but rather a distant memory.

"The strong man found out about it and went into a rage. He was sweet on that particular girl, you see. He took matters into his own hands. He beat the man so that he nearly died. The management wanted to call the police but no one admitted having seen what happened."

"Were you there?"

"No, I was performing. I knew something had happened though, even as I worked with the lions. I could see it in the faces of the other crew members." She shrugged. "I can't say I was sad."

"Did he leave the circus?"

"Oh, yes. Even after his bones mended he was too weak to work at his job. That was part of the revenge, you see. The man didn't have an education that would have enabled him to go work at something and now he couldn't rely on his back for labor. How was he going to feed himself?"

The three of them sat quietly. Talia considered the strange justice. She couldn't have said what she would have done in the same situation. A life in a circus was a hard life and so unlike other occupations. She supposed you had to rely on the culture if you were going to live and work in such an industry. It seemed kind of brutal, though. Still, it had, in a convoluted way, led to her own rescue and for that she was grateful.

"You look exhausted. Why don't you have a lie down?" The doctor took the stack of papers and stood. "You can look at these more closely after you have rested."

"I think I'll sit here for a bit, if you don't mind."

Chloe disappeared inside the house and returned with a lightweight blanket. She spread it over Talia and tucked it around her legs.

"Thanks."

Sliding her hands between her knees, she admired a yacht anchored not too far offshore. It belonged to one of the neighbors, a celebrity of some sort. Chloe thought it was an actress but since everyone in the area valued their privacy, she couldn't be certain.

Talia loved the water. When she'd lived in the Eastern US, she'd spent most of her vacations on the New England coast. Prior to that she'd lived on a farm, miles away from lakes or oceans. It was, in her opinion, some of the most boring landscape in the country.

It hadn't always been that way. She'd lived the first eight years of her life in Chicago where she could gaze out at Lake Michigan and dream of a day when she would travel the world. Although that dream had come true, she couldn't say it had been anything close to what she'd hoped for.

When she was seven, her father, a pilot in the reserves, had been killed when his helicopter crashed during a training mission. Wallowing in grief, her mother had bounced her from relative to relative, telling anyone who would listen that she didn't have what it took to be a single parent. The stress of raising a child alone was just too much.

After a year and a half moving from one relative's to another in an effort to keep her in the same school, she'd been shipped off to live with her maternal grandmother in Iowa. The woman had done her best to make the lost little girl feel loved but nothing could make up for the rejection of her own mother.

"You have to understand, Talia," the older woman had tried to explain. *"She just isn't strong. Not like you are."*

She'd been baffled by the idea that as an eight year old child, she could be stronger than a grown woman but she hadn't argued. Her grandmother had arthritis that flared up when it got damp which, in Iowa, was most of the year. Whether the humidity of summer or the brutal snows of winter, the damp made the farmer's life difficult. Widowed long before Talia was born, her grandmother had a staff to run the farm but when her arthritis flared up it was all she could do to get out of bed. The little girl didn't want to make things more difficult so she'd generally remained quiet on the subject.

A clever business woman, her grandmother had opened her home to students studying agriculture and veterinary medicine, providing room and board in exchange for working the farm. One of the students had taken an interest in Talia, seeing that she was not only bright and independent, but that she had demonstrated an uncanny ability to understand animal behavior.

"I would like to see your granddaughter kept out of school," he'd told her grandmother one fall afternoon. "She would do much better with homeschooling, I think."

"There's nothing wrong with my granddaughter," the older woman had snapped.

Talia had been in the kitchen washing dishes and had tiptoed closer in order to better hear the adults talking. She liked the handsome guy who was doing residency with the local vet. He always had time to answer her questions.

"I think you misunderstand. Your granddaughter is exceptional. She probably finds school boring but doesn't want to complain."

"What makes you think you're an expert on my granddaughter? You've lived here less than a quarter, you aren't married and have no children of your own."

"I have eyes, Mrs. Bryant."

"What are you talking about?"

"You've probably noticed that Talia spends a great deal of time around the students on your farm?"

"She's a helpful child."

"She most certainly is, and every one of us is grateful for her. I noticed her reading some of the textbooks."

The students had turned part of the barn into a library where they could share resources. Even in the digital age, colleges required the purchase of expensive text books and since many students shared the same curriculum in different order, they shared the costs by sharing the books.

"Is it upsetting the students?"

The man smiled. "They are, as am I, delighted. But it proves my point. She's not only reading the books, she's helping some of the students with their homework. I am beginning to suspect she has an unusually high IQ and may be something of a prodigy. I think that she would do better if she was homeschooled where her exceptional talents could be developed."

The bluster had gone out of Edna Bryant. "I cannot afford to hire a tutor and I am nowhere near smart enough to oversee her education."

"We could buy you some time until a better solution presents itself."

'I don't understand. How?"

"The students and I were discussing it and we're willing to get her started. Your co-op program has been so successful you'll have a steady stream of students even after the ones who are here move on. It will buy you some time."

"But -."

He held up his hand. "If I might continue?"

Her grandmother had nodded.

"Your granddaughter has been through a very difficult time these last years. Fitting in with farm kids in a small town after growing up in Chicago has not been a successful transition, I'm afraid."

"Has something happened at school? Are the kids being mean to her?"

"Kids can certainly be cruel but you have to understand, there are more than cultural differences keeping her apart from the other students. Her intelligence means that she outscores and outperforms everyone else in the class, including the ones who, before her arrival, had been considered the brightest."

The older woman had let out a defeated sigh. "I see."

"It isn't a long-term solution of course but I honestly think pulling her out of school would be in her best interest. We have come up with a preliminary program to ensure she doesn't lose a beat."

"I don't know. This is a big step. I'd like to talk to my granddaughter first."

"I understand. I can leave these with you." He'd set a pile of papers on the coffee table. "It's a program that adheres with state laws. We noticed you have a computer. Online courses will ensure she is in total compliance even in the absence of a certified teacher."

"Thank you for your concern. I love my granddaughter. I hate that she's had to suffer like this."

"You're doing the best you can, Mrs. Bryant. You cannot be faulted for that."

In the end, homeschooling in Iowa was not necessary. Shortly before Christmas, two events altered the course of her young life.

The first was learning that her mother was not coming home for Christmas.

"She took a bunch of pills, you see. They made her sick and now she's in a hospital where they can take care of her. I'm sorry, Talia."

She'd barely digested that horrible news when another, more disruptive development presented itself.

"This is your dad's younger brother, Cole."

The handsome man looked a lot like him. He'd also looked as nervous as the farm animals just before a violent thunderstorm. Wanting to put him at ease, she'd smiled shyly and shook his calloused hand.

"Nice to meet you, Uncle Cole."

Little did she know, he'd come bearing a precious gift. The gift of stability. He'd come to take her home with him.

"You understand I'm not sending you away, don't you?"

"Yes, grandma."   And she had.   The woman had struggled to make the little girl a priority even as she tried to run a farm.

The business was in transition, she'd tried to explain.

"It seems like it's always transitioning," Talia had pointed out.

"You're such a bright girl. You're right. First, I was forced to grow corn for ethanol or the state would punish me financially. Now, the state wants us to cut back on production. Says there's evidence the aggressive agricultural practices are contributing to environmental damage."

"What will you do?"

"Well, I'm going to focus more on dairy. I've decided to lease out some of the land and use the money to buy more Bos," she'd said, referring to *Bos Taurus*, the species name for dairy cows.

Talia had known her grandmother would have her hands full, even with all the help she claimed to have. She knew going with her Uncle Cole would be better for her grandmother, and the man did make a hard sell.

"I hear you have a way with animals."

"I can tell how they feel."

"That's a good skill to have. It's called animal husbandry and it's a skill you can put to good use on my farm, too, but with horses instead of cows."

"Horses?"

"I kept back part of the property for ranching. A river runs through it and I have some great grazing land."

He'd pulled out his smart phone and showed her numerous photos.

"Who's that?"

He'd smiled.

"That's Billy Truex."

His family lived on the farm next to her uncle's. In exchange for farming part of their property, her uncle gave part of his for their horses to graze on.

"Young Billy works with the horses when he's not at school."

She'd seen something in the boy's clear blue eyes that left her feeling warm inside. She smiled up at her uncle. "When do we leave?"

The man had given her the first of many hugs.

"I'll bring her back any time, Edna."

"I know you will."

The adults had exchanged a look she hadn't understood but she was too excited about moving to Kansas to give it much thought. Her grandmother shared the details of the conversation with the veterinary student with her uncle.

"I'm not surprised," her uncle had replied, eyeing her affectionately. "Her father was just the same." He had then explained his plan.

"I live in a rural area, much like this. The school district has its challenges. The neighbors send their kids to a very fine private school. I'm planning to send you there. You won't be bored, I promise."

And she hadn't been.

CHAPTER 8

Talia only realized she'd fallen asleep because someone was gently shaking her awake.

"Come inside," Christoff urged, "it's time for dinner."

"How long have I been asleep?"

"For over two hours, but do not worry. You needed it."

"But the files -."

"Will keep another day. Let us enjoy the evening. My sister has graciously left us a meal she prepared before leaving for the sanctuary."

"That was sweet of her."

"I thought we'd eat in the library. It's more intimate than the formal dining room and the view is much better."

That would be difficult, she thought, since the dining room had incredible views of the lake. Smiling, she followed him up the stairs.

"Be prepared to be delighted."

"If you do say so yourself."

"It isn't boasting to speak the truth," he replied, then pushed open the doors.

"Wow."

The view from the second floor room was indeed spectacular.

"See? Come, have a seat."

He led her onto a balcony overlooking the lake where a table had been set with china. He held out a chair.

"The grill is almost ready. Will you have a glass of wine while you wait?"

"If you'll join me."

"Of course. Red or white?"

"What are we having?"

"Salmon."

"White please."

"Excellent." He poured pinot gris into beautiful crystal goblets, then raised his. "I'm delighted to have you here."

"Thank you, Christoff. For everything. I could never -."

He waved her off. "You will make it up to me, and more, by helping me unravel this mess."

❧ ♪ ♫

In spite of having just spent the better portion of the last twenty-four hours on a plane, Juan felt anything but tired. He'd slept most of the way and woke more determined than ever to complete this assignment. That she'd escaped him still irked the hell out of him but he put a lid on his irritation and focused on next steps.

The message from Tim had been brief. He was to be at the airport café by ten and wait to be contacted.

"Senor Hernandez?"

Juan looked over to see a young man in a navy suit walking toward his table.

He stood and shook the man's hand. "Aye, that's me," he replied in a thick Australian accent.

The guy sat across from him. "Damn mate, that's incredible."

One side of Juan's mouth went up in amusement.

"How the hell -?" The young man paused while a waitress poured coffee into his cup.

"If I hadn't known -." He let out a breath. "How do you do that? I've lived here since I was fifteen and people still peg me from New York, even with diction lessons. You sound like you were born here!"

He picked up his coffee, sipped. "It's a gift."

It was one of the characteristics that made him a top field agent. Not only could he blend perfectly into a number of environments, he could ape dialects to the degree it was impossible to tell him from the locals.

"Must be," the young man replied, his admiration evident. He flagged the waitress, ordered a sandwich. He watched the server walk back to the kitchen before giving his update.

"I've got bad news for you, mate. She never got off the plane."

Juan pursed his lips. When he'd landed and there'd been no update from Tim, he'd felt concern for the first time since he'd lost the research scientist. He studied the young agent. He didn't want to insult him by asking if perhaps he'd gotten to the airport a little too late and had missed her, but -.

"I can guess what you're thinking but no, I was there before the plane landed."

"No offense, mate."

The young man smiled. "None taken. I'd have wondered the same thing. We used our connections to see if she had a passport in another name." He shook his head, took a bite of fish sandwich. "The facial recognition program they use is pretty top notch. Nothing came up."

"Which means someone else is protecting her. Someone with connections of their own."

The man nodded. "We came to the same conclusion."

Juan drummed his fingers on the table. He wasn't going to get any further at this point. He had to let the wheels of tracking stay in motion.

"May I offer you a bit of advice?"

He looked at the agent in surprise. He'd been so lost in thought he'd forgotten he wasn't alone. "Sure."

"Find out what she's afraid of."

He nodded, considered. She hadn't seemed frightened, only arrogant. Was it a bluff? The agent continued.

"I read her file. There's obviously more to the story. The fact that she's gone to such lengths to avoid being brought in suggests she has something to fear."

He nodded but didn't comment.

"Any idea what Brightman wants with her?"

"No. He's been pretty tight-lipped about it."

"Is he acting for someone else, do you think?"

"I don't think so, no. I think he wants to talk to Ms. Blackmoor personally."

While his boss had been adamant that sooner was best, he hadn't seemed overly concerned at the unexpected hiccup. Either he was letting Juan know he had faith in his ability or he was comfortable waiting. Either way, Juan hadn't detected any urgency or panic.

The other man finished his sandwich and took a sip of water. "If you find out who else is looking for her, you should be able to figure it out. In the meantime, here." He slid a receipt jacket across the table. "Money to cover my lunch, but don't open it until I'm gone."

It took a lot of effort not to react. If there was something in there the agent didn't want to discuss it meant it was off the record, which meant the young man wasn't just a local field contact.

Juan waved off dessert and glanced over to see that the agent had disappeared into the airport crowd. That wasn't surprising. With short hair and a saunter that bespoke confidence, he'd looked like just another business traveler.

Juan slid a credit card into the restaurant receipt holder and slipped the other into his lap so he could transfer the contents into the briefcase at his feet.

Tim never said exactly who would be meeting him in Sydney. Still, he'd been shocked to discover the contact was not primary to their side. A double agent.

He'd been able to tell the guy wasn't native Australian but he didn't think he was American either. Russian? More likely than European. He wasn't built like a European.

While learning to blend into different environments, Juan had conducted in-depth studies of different nationalities, focusing more on physical differences than cultural ones since those couldn't be faked without plastic surgery. He'd learned to interpret subtle differences in facial features, height and weight, and bone density. Just as Europeans could spot American tourists a mile away, he could tell someone's physiological heritage, even two or three generations back.

"Thank you, Mr. Gonzales," the waitress said, returning his bill for signature. "Have a nice day."

"And you." He fought a smirk at her reaction to his accent. She blinked in confusion, tried and failed to smile, and finally scurried away.

He brought up a mental image of the agent. He was pretty sure the guy was Russian, though it was probably true that he'd been in Australia since he was fifteen. There was no reason to lie about that. One belief agents held in common was that to tell some truth was a relief. It kept them from losing themselves in the lies that their lives had become.

He picked up the briefcase. Depending on what the man had passed along, he would be grateful or not.

He walked toward the men's room where he could examine what had been given to him. The room was empty. He went into the lone stall and locked the door. He wasn't worried about taking too much time since anyone needing a stall would see there was only one and would find another bathroom.

He reached in and pulled out a flash drive. It had been encrypted to match his thumb print and held a self-destruct code that would wipe whatever information was on it once he'd viewed it. That the agent who'd passed this on to him had gone to the trouble of customizing the security for Juan sent a clear message. Double agent or not, they were on the same side. At least at this juncture.

Juan stared at the screen in consternation. The sedan had been registered to the Chinese Consulate. The thugs driving it were reputed to be working for the South Koreans.

The South Koreans and Chinese working together? Or working to double-cross each other? That the information hadn't come from Brightman was significant. It meant his organization didn't have all the pieces. He had to talk to Tim.

"This is a first."

Juan grunted. He hated calling in when on assignment but the exception was necessary.

"Why did you give me this assignment?"

Tim sighed. "We've gone through this before -."

"Tell me again," Juan snapped.

"You're the ideal agent for the job, that's why. I told you that before."

Ideal, huh? His mind raced. *Why?*

"You should have put Foster on it," he said abruptly.

"I didn't want to pull him in. I need him where he is."

"That's not what I'm talking about, Brightman."

"Oh, come off it, Hernandez. If I thought your being Latin American would in any way negatively impact the outcome of this assignment do you think I would have hesitated to put someone else on it? Do you forget where she was when you -."

"That she was there simply tells me she is willing to go to great lengths to ensure she isn't found."

"A lone white woman, an American no less, picking coffee on a Costa Rican plantation? You're giving her more credit than she deserves."

Juan closed his eyes. He hadn't thought of that. The fact he hadn't told him he was losing perspective. Not good.

"That plantation is connected to an exclusive resort owned by other Americans," he countered. It was a feeble argument, he knew.

"She stood out," Tim replied, "trust me."

"Why are the Chinese and South Koreans looking for her?"

"What makes you -?"

Juan snorted. "You mean you don't know?"

He told him what was on the flash drive.

"Shit."

Juan's eyebrows shot up. He'd never heard his boss swear, even when it was more than justified. The man just didn't lose his cool, which was partly why he'd been put in charge of such an elite group at a relatively young age. Could it be that he had a personal interest in this case?

"Hold on a minute, Irena just walked in."

Juan waited while Tim talked with his secretary.

"We got something."

Juan listened in disbelief.

"She's where?"

"You want me to go where?"

The good doctor poured wine into her glass. "Please hear me out."

"I've trusted you this far, but this makes me doubt your sanity." She grabbed the glass, began to sip but stopped and began using it to gesture with. "You pluck me out of one danger only to set me in the middle of -."

"You were not in danger."

Her sip turned into a gulp. "Easy for you to say. You weren't about to be taken to Santiago against your will. I've no doubt that agent would have used force."

"Talia, if the man who wishes to talk to you meant you any harm whatsoever, I would not be suggesting this plan of action." He sipped his wine. "I have looked into this situation -."

"Meaning you know more than you're telling me."

"I'm telling you what you need to know. If I tell you more than that it will put my plan and your life in danger."

"Okay, I accept that. I don't like it but I accept it."

He closed his eyes briefly. "Thank you. Having your trust increases our chances of success." He refilled her glass and then his own. "I looked into the backgrounds of those involved. The man who was tasked with bringing you to his superior is a very capable agent."

"You're more so," she quipped, working to keep the hand holding her wine glass steady.

"Your faith in me is appreciated. And not without merit. It was our good fortune that the agent underestimated your value. If he hadn't, I might have had a more difficult time getting you here."

She met his gaze. "But you would have."

He sighed. "Of course. They may be good but I'm better. I make it my business to be better."

"So, you know who *they* are and why they want to talk to me?"

"The world of espionage is a small world indeed. You know, you could figure it out on your own if you were able to quiet your mind long enough to think on it."

Ignoring the implication that she was being overly emotional, which she was, she backtracked. "So, tell me again why I need to get on a plane and fly to Hong Kong?"

"Well, if it makes you feel any better, you only need to go to the airport."

"To the airport," she repeated. "Why in the world do you need me to get on a plane and fly to the airport?"

"I need you to pick up a package. A very important package."

"You have dozens of people in your employ. If this package is so important, why would you send a neurobiologist who's had a crash course in espionage and self-defense to -?"

"They have your prototype."

She stared at Christoff in disbelief. She was glad he hadn't shared the news while she'd been sipping wine. If he had, he'd be wearing it.

It has to do with Kyle.

"How did they get their hands on it?"

"It's a long story."

"Did Kyle -?"

He waved a hand dismissively. "The details at this point are unimportant. What I need is for you to go to Hong Kong and retrieve the prototype."

It has to do with Kyle.

"There has to be more to this. Anyone could pack it into a crate and smuggle it out of the country, Chinese government or no."

"Talia, I'm asking you to do it."

Whether it was his tone or the combination of fear and desperation she saw in his eyes that silenced her when she would have argued further, she couldn't say.

She stared out at the lake. Lights from a sailboat making its way to a nearby dock made her wish for a simpler time. However, the truth was that if she was to ever have any peace in her life, she had to see this through. She looked up to see Christoff watching her intently.

"What time is my flight?"

He closed his eyes and breathed in deeply. His shoulders slumped with relief.

"I assume I'm going to be working with someone?" she asked quietly.

"I've arranged it so that Senor Hernandez will be there, waiting for you."

"Senor Hernandez?" she asked, her brow furrowed.

"Before we discuss the particulars, let us return to the veranda and enjoy a cognac, shall we?"

"Are you trying to get me drunk so I'll agree to anything you say?"

"If that were my plan, my dear, I would have plied you with liquor the moment you got to my house. You were asleep on your feet."

She blew out a sigh, stood. "Lead the way." At the door she kissed his cheek. "It's a good thing I like you so much."

"And you are the daughter I never had. I won't let you fall into the enemy's hands. Now, let us go."

As she followed him out to the porch with sweeping views of the coastline, she thought on his words. He was asking her to walk into the lion's den. She would be risking her life. He must have an awfully good reason for wanting her to do so.

"I want you to know that I have called in every favor owed to me in order to put the best of the best on this." He handed her a snifter filled with amber liquid. "There are multiple governments working to ensure you will be successful."

She'd been moving the glass in small circles, gently warming the cognac against her hand to buy some time. As his words sank in she looked up in shock. "Multiple governments?"

"Let's just say that while not everyone agrees with the direction biotechnology is taking, they have accepted that there are certain -." He paused, sipped. "Inevitabilities, shall we say?"

She had no intention of getting into a political discussion on her life's work so she changed the subject. "Who is Agent Hernandez and when do I meet him?"

"You already have."

"Carlos?" She'd always suspected there was more to the man who had been protective of her from the moment they'd met.

Christoff shook his head. "He is who he appears to be. A hardworking man with a good heart and an eye for pretty women."

She wanted to look anywhere but at her host. The man took the phrase *in-the-know* to new and sometimes unbelievable heights. "Okay, if not him, then who?"

"You call him Jorge Gonzales."

"Him?"

Shock and resignation set in and she fell into a nearby chair. The sudden jolt sent cognac splashing onto her jeans. She considered the irony of it all. The good looking agent was supposed to protect her?

"Oy."

CHAPTER 9

~~~~~~

Juan stared at the movie screen in frustration. Another goddamned plane. Although the flight to Hong Kong was shorter than the one from Costa Rica to Australia had been, it still forced him to sit for hours. Another wasted day. Nervous agitation didn't begin to describe the jumpiness coursing through his body.

Shifting in his seat only sent painful needle sensations down his leg. Coach class seats had little to recommend when you were dealing with scar tissue. The bullet near his knee had been removed years ago but whenever he had to remain in the same position for extended periods of time it ached like a bitch.

There was another problem. Due to his recent injury, he hadn't been able to run and though he was well enough now, he hadn't found the opportunity. It was starting to wear on him.

For most of his life, he had been a passionate runner. He'd completed his first marathon in junior high. Even when on an assignment he tried to run several miles a week.

In addition to keeping him fit, running kept his mind sharp. The endorphins that coursed through his body calmed him in the midst of chaos and enabled him to think clearly. The think time he got in while running had been responsible for more than one successful assignment. He glanced around. Jogging up and down the narrow aisles would get him nowhere but into hot water, with passengers and airline employee alike.

He looked at his watch, accidentally jostling the elderly lady next to him in the process. He smiled in apology and ignored the dirty look he got in return. They would be landing at Hong Kong International in ninety minutes. He flagged a stewardess. It was time for a beer.

As he was taking his first sip, the captain updated everyone that they were changing altitude to avoid turbulence. He asked the stewards to secure the beverage carts and themselves and informed the passengers that flying at the new altitude meant they would arrive at their destination a half hour early.

The news and the beer left Juan a lot less agitated. Happy at the prospect of being able to stretch his legs that much sooner, he finished the Fosters and thought back to his conversation with Tim.

Talia Blackmoor was on the radar of both the Chinese and South Koreans because of her work in brain research. Specifically, with the human brain after a stroke. She'd been working on a device that showed promise in facilitating communication with patients who had fallen into a coma brought on by a stroke.

Juan could certainly see the advantage. Families could do more than stand helplessly by and wonder if their loved ones knew they were there. Staff could find out what the patient needed, perhaps help them feel less afraid. He could understand why the Chinese or South Koreans would want to talk with her, perhaps see if they could bring her over to work for them. He remembered she had been fired. Maybe someone at the company found out she was thinking of going to a competitor.

"We need to get to her first."

Tim's tone spoke volumes.

"She's in danger from them?"

"A great deal, for reasons I can't go into right now. I need you to bring her to me as soon as you're able. There's a ticket waiting for you at the Qantas counter and someone will be at Hong Kong International to provide you with up to date information."

He was tempted to check his watch again but didn't want a repeat with the lady to his left. She was likely to stab him with one of her knitting needles in repayment. He mentally reviewed the information passed to him in Sydney. He could understand the Asian governments wanting to get their hands on the technology but he couldn't understand why that translated to danger for the woman. Yes, millions, if not billions of dollars were at stake, but if they killed the researcher, they lost the technology for sure.

It was more likely they wanted to use her as a political pawn, some type of bargaining chip. That certainly made sense. He shook his head. It would have been too easy to kidnap her from that hovel she was living in. Unlike most of the shacks, hers had a door but it was more for show than any security. If they'd wanted her, they could have easily had her by now. Unless it was early in the game?

That didn't make sense either. She'd been out of the US for almost two years. If they'd wanted her for her intellectual capital regarding this device, they wouldn't have waited this long to try and talk to her. Something must have changed. Some variable introduced that spurred the Asians to act now. He brushed a finger thoughtfully against his lip, then tapped it.

The head stewardess asked the passengers to prepare for landing. He slid his seat back into the upright position, gritting his teeth as a sharp pain shot up his leg.

"Might I suggest flying First Class next time?" the lady next to him said suddenly.

"Good idea," he ground out, massaging his leg. He shook his head. Wouldn't the tax payers love to pick up that tab?

Fortunately, the plane was large enough that multiple doors were used to funnel passengers toward the jetway. It wasn't long before he was accepting a small package from his contact.

"Time is, I'm afraid, something we don't have much of. You need to get Ms. Blackmoor on a flight to Santiago as soon as possible. Your tickets are in that packet."

"Where is she?"

"Her flight from Managua arrives shortly before seven this evening. "

"Wait a minute. Managua? As in Nicaragua?"

"You'll have a little time, enough to get something to eat perhaps."

Another goddamned flight. *Oh joy.* Brightman was going to pay for this.

"I don't understand. How is it she was in -?"

The agent blinked.

"Forget it. Not important. Okay." He let out a breath, tapped the packet. "I take it her flight information is in here?"

"Yes."

"She isn't going to be happy to see me. What's to stop her from making a scene?"

"I'm going to be waiting for her at the Arrivals Hall. I will deliver her to you."

"And just where am I supposed to be?"

"At a restaurant."

Juan counted to ten. If he sat any longer his legs were going to be useless. "Is there a fitness center I can use?"

The agent cocked her head. "A fitness center?"

"I would like to run. I've been on a plane for too many hours."

"I would think your time would be best spent resting -."

"No. No more sleep. I've slept enough, thank you very much. What I need is to run."

Juan wanted to shout at the woman but refrained. How he spent his time before the flight landed wasn't important. As long as he was at the restaurant on time, what did she care if he slept or ran or went dancing? He was beginning to suspect she was an agent in training, else she wouldn't have been thrown off by the request.

"There are shower, fitness, and spa services at the local hotels but there is nothing at the airport."

He looked at his watch then back at the agent. "Do you have any suggestions?"

A mercifully short time later, he was on a treadmill. He had no idea where the woman had gone. The agent, who had introduced herself simply as Ju, promised to deliver Talia Blackmoor shortly after seven. He shook his head. "Fool me once," he grumbled, then considered how he might avoid a scene with the researcher when she saw him. At the Arrivals Hall, of course.

🌶 🌶 🌶

The sound of tray tables being pushed against seatbacks woke her. Blinking, Talia looked around. Passengers were preparing for landing. A glance out the window revealed a sea of lights. Hong Kong International Airport was clearly visible which surprised her since she'd expected a haze from pollution to act as a curtain.

She checked her seatbelt, using the opportunity to run a hand over the passport she wore in a waist pack. A backup was shoved down her boot. The whine of the landing gear coming down was followed by the sensation of being pushed back against the seat as the Captain began their descent.

Thanks to sleep, a hearty meal, and a protein drink Chloe promised would leave her wide awake and energized, Talia felt more prepared than she could hope. It didn't hurt that she'd spent hours going over the plan with both Christoff and his sister.

She was flying into the mouth of danger but she could take heart in the amount of thought that had gone into the plan. The siblings had laid out several backup scenarios in the event any of a number of wrenches were thrown into the mix. If Murphy's Law showed up, they would have a way to deal with it.

And they'd assured her that she could trust Agent Juan Hernandez.

"He is one of the very best, if not the best in his unit."

"Since I have nothing to compare him to," she'd thrown back at him, "how can I find comfort in that?"

In response, Chloe had handed her a report. "Read this."

At first glance, it looked like nothing more than a marketing pitch for Senate appropriations time. The success rate of the small elite group was the highest. The metrics were all above standards. She was about to roll her eyes and return what she was certain was propaganda when something got her attention.

Each of the unit members had unique abilities that enabled them to perform under incredibly difficult and uncertain circumstances. That wasn't what got her attention since it was just more marketing. What drew her eyes to each member's profile was how much of it was whited out.

"You do not have clearance," Christoff had explained.

She studied the profiles. An agent may have experience in a specific location or with a particular group of terrorists, but the details were whited out. Another column showed unique characteristics and scoring on various tests but again the details had been covered up. Except Juan's.

"I thought I didn't have clearance?" she asked, not looking up.

"I believe you should know the man who will be protecting you."

Something about the way he'd said it had her looking up, but only to see a neutral expression. She replayed the sentence but couldn't say with any certainty what hidden meaning was in it. She looked back at Juan's profile.

His IQ was off the charts.

"Okay, so he's intelligent. That doesn't always translate, you know."

"Keep reading," Chloe replied patiently.

He was an avid runner which probably meant he could work in different climates, including variances in altitudes, without needing much time to acclimate.

He had scored highly enough in several assessment tests that it was theorized he had high psi abilities. She looked up.

"Psi abilities? As in he's a psychic of some sort?"

Christoff nodded. "He refuses to be tested but his performance in assessment tests suggests he has several extraordinary, if not extrasensory, abilities."

"Why won't he allow himself to be tested?"

"He has some very strong beliefs when it comes to the supernatural," Chloe supplied. "They tend to be negative."

"Huh, get a bad tip on s horse?"

The siblings hadn't responded other than to ask if she was satisfied.

"Does he know I need to retrieve this package? I mean won't he want to drag me to the first plane headed to Santiago?"

"I have reached out to his superior. We are in sync."

"So, you guys are on the same side?"

Chloe was shaking her head. "No two are ever on the same side. They simply have the same objectives."

She looked at her host. "Whose side are you on?"

"Yours."

She glanced at his sister. "Or is it that we just have the same objective?"

"I think you need to get to bed. You have a long day tomorrow."

She hadn't missed the look that passed between the siblings at her remark. She would have to accept that they were all trying to accomplish the same objective. It would have to be enough. For now.

As the plane descended, she fidgeted, toying with the buttons of her blouse and crossing her ankles. Dressed for hiking had advantages and disadvantages. It enabled her to travel light but left little room for hiding anything. Still, Christoff and his sister were nothing if not creative. Her boots enabled her to hide various items wrapped in shielding to get through a metal detector. The back and waist packs helped her appear as a tourist traveling on a budget.

The wheels touched down smoothly and the plane rolled to a stop.

"Welcome to Hong Kong," the stewardess spoke. "Please remain seated with your seatbelts fastened while we taxi."

The sound of seatbelts unbuckling made her smile. Especially since hers was one of them. She stared out the window and tuned out the mundane information coming over the speakers. While the captain informed the passengers of weather conditions, local time, and customs procedures, she considered her reasons for being there.

She owed Christoff a great deal but that wasn't why she had agreed to help him. In reality, she was only a small piece of the puzzle. It was the bigger picture that mattered. At least that's what she told herself.

Kyle.

She closed her eyes against the stab in her gut. Who was she kidding? Big picture, hell. There was only one reason she'd agreed to this. Kyle.

She wouldn't have even known he was in any way involved if she hadn't come out and asked. The shift in Christoff's eyes as he answered had been so subtle most people would have missed it. But most people hadn't spent a lifetime studying the subtle nuances of body language.

It was hard to fathom how the brilliant researcher had become entangled.

"He would never have sold me out," she'd said when she finally found her voice.

"He didn't. But please don't ask me for any more details."

"Why not? I think I have a right to know -."

"Do you?" he'd snapped, shocking her even more. The man had never raised his voice to her. "You left without a word -."

"You know damned well why I left."

"I know you think that was your only choice but -."

"How dare you judge me for something you know nothing about! You weren't there! What, you think because you read some goddamned report slipped to you by one of your spies that you understand the position I was in? The choice I had to make? You know nothing."

Emotionally drained, she'd slumped against the back seat and stared out at the passing scenery. The remainder of the ride to the Managua airport had been short, and, mercifully silent.

Her thoughts were interrupted by the voice of a stewardess urging passengers to check around their seats and in the overhead compartments before getting off the plane. In no hurry to deboard, she pulled the backpack over her shoulders and allowed several passengers with families to go ahead.

"Have a good day," a crew member chirped, startling her so that she tripped. Another passenger reached out to steady her but in her heightened state she overreacted and actually fell back and would have knocked over a child if another man hadn't quickly stepped in and swept him out of the way.

She apologized and continued down the carpeted hallway. Blowing out a breath, she reminded herself that most of the people around her were innocent bystanders. She needed to be alert but she couldn't look at every individual as if they were the enemy.

Getting through customs was mercifully uneventful. She made her way to the Arrivals Hall where several people stood holding placards. Talia was shocked to see her name on one of them. For several seconds she pondered what to do. If the woman was holding a placard then there was a chance she didn't know what Talia looked like. Then again, if she did and she approached her, it could get awkward since Talia had no intention of going anywhere with her.

Christoff hadn't said anything about a female.

Where was the agent?

Juan stood up the moment he spotted the research scientist. Ignoring Ju, he pasted a smile on his face and stepped forward. "Ms. Blackmoor?"

At the sound of his voice, she turned. Her expression went from confusion to relief the moment she saw him.

Interesting.

If he didn't know any better, he'd say she was happy to see him. She smiled and shook his hand.

"It's good to see you again, Senor Gonzales."

"Forgive the casual attire. I -."

Ju disposed of the placard and came over to stand beside him.

Talia shook her head and swept a hand down her person. "I'm not exactly dressed for dinner."

Juan turned so that he was facing both women. "Ju, this is the woman I told you about, Ms. Blackmoor. Ms. Blackmoor? This is our local representative, Ju."

He studied the interaction between them as they shook hands, paying close attention to the other agent. She'd never explained what she'd intended to tell the researcher when she got off the plane, and he wanted to see how she was handling his explanation.

While on the treadmill that afternoon he'd mentally replayed his meeting with the other agent. Something about her didn't add up. That she'd been so thrown off by small details meant she was either a novice or she was playing for the other side.

Tim would never have sent a novice to meet with him. The researcher was too important. Which meant whoever Tim sent had been disposed of. There was no other explanation for how Ju had gotten so close.

He needed to find out what she was up to. He didn't have all the facts so it was best to keep the game in play. He'd cut his run short so he'd have enough time to shower and change before heading to a restaurant. He wanted to eat before getting to the Arrivals Hall.

After ordering a burger, he'd pulled out his laptop and confirmed that the research scientist had indeed gotten on the plane in Nicaragua. He put away the computer and glanced around the airport. Nothing seemed out of place. He concentrated on his meal. One thing he knew in his gut. The woman waiting to meet Talia Blackmoor at the Arrivals Hall had no intention of delivering her to him.

He'd sent a quick beacon to Tim. Normally, he would have maintained total silence during this phase of the operation but reaching out served his purposes in two ways.

One, it let his boss know that everything was proceeding. Since he knew the man had multiple andirons in the fire, he figured easing his mind a little couldn't hurt.

The second purpose was to keep the ball in motion. He needed whichever organization Ju was working for to believe he thought she was on his side. If she'd been alerted in any way to his intentions, things could get ugly. At this point, his primary objective was to get Talia Blackmoor and the package she was retrieving safely to Chile. He could worry about betrayal and double-cross later.

Juan smiled at the Asian woman.

Your move.

"Ah, yes. I have a car outside."

Really? I thought I was supposed to get her on a plane as soon as possible?

CHAPTER 10

〰〰〰〰〰〰〰〰〰〰〰〰〰〰〰〰〰〰〰〰〰〰〰〰〰〰〰〰〰〰〰

Juan fought the urge to smile. It was clear by Ju's expression that she hadn't planned on his tagging along. Damn if he wasn't starting to enjoy himself.

"Do you have any luggage?" he politely inquired.

Talia jerked a thumb over her shoulder.

He nodded and indicated that they should follow Ju. "Useful things, aren't they?" he said, referring to the backpack. "I like to travel light myself. Especially when traveling internationally.

"I hope you had a pleasant flight?" Ju tossed over her shoulder.

"Yes, thank you."

Juan was glad the research scientist was walking behind the other agent. By keeping in step with her he could easily observe Ju's actions. It hadn't escaped his notice that she'd shoved her hands into her pockets. He suspected there was a communications device of some sort in at least one of them. She would either text a message or open a channel that would enable someone somewhere to hear every word spoken. He shook his head and revised his earlier opinion. He definitely wasn't working with an amateur.

"Is everything alright, Senor Gonzales?"

"I thought we'd agreed that you will call me Jorge."

"Did we?"

Damn, but she was feisty! He couldn't help it, he smiled. Yep, he was definitely beginning to enjoy his assignment.

Talia fought the urge to take Juan's hand. Something was wrong. Unfortunately, it was too early to tell what. Christoff hadn't said anything about a woman. So, either Ju was sent by Juan's superiors to work with him or she was working for the enemy. She didn't consider herself racist but Ju's Asian heritage didn't give her confidence. Not when the people behind this mess were also Asian.

"My boss didn't give me any details," Juan said suddenly. "Where are we going, exactly?"

Talia worked to keep her expression neutral. If she didn't know any better, she'd think the man at her side was alerting her to the fact he was not in charge. That he might have lost control of the situation wasn't the best news she'd heard but she was far from panicking. For one, they were in a public place. More importantly, Juan didn't act like a man who was worried.

If there was one thing she could count on, it was her ability to read people. He may not have all the information but his posture and his gait told her that he had complete confidence in himself.

Early in life she'd learned that how people carried themselves and how they acted provided more information than what might come out of their mouths.

Shortly after arriving in the small agricultural community that her uncle called home, Talia had been given a lesson in human behavior. Or the cruelty of children, which wasn't necessarily mutually exclusive.

Eager to make friends, she'd fallen in with a group of girls who'd seemed pleasant enough. However, after a short time, she realized all was not as it seemed.

Wanting to make her feel comfortable, if not to distract her from some of life's harsh realities, her uncle had invited the neighbors over for a welcome dinner. Among them was the Truex family. With three rambunctious boys, the family that lived nearly three quarters of a mile from their farmhouse had been her favorites. And the youngest in particular.

Blonde with blue eyes and a shy smile, Billy Truex had put her immediately at ease with his sense of humor and a promise to show her his tadpoles. Two years older, he had quickly become a trusted friend. Before long, she'd introduced him to the girls at school.

"Oh, we know Billy already," they'd explained, which made sense. What hadn't was what happened after.

They began avoiding her, always providing some flimsy excuse about why. They smiled readily enough but it was coupled with a tension she didn't understand. They passed notes and giggled when she was nearby, and exchanged covert glances that left her wondering what she'd done wrong.

Not wanting to bother her uncle about it, she'd decided to try and figure out for herself what was going on. She began watching the girls closely, observing how they interacted with teachers, parents, and other kids. She'd quickly come to see that what came out of their mouths rarely matched their thoughts and feelings.

She would see them smile at someone but later, when they didn't realize she was nearby, would hear them saying unkind words about that same person. Over time, she'd learned to rely on their expressions and not their words to judge a situation. It helped her avoid unpleasant confrontations but it did nothing to ease her confusion or relieve the pain of their rejection.

Sometimes at night, when she lay awake staring out at a full moon, she would wonder if they meant to be mean to her. If they knew what they were doing.

"Oh, they knew alright," Billy had explained later.
Much later.
They were up in his hayloft. She'd just graduated from high school and he was home for a visit before starting his junior year of college.
"I don't understand," she'd said quietly, trailing a finger down his bare chest. One of his thighs rested between hers. She'd stared into beautiful blue eyes and listened as he explained.
"Before you moved to town, I hadn't looked at a girl for more than two minutes." He slid a piece of straw along her jaw. *"I certainly never paid attention to any of them."*
"We were just friends. You weren't sweet on me."
He stroked a finger down her nose. *"No, I wasn't, but you weren't throwing yourself at me like those girls were."*
"But they were only ten years old!"
He'd laughed at her, the hair on his belly tickling her soft smooth skin. She'd shivered and demanded he explain himself.
"You're in farm country. Life here isn't like it is in the big city."
"Well, no shit, Sherlock. Is that the extent of your wisdom or do you have anything useful to say about it?"
"The girls here aren't like you. For the most part they don't plan to go off to college and get an education so they can have a career. Their life's aspirations are a little closer to home."
"You mean marriage."
"And the sooner the better. Haven't you noticed the number of classmates who end up married not long after putting on that cap and gown?"
"Yeah, I noticed," she'd replied dejectedly.
It had been a point of contention since she wasn't able to talk to the other high school seniors as peers. The girls tended to avoid her, but the boys hadn't been too keen on

being friends either. That was partly because they'd become wary of girls looking for a husband, and partly because she outscored them on AP tests. When she entered college that fall, she would be halfway to graduation.

"When they saw me hanging with you, they decided I was off the market. You'd stolen a prospect out of a very small pool."

"But we never planned to get married." She paused. *"We still don't."*

"No, but like I said, you're different."

He'd kissed her sweetly and then made love to her for the second time in as many hours.

"Ms. Blackmore, are you okay?"

She was so surprised by Juan's voice, she stumbled and would have fallen if he hadn't steadied her.

"When was the last time you had something to eat?"

"On the plane. It was quite good, actually."

"Sleep?"

"I've had enough. Really, I was just lost in thought."

It was obvious he was dissatisfied with her answer but he kept quiet.

"Where are we going?" she asked Ju.

"I've been instructed to take you to our resort where you can recover from your jet lag. I understand you've spent a great deal of time on an airplane recently."

"Where is this resort?"

"It is not far," she replied and led her toward the airport exit.

Juan was torn. If he asked Ju to explain exactly where the resort was located he would set in motion events that would likely include running and shooting. Not a good idea in an airport filled with innocent bystanders. At the same time, he had no intention of getting in a car with the agent.

"It was nice of Tim to think of my comfort," Talia replied, following Ju through the airport doors.

Juan had spent the last several years living in South America, so he was used to tropical climates. However, stepping into Hong Kong's heat and humidity left him wishing for something cold to drink. He was dressed casually but he was wearing far more than was comfortable. He envied the research scientist for her attire.

Ju led them past the main parking areas toward a smaller group of parked cars. He glanced at Talia. She was studying their surroundings with the same intensity he was.

The whole area appeared deserted. He shook his head and gave thanks for fools. The agent obviously hadn't considered that her advantage was also his.

The lot was near a cluster of what looked to be maintenance hangars. If it had been just the two women the location would have served, but his presence changed things. The agent was either bordering on incompetent or she had something up her sleeve. Which, as it turns out, was exactly the case.

The first hint of trouble was Talia's gasp. The next was the blinding pain that tore through his ribs. Clutching his side he fought to keep from blacking out which was probably a losing battle since he was pretty certain he'd been shot with a poison dart. Through the ringing in his ears he picked up the sounds of a struggle. He wished he could see what was happening. Unfortunately, it wasn't to be. Losing consciousness, he hit the pavement face first.

Because she'd been watching the woman who called herself Ju so closely, Talia had seen the attack coming. Unfortunately, there hadn't been enough time to warn Juan. However, there had been enough for her to defend herself. The Asian woman had grabbed her wrist, using her thumb to press against a nerve that would have incapacitated her if she hadn't been prepared. The precious seconds her awareness gave her enabled her to swing her fist at the woman's throat with all her might.

Talia fought not to throw up as the key she'd been holding jammed into flesh and sent blood spurting. The woman clawed at her throat as she fell to the ground and began convulsing.

Talia glanced around quickly. Not only was no one in sight, it was eerily quiet. She wasn't sure what scared her more; that the area was so deserted or that no one had come running once the fight started.

She backed away from the blood pooling on the ground. The woman was no longer moving. She bent down and emptied Ju's pockets, quickly shoving everything into her waist pack.

Another look around showed her to be alone. She frowned. Hadn't anyone seen what happened? They were a good distance from the main parking area, but still.

She knelt and touched her fingers to Juan's neck. His pulse was weak but there. If she was going to help him she needed to know what had happened to him. She didn't see any blood but she knew he'd been hit somehow.

She couldn't exactly turn him over. Not without knowing where he was hurt. She might very well make it worse. Did she dare call for help and if so, from whom?

"Freeze."

Something cold and hard pressed into the back of her head.

"Get your hands up or you're dead."

Talia closed her eyes and blew out a sigh. *We're fucked.*

🌶 🌶 🌶

Tim set down the phone and pinched the bridge of his nose. As a general rule he didn't take aspirin but he was damned tempted. Their contact in Hong Kong was dead.

He walked over to the sliding glass door and stared out at the small garden he'd requested the embassy put in. Zen in design, it served as a visual refuge when chaos threatened to overwhelm. At that moment, however, he was finding very little comfort in it.

It was amazing how quickly a situation could get out of control, even when you put the best people in to handle it. He mentally reviewed every step he'd taken but could find no weak link. As far as he knew, other than the man in Sydney, no double agents had been directly involved with this operation. That wasn't much of a comfort though, since it meant the other side had likely been involved from the beginning. Which meant he was being played. It was time to call in reinforcements.

🌶 🌶 🌶

Dan Foster adjusted the semi-automatic so he could glance down at his wrist display.

Now? You gotta be kidding!

Keeping an eye on the cave entrance and a finger on the trigger, he answered.

"Foster," he hissed as quietly as possible.

"I didn't catch you at a bad time, did I?"

A shadow slithering up to the mouth of the cave kept him from answering. The angle was bad but it would be worse if he remained a sitting duck. Rolling onto his knees from the squatting position he'd been in, he eased his finger back. When the shadow collapsed he looked down at the gun in confusion. There was no way the bullet could have found its target. Not at that angle. His shot had been a pure Hail Mary.

He aimed the gun as another shadow fell across the entrance, but relaxed once he saw its shape.

"Kaila," he breathed.

The blonde agent blew on the end of her gun and smirked at him. Combined with her green eyes, the expression reminded him of an impish fairy sheriff.

"Ready to admit there might be some redeeming value to psychics after all?" she drawled.

Rolling his eyes, he held up a finger and spoke into a mic. "Yeah, you could say that. "

Kaila cocked her head. Knowing there were plenty of bad guys still around, he decided to mouth the answer.

"What's Tim want?" she whispered. "Hell of a time to call."

He shook his head, waiting for his boss to talk. He'd think the guy'd hung up but he could hear breathing. Kaila waved and went back outside, taking up position in some bushes at the base of a tree.

"Can you get in touch with Sean Andrews?"

The unexpected question caught him off guard and he stumbled. Righting himself, he crept toward the entrance.

"Since I'm planning to marry his sister-in-law," he whispered, "I'd better. What's up?"

"Juan's in trouble and I need his help."

Outside, Kaila had gone stock still. He took a deep breath and quietly pulled a dagger from his boot. Keeping an eye on her, he took one step forward and let it fly, exhaling as he did so. The first thump let him know he'd hit his target. The second one let him know the hit was successful.

Kaila crawled out of sight, gun at the ready. When he didn't hear anything he angled his head in an effort to see outside. When that didn't work he took a step forward only to yank back again when he saw Kaila's arm go up to shoot someone he couldn't see. She was obviously successful. The bullet meant for him ricocheted off the cave wall, sending pieces of rock in all directions, including into his cheek.

"Look, this isn't the best time -," he said, his hand to his torn cheek. Blood mixed with dirt as he worked to get the debris out.

"Let me," Kaila said, walking up.

"What was that, Tim?"

"I said it's a bit urgent. Can you have Sean call me as soon as he can?"

"Tell him I'll call Kian," Kaila murmured, ready to place a cloth against his cheek. "She has Tim's number on speed dial."

"What's on that?" he quietly asked, pointing to the cloth.

"Don't be such a baby, it's only hydrogen peroxide."

"I was just curious."

"Uh-huh, sure you were. Hold it against your cheek to staunch the bleeding. I'll go outside and call my sister."

"Tim? You get that?"

"I did."

"What's going on?"

While Kaila phoned home, Tim briefly explained the situation.

"Well, based on what you've told me, Sean's your man. You do realize of course that he doesn't work for you?"

"I'm hoping he'll consider a contract arrangement."

The line went dead as Kaila walked back into the cave. "Kian's calling him right now. Oh, by the way, we got all the bad guys."

"You sure?"

"Yeah, I walked the perimeter. Our backup was useless."

"Good thing we didn't need him. Where is he by the way?"

"On his way to the hospital."

He kissed her nose. "Juan's in trouble. Tim wants -."

"I know."

He frowned, squinted at her as if trying to see inside her head. Were her psychic abilities *that* good?

She tapped her temple. "I'm tuned to your channel, or did you forget that?" She began gathering their equipment. "Obviously, you did."

I'm planning to marry -.

Dan closed his eyes. When he opened them again it was to see her looking over her shoulder at him, a knowing smile on her face. Shaking his head in defeat, he reached into his pocket and pulled out a small metal object. He handed it to her.

Kaila looked down at the hammered metal then back at him. "I'll expect you on your knees with a proper proposal later." She slid the ring on her finger and went back to gathering their belongings.

"Did I interrupt something?"

"Tim? I thought you'd hung up."

"Not until I made sure you two were okay."

"We're packing up and headin' out."

"Listen, why don't you guys plan on taking the next two months for a break? I don't have anything pressing right now -."

"Except Juan's situation."

"Except that."

Kaila scoffed. "If you think I'm going to get married and honeymoon in two months, Brightman, you're crazy."

"I rather thought you might like to go home and tell his parents? Maybe yours?"

Dan laughed. "You call time with family a vacation?"

"If you tell your mom you're finally marrying Kaila, yeah. It might even get her off your back about grandkids."

Dan slung a backpack over his shoulder. "I wouldn't count on it."

"Listen, I gotta run. I'm glad everything went well. Take two months."

"And your report?" Kaila asked.

"That, I'll expect on time."

"If I'm typing I'm working," she replied in a sing song tone.

"If you want an extended honeymoon in a place you aren't likely to get shot you might want to reconsider." He hung up.

"We'll negotiate the details later."

She walked up and wrapped her arms around Dan. "I like the ring."

"Do you?"

"You know I'm a sucker for antiquities."

"It's a replica."

"I figured."

It wasn't that he couldn't have afforded an authentic one, it was that her line of work made it likely an antique would be stolen or badly scratched.

"The real one is waiting to be claimed."

"The real one?"

He kissed the top of her head. "Do you honestly think I would have you go around in nothing but a cheap imitation?"

"But I can't wear a ring while I work, you know that."

"I do, which is why we'll keep it in a safe deposit box at home. You can wear it between assignments. Would you like to see what it looks like?"

He pulled out his cell phone and turned it on.

"Oh, my god. That's – that's." She let out a breath. "Wow."

"So that's a yes?"

"That was a proposal?"

He looked around the Malaysian cave. "Honestly? I'd rather do it right."

"Then I'll wait."

"And my answer?"

"You'll wait, too." She pointed at the phone. "It's incredible. Thank you."

"Kian helped me find it."

She slung a backpack over her shoulder and grabbed her semi-automatic from where it had been propped against a wall. "How's the cheek?"

"Fine. The bleeding's all but stopped."

"Do you think we should go play backup?"

"You mean for Sean?"

"And Juan."

"Tim didn't ask."

"And?"

He sighed. "Is the prospect of facing my parents as my fiancée that daunting?"

"We aren't engaged, yet."

"Do you know how long it will take us to get there?"

"About two days." She left the cave. "We can sleep on the plane."

"Let me think about it, okay?"

"Okay, you think and I'll buy our tickets."

Not bothering to reply, Dan shook his head and followed her out of the cave.

CHAPTER 11

"Are you sure you're alright?"

Setting the wine glass on the tray, Talia swallowed, nodded. 'This is helping restore my nerves."

"I'm sorry I had to go all military on you."

"I understand, really. If you ever want to make a living as an actor, though." She stopped. "I suppose you already do." She glanced toward the back of the plane.

The man sitting across from her followed her gaze. "He's in good hands, I promise."

"His breathing was so shallow."

"It was lucky that the dart just glanced off the skin. If he hadn't been wearing that vest he'd be dead right now." He smiled. "Why don't you try to rest? We have a long flight and you won't do yourself any good worrying about what isn't in your control."

"Can I go back there, do you think?"

He held up a finger and pressed his hand to where a thin black cord disappeared beneath his sweater. "Okay." He smiled up at her. "The doc says he's awake and asking about you."

She unbuckled her seatbelt and walked to where Juan was strapped to a gurney. Sporting a scraped nose and a black eye he looked the worse for wear. She stopped a few feet away and studied him. He may look as if he'd lost a bar fight but his eyes were clear.

"How are you feeling?"

"All things being equal, I'd rather be watching a football match."

"Who's your favorite team?"

"Colo Colo."

"Oh, you mean that kind of football."

"Is there any other?"

"Well, I'm partial to the Chiefs myself."

"I'm glad she didn't get you."

"I could say the same." She looked over to see the doctor watching her thoughtfully. "How is he, really?"

"Better. He's going to be pretty sore but he'll make it."

She smiled at Juan "I'm glad to hear that."

The doctor stood. "I'm going to stretch my legs. Why don't you have a seat?"

"Thank you."   She stretched out her hand.   "Talia Blackmoor."

"Dr. Akio Ito. You may call me Akio."

"A pleasure and please call me Talia."

The doctor gestured toward the agent. "Feel free to answer his questions." Without another word he walked toward where the other man sat staring at a laptop.

Talia sat in the doctor's chair and turned to look at Juan. "What did he mean by that?"

"He means that I want to know how it is that we're here and I'm not dead."

"Excuse me." The doctor stood in the aisle. "I thought you might like this. I took the liberty of topping it off for you."

She accepted the wine. "Thank you."

He smirked at the agent. "You don't get any."

"I prefer beer," he replied. He looked over at her. "Spill it."

"Are you kidding? This is a nice merlot."

"Very funny, Ms. Blackmoor."

"Talia."

"What?"

"Don't you think that after everything we've been through, you could call me Talia?"

"Not until you call me Jorge."

"You mean Juan, don't you?"

She almost laughed at the look he sent toward the front of the plane. "Les didn't tell me your name."

He studied her before speaking. "I'm afraid you have me at a loss, Ms. Blackmoor, since I was unconscious when you were dealing with Ju. Would you please explain what it is that we've been through together?"

Tamping down her disappointment at his refusal to use her first name, she tilted her head. "Very well. Since you said please." She took a deep breath but he interrupted her before she could begin.

"Are you a spy?"

"What?"

"I know your file says you are a neuro-bioethicist, but you've had training."

"What makes you so certain?"

"Because we're here and I'm not dead."

"I'm not a spy."

Wine sloshed as the plane hit a patch of turbulence. The pilot instructed them to buckle their seatbelts. After a few minutes the flight smoothed out.

"But you've had training."

"I've had some intense self-defense training, yes."

She'd had more than that but he didn't need to know.

"Why?"

"Because I lived in New York."

"That's not the whole story but I'll leave it for the moment. What happened with Ju?"

She related the details of the attack. "I'm sorry I couldn't warn you sooner."

"It was enough. When I heard you gasp I turned. Between the angle and the bullet proof vest I had on, the dart glanced off the skin. Only a small amount of poison penetrated. I owe you my life. Thank you."

"I'll be right back."

She handed him the wine glass and went to retrieve her waist pack. She smiled when he handed her an empty glass.

"Would you like some more?"

"You aren't worried Akio will frown at you?"

She reached into the pack. "If I was intimidated by frowns I would have never left the coffee plantation with you." She glanced toward the front of the plane. The two men were deep in discussion. "Here."

Juan tried to ignore the warmth of her fingers as she deposited a few small objects into his hands. The feathery motion sent an electrical jolt up his arm. Rolling his shoulders to cover the shiver, he examined what she'd given him.

"Those were in Ju's pockets," she supplied.

He stared.

"What?"

He looked up the aisle to where Les and Akio were laughing over something. "Does he know you brought these to show me?"

"He doesn't even know about them," she said placidly.

"You mean you took these from her? When?"

"After she was dead."

Juan wasn't sure what shocked him more, that the research scientist had had the presence of mind to rifle through the dead agent's pockets or that she talked about it as if it was no more than buying a Hallmark card.

"I thought you might want to know who she was."

"How did you know she wasn't working with me?"

"When you asked her where we were going I knew you were no longer in control of the situation."

"I was always in control of the situation," he snapped.

She smirked. "Yes, I can see that."

"What happened after you rifled through her pockets?"

"I shoved everything into my pack and went over to see if you were breathing. Before I could determine what had happened, Les had come up and pressed a gun to my head."

"Did he identify himself?"

"Only as military police. I figured he was sent by airport security and he had the gun so I didn't do anything other than to put my hands in the air."

"That wasn't all you did."

She looked over to see Les standing nearby. He smiled at Juan.

"How are you feeling?"

"Not bad."

"He just got out of the hospital a few months ago, you know."

"No," Talia replied, looking at Juan, "I didn't."

"What else did she do?" Juan asked, wanting to change the subject.

The other agent plucked one of the items out of his lap before answering. "She insisted we provide immediate medical attention," he murmured, examining the small black device. He glanced over at the research scientist. "She told me you were from the Chilean consulate and I'd better get an ambulance or I would be responsible for an international incident."

He set the device back and picked up the small phone. He looked over at Talia. "You got these off Ju?"

"I did."

"Interesting," he murmured.

"Interesting doesn't begin to explain it," Akio said, walking up. "I've gotten word from your benefactor, Ms. Blackmoor. The package is safe."

The silence in the small area was thick enough to cut. Talia ignored Juan's eyes boring into her and considered. She had absolutely no reason to trust anyone other than Juan and even that was tenuous. She'd only given him the benefit of the doubt because *her benefactor* insisted she could trust him.

It had nothing to do with captivating eyes that steadily returned her gaze. Nothing.

She looked at the men standing. Akio may be caring for Juan's health and Les may have gotten them out of Hong Kong, but it remained to be seen if they were out of trouble.

"Where is it?" she asked, finally.

"It's waiting to be picked up."

"Did he mention -?"

"He did. We're on our way."

"I don't understand. He told me it was in Hong Kong, at the airport."

"This may help?"

The doctor handed her a transport slip.

"May I?"

After reading it she handed the paper to Juan.

"So, it was moved?" He looked at Les. "When was she going to be informed of this?"

He shrugged. "When Osiro didn't check in, Brightman had it moved to Tokyo."

"One of my associates is with it now," the doctor explained, "safe guarding it."

"Where?" Juan asked.

"Misawa Air Base"

Located in the Aomori Prefecture in the Tohoku region of Japan, Misawa Air Base was a US military facility. Housing the US Navy, Army, and Air Force as well as the Japanese

Self-Defense Force, it was the only combined, joint service installation in the Western Pacific.

Talia closed her eyes in defeat. "The US government has it?"

"I'm sure they don't know what it is they have," the doctor replied.

"Isn't Misawa near Fukushima?" Juan asked.

"We won't be there longer than the time it takes to load the package and take off again."

The pilot asked the passengers to return to their seats and prepare for landing. Talia stood, glanced at Juan. "I thought you said you didn't have a private jet?" Without waiting for a reply, she went to sit down.

Juan couldn't help but smile at Talia's words. Damn if he wasn't enjoying himself.

Akio secured the empty wine glass before strapping himself into a seat opposite the gurney.

"Why don't I get a seat?"

"Your wheels are locked and you are securely attached to the plane."

"I'd rather -."

"Do not worry, you will be up and about soon enough." The plane shook as they passed through turbulence. As they began their descent they hit an air pocket.

Juan sucked air through his teeth. The force of being pushed against the belts holding him to the gurney was causing intense pain as it pressed on fresh scars. He closed his eyes and grit his teeth.

"I'll give you something for the pain when we land."

"No," he ground out. 'No more drugs."

They touched down and began taxiing. The pilot apologized for the rough landing and applied the brakes.

"Why did we stop?"

The doctor unbuckled himself and stood. He leaned over and began undoing the straps. "I need your bed."

"What?" He glanced over to where the research scientist was talking to Les. Judging by the look on her face, he guessed she had just received some shocking news. He looked at Akio. "The package?"

"Yes, we need it on board. It is going right here."

"What is it?"

"You will see."

He would have looked back at the research scientist but Akio was blocking his view. "Give me your hand. I need to get you over to that last row. You can lay across the empty seats."

"We're not getting off the plane?"

"No."

"Where are we going?"

"To deliver the package."

"Excuse me, Akio." Les moved past them, jostling Juan's injuries in the process. "Sorry about that."

"Right," he grit out.

"Are you sure you don't want something for pain?"

"No!" He blew out a breath. "I'm sorry. No. I hate the way that shit makes me feel."

"I understand. Can you get yourself settled in? I'm afraid I need to assist Les with the -."

"I can help him," Talia offered from where she stood in the aisle.

"Excellent, thank you." He went back to where Les was directing the loading of the package.

"I don't need any help," he hissed.

She stepped forward and took a hold of his arm. "Yes, you do."

He tried to jerk away but only succeeded in causing himself more pain.

"Would you swallow your damned pride and let me help you? It's obvious you're in a lot of pain."

He bit down on a reply and allowed her to help him lay across the seats, his back to the window. She shoved several small pillows behind him and set a blanket in his lap.

If Juan hadn't been so curious about their package he might have been looking in a different direction and missed the subtle change in Talia's posture as she stiffened. He thought he heard a gasp but with all the noise the men loading the package were making, he couldn't be sure. What he was sure of was that all the blood had drained from her face. She swayed and he could have sworn he heard her whisper a name. *Kyle.*

He reached out and took her arm to keep her from falling. Or fainting. Because he was trying to avoid further injuring himself his movements were clumsy. In the end she fell on top of him.

"Shit," he hissed as her elbow landed between his legs.

"Juan, I'm sorry." She tried to push off of him but only managed to land in the tiny space between the rows.

"Akio?" Juan called. "A little help here."

Les walked over and hauled her, none too gently, to her feet. "They need you."

"Wait a minute -." Juan called but they had already walked away. He tried to situate himself so that he could see what was going on but it was futile. Several men in fatigues blocked his view of the rear of the plane. He may not be able to see what was going on but he could certainly hear.

"Oh, Kyle, what have they done to you?"

He frowned. *Kyle? The package was a man?*

Swiping at her eyes, Talia knelt by the gurney. A handful of men wearing army uniforms towered over her. Two of them were securing straps to the gurney and two others were securing carts upon which equipment rested. Akio pressed a stethoscope to the man's chest and another doctor shone a light into his eyes.

The uniformed men continued working with the doctors to secure everything. After several minutes, all but a few who were heavily armed exited the plane.

Les helped one of the men secure the rear door before returning to the front. Two armed officers took up posts, one at the back and the other in the aisle across from Juan. A third man stood near the cockpit.

"Ma'am? I need you to return to your seat until we're in the air and the pilot has reached cruising altitude."

She considered arguing with the young man but one glance at Akio and she relented. Juan called to her as she walked by but she ignored him. It was all she could do to breathe.

She managed to get herself to her seat and buckle herself in. She stared out the window.

Something tickled her face. She jerked her head around to find Les holding out a handkerchief. Snatching it she turned away and let the tears fall.

Oh, Kyle.

"Turner!" Juan yelled. "When we're at cruising altitude you'd better get your ass back here!"

The man across from her smirked into his laptop. He glanced over at her. "You gonna be okay?"

Not trusting her voice she turned and watched the ground disappear beneath them. Knowing there was nothing to be done until they were at cruising altitude, she focused on breathing in and out. She couldn't help Kyle if she was unconscious and as light-headed as she felt, she didn't think she was too far from it.

What in the hell had happened?

The moment the pilot started talking she yanked the seatbelt open. She jumped out of the seat only to collide with one of the men in uniform. The apology she was about to give died on her lips at his expression. Compassion, and understanding.

You cannot come apart.

Not now.

Not ever.

Willing the tears away, she ruthlessly shoved her emotions deep inside and fought not to hyperventilate.

"I'll take you back, ma'am."

Her eyes on the officer's back, she stalked past Juan without saying a word. The doctor helped her into a seat next to the gurney.

"May I introduce my associate? Dr. Keiji Nara, neurosurgeon."

She shook the man's hand and smiled weakly. "This comes as a bit of a shock. I – I had no idea -."

"We understand," Dr. Nara replied.

In spite of her best efforts, she began to cry. "What happened to him?"

"He was taken by force."

She nodded. She'd known he would never have willfully betrayed her.

"Why is he like that?"

"He wasn't a very cooperative hostage and I'm afraid they punished him."

"Punished him? Punished him how?"

"They induced a stroke. The damage was extensive, I'm afraid."

"How did he get here? Why is here?"

"I do not have all the details. I was the doctor on call when he was brought to the hospital. I checked him into the intensive care unit and contacted the US embassy. They sent someone to investigate and a short time later he was moved to the military base. I was asked to remain with him."

"By who?"

"By a Tim Brightman."

"My boss?"

She looked up to see Juan leaning against the rear wall. He looked very pale.

"I don't think you should be standing," Akio said, guiding him back to his seat. He looked at the soldier sitting across from him. "Please make sure he remains here. If he falls on the other patient it will probably kill him."

The young officer acknowledged by lowering his weapon slightly. Juan got the message. He didn't like it but he sat down.

CHAPTER 12

~~~~~~

Talia looked back at Dr. Nara. "Do you work for the embassy? Or the military?"

"I do not. All the communications went through the embassy. I accompanied Dr. LeMonde to Misawa and have been caring for him while arrangements were made to locate you."

"How long ago did this happen?"

"Two weeks."

She pointed to the prototype. "How did you get that?"

"I did not."

"Ms. Blackmoor?"

She looked up at Les.

"If you would join me up front I may be able to provide you with some of the answers you need." He glanced at the two men. "That is, if you don't need her here."

"No, she is free to go."

"Can Juan come with us?" She looked at Akio. "I heard him say Brightman was his boss and I -."

"He can go."

The soldier followed them forward.

"Thanks," Juan said, taking the seat next to her.

"You're welcome." She looked over at Les. "Talk."

"Your benefactor -."

"Who is that?" Juan asked.

"It's not important," she snapped.

"The hell it isn't -."

"I said it's not important, Juan."

He fumed but kept quiet.

"Your benefactor reached out to my boss."

"So, you work for this Tim Brightman also?"

"I do. He reached out to my boss and asked if we could bring you in."

Why hadn't Christoff reached out to her directly? She knew he bore no love for the arrogance of western nations. She couldn't imagine what motivated him to contact the US Embassy.

No.

He'd contacted Tim Brightman. The man might work at the embassy, but he was not just an administrator. She looked over at Juan.

"Did you know why Tim wanted to talk to me?"

"No, I don't know why he wanted to talk to you." He jerked a thumb toward the rear of the plane. "Who is that?"

"My former research partner."

"He was working with you on that brain wave machine?"

"I thought you said you didn't know why Brightman wanted to talk to me."

"I don't. I know what you did for a living. Before you were fired, that is."

One side of her mouth went up. *Fired, eh?*

"Why did this guy care, this Tim Brightman?"

"He is plugged into the military," Les answered. "The US government doesn't look kindly on the idea of another nation stealing our biotechnology."

"So, they wanted him to get the machine? I couldn't have helped him with that. I didn't know where it was."

"Your benefactor had someone else working on recovering the machine. Mr. Brightman was bringing you in for his own personal reasons."

Talia dragged a hand over her face. Too many missing pieces.

"Is it possible Brightman knows your colleague?" Juan asked. "What's his name?"

"Kyle. Dr. Kyle LeMonde." She shook her head. "As to whether or not he knew your boss, I have no idea. I guess anything's possible."

"Les, could I talk with Ms. Blackmoor alone?"

"Only if you call me by my first name," she snapped.

Juan smiled. "I would like to talk with you alone, Talia. Please?"

She glanced at Les, nodded.

"I'll go talk to the pilot, get our ETA."

Juan leaned closer, lowered his voice. "I have a few theories if you're interested."

"I would appreciate that very much."

"Answer one thing first. You weren't expecting that guy, were you?"

It was obvious to him the unexpected shock hadn't worn off.

She shook her head. "I was told I was to pick up the prototype."

"This benefactor of yours knows Dr. LeMonde, correct?"

"Sure. We all know each other very well."

"Is he another researcher?"

She looked at him in silence. Her benefactor may have asked her to trust this man but as far as she knew, he hadn't had any direct contact with him. It was probably best if she said little about his identity.

"I can find out, through my own channels. After all, he reached out to my boss."

"He's a researcher. We weren't working on the same project, though."

"Were you competitors?"

"No. In fact, we sometimes cooperated. We also hooked up at conferences and through various academic programs." She smiled. "When you get to that level of specialization, the community of researchers becomes incredibly small."

"How small?"

"I don't know what you're asking."

"Small enough that there are only a few elite members?"

"Yeah, I guess you could say that."

She wondered if he was comparing it to the group he was in, the group that he worked for, headed by Tim Brightman.

'That certainly narrows down the suspects, doesn't it?"

"I suppose you could look at it that way." She glanced toward the rear of the plane. "It sounds like they know who did this, though."

"Do you know?"

"I haven't been told who they are but I know they are Asian."

Christoff had told her that much.

"Chinese or South Korean."

She looked at him in surprise. "Yes, that's right."

"Okay, so your benefactor cares about your colleague, and about the project not falling into the wrong hands. For whatever reason."

She knew the reason but didn't think it was necessary to share that with Juan. Not at this point, anyhow.

"He probably reached out to my boss after your colleague had been hurt."

"My colleague's name is Kyle."

"So, that did mean something to you."

"Is this about your wounded ego because I didn't behave like you expected?"

His eyes widened but he didn't respond. He looked over to where Les was chatting with the armed soldier standing near the cockpit, then back at her. "Forget it. Okay, so he finds out your colleague has been kidnapped, harmed, and reaches out to Tim to bring you in before the same thing happened to you."

"Then why not go through the embassy in Costa Rica?"

"Because Tim doesn't work in Costa Rica."

She recalled what she'd read about Tim and the members of his organization.

Christoff's words came back to her.

"I want you to know that I have called in every favor owed to me in order to put the best of the best on this."

"I wonder how they got the machine?" she murmured.

"Les said your benefactor put someone else on that. I'd say they were successful. Any idea who is behind this?"

"There's a company. It's one of those new Chinese hybrids, where the Chinese government tries to convince the world they're progressive, allowing people to own a business?"

Juan nodded.

"A couple of years ago, they reached out to Kyle and me at a conference in Europe and tried to lure us away. To work for them. We both refused."

"Who reached out to you, the Chinese government or people from this company?"

'As far as I'm concerned it's one and the same given the government was bankrolling the research. Anyway, we refused."

"Based on current events, I'd say that didn't go over too well."

"They got to our supervisor. Blackmail or bribe, who knows? All I know is that he came to me and told me I was being transferred to Beijing."

"And Kyle?"

"I, uh -." She took a deep breath. "I never got the chance to talk to him about it."

"Okay, so your boss tells you you're being transferred and you tell him no?"

"Sure, you could say that."

She'd told her manager, in no uncertain terms, to go to hell. She also told him she knew the truth; that he was selling out to the Chinese, and she planned to go to the authorities with that knowledge. He'd responded by threatening to hurt people very close to her. So, she'd run.

"So, you ran."

"Well, it wasn't that simple. He told me that Kyle had already agreed. I didn't believe him but he told me that he'd been persuasive."

Which meant they'd threatened Kyle in the same manner they'd threatened her.

"Then you ran."

"Not exactly. Running implies quitting and going to another company or something. I knew that would never be enough. I knew that they would come after me unless they thought I was dead."

"You were easy enough to find."

"You were looking for me. They had no reason to. They thought I was dead."

"How did you do it?"

"My benefactor."

A year before the Chinese company had approached her in Europe, Christoff had flown to New York for a medical research conference. He'd asked her and Kyle to join him and his sister for dinner where he proceeded to tell them he'd gotten word that a Chinese company wanted their project.

"Well, they can't have it," she'd replied. Kyle had reached over and taken her hand.

"I don't think you understand," he said quietly.

"Indeed," Christoff had agreed. "This is not a corporate takeover. The Chinese government is behind this."

"The Chinese government? Then we'll just go to our government."

Kyle had exchanged a long look with Christoff. *"Talia, do you think we'd be allowed to continue our research if DC gets wind of this? They'd appropriate it and we'd be removed."*

"But it's our project! It's our work!"

"If they felt it could be used as a political bargaining chip we would lose it."

"Kyle, it's not like we're talking about an espresso machine. They can't just put an engineer on it and call it a day. They need us."

"My dear," Christoff had countered, *"while your work has been considerable, there are a number of others around the globe who could pick up where you two left off."*

"Not to mention," Chloe had put in, *"you're assuming the US government wouldn't turn it over to the Chinese anyway, in return for something else."*

That was the day her innocence had died. In more ways than one.

Kyle had seen how devastated she was by the news. He'd quietly thanked the siblings for coming to them in private and hailed a taxi. Normally, when she was upset Kyle would have made jokes or in some other way tried to cheer her. His silence on the ride to their hotel had been greatly appreciated.

He'd procured a bottle of wine and suggested they drink it upstairs. Not wanting to be around people or noise, she'd readily agreed. Once in her room, however, rather than pouring the wine, he'd pulled her into an awkward embrace in an attempt to comfort her.

Somewhere, in the middle of holding her, his lips had found hers. Fingers that had been rubbing her back slid beneath her blouse, unhooking her bra. A tongue that had been whispering comforting words slid first into her mouth, then down her skin. Following the slick trail, his fingers found their way between her legs where he stroked her first gently, then with growing speed and force until she'd come in his arms.

One moment he was holding her trembling body and the next he was wonderfully, comfortingly, inside of her. Feelings of pain and betrayal had warred with passion and a need to drive the hurt out at any cost. In the end, the need for comfort won out and she gave herself to him with abandon, taking as much pleasure as she gave.

"Ma'am?"

Swiping at her eyes, Talia smiled up at one of the officers.

"I was asked to give this to you. Dr. Nara and Dr. Ito asked that you read it carefully."

She accepted a manila folder.

"Sir? I was asked to escort you back to your seat."

Her feelings raw from the memory, Talia was only too happy to be away from Juan's scrutiny. When he looked ready to protest she encouraged him to go lay down.

"You need to recover and I need to read some pretty chewy stuff." When he continued to hesitate she smiled. "I'll update you later."

Waiting until the agent was back in his seat gave her time to push the remnants of the memory away. Ripping open old wounds wasn't going to help. If she wanted a life of peace, she had to keep her face turned to the future, not the past. Blowing out a sigh she opened the folder and began to read.

My dearest Natalia,

I am sorry I wasn't able to tell you about Kyle. His condition dictated that I wait until confirming he was stable and by then you were on your way to Hong Kong.

I have included scans for you to examine. I imagine you will see, as I do, the potential to help your beloved Kyle. More than anyone, you are in a position to speed his recovery.

Surely, he didn't mean for her to use the prototype? It was months, if not years away from being ready for trials.

I have taken steps to ensure your safety and to keep the prototype from falling into the wrong hands. I will contact you soon with next steps. Until then

Christoff

"Buckle your seatbelt and prepare for landing."

Les had explained they would be landing in Hawaii long enough to refuel and take on a new crew before proceeding to Santiago. Knowing there was nothing to do but wait, she began looking over Kyle's brain scans.

When the sounds of raised voices began, she didn't look up. Assuming some maintenance guy was yelling in order to be heard over airport noise, she continued reading. It was only as she was being yanked from her seat at gunpoint that she realized something was horribly wrong.

The soldier pulled her to the service station just behind the cockpit and shoved her to the floor. He positioned himself so that he was in front of her, gun at the ready. She craned her neck in an effort to see what was happening, only to find herself pushed back.

"For your safety, ma'am."

The sounds of fighting carried easily in the relatively small cabin. She heard a grunt. Juan? God, she hoped not. Hadn't he been through enough?

"Clear!"

The soldier stood but gestured for her to remain where she was. He turned. "You can stand but remain behind the wall until I tell you otherwise."

Talia's heart pounded. Was Juan okay? She knew he'd been hired to keep her safe but she hated the idea he might have been badly hurt in the process of doing so.

Agent Turner poked his head around the wall. "Be just a minute, Dr. Blackmoor. We're getting you off through the front."

"Is -?" She was talking to thin air.

Two soldiers escorted her to the front door where a ladder had been wheeled up. She looked to the rear of the plane. A small group clustered around two bodies on the asphalt.

"Please don't be Juan," she whispered. She continued to pray silently as she followed an armed soldier over.

"Let me through!" she snapped, shoving him aside. "Oh, Juan."

He was looking in her direction but she doubted he was really seeing her. His eyes were glazed over with pain and he looked to be having difficulty breathing.

Two marines were guiding Kyle's gurney down a ramp.

"Dr. Blackmoor?"

She looked up to see a tall man with black hair standing at her side.

"There's been a change in plan. My wife and I are going to escort you and Dr. LeMonde to a safe location."

"What about Juan? We can't leave him here!"

"These men have been instructed to look after Agent Hernandez."

"No! I don't want to be separated from him!"

On the ground, Juan struggled to sit up. She moved forward but a soldier stepped in front of her.

"Get out of my way! I need to help him!"

"The doctors will take care of him, ma'am. Our orders are to get you and Dr. LeMonde to a safe location. Please follow me."

She could hear Juan calling her name.

"Juan! Find Christoff! Find him! My benefactor! Find -!" She stared in horror. "Dr. Ito, no!"

The doctor injected something into Juan's arm. He went limp and would have fallen if one of the soldiers hadn't caught him.

"Ma'am? I need you to follow me."

She stood frozen.

"Ma'am? We would prefer not to sedate you. Please follow me."

She reluctantly followed the man, stopping briefly to look over her shoulder at the group standing over Juan. A petite blonde was yelling at her. In Spanish.

"Todo va a estar bien!"

It's going to be alright.

CHAPTER 13

The sound of voices broke through the haze and Juan opened his eyes, blinking to clear his vision.

"You're awake. How do you feel?"

"Andrews?"

Sean shook the agent's hand and smiled. "It's good to see you."

"How -?" He tried to sit up but couldn't.

"You're restraints," Sean explained. "Let me get the nurse."

"Nurse?" He looked around in confusion. "Where are we?"

"Just a minute." He left the room.

"Are you in much pain?"

"Kian? What's going on? Where are we?"

"You're in Talca."

"*Chile?*"

She nodded and leaned over him. "I'll be careful not to jolt the IV tube but I think you'll be more comfortable if I undo these."

She reached out and unbuckled the black straps holding him down. "I don't know why someone didn't undo these when they rolled you in here." She looked at him. "You don't remember anything, do you?"

"I remember landing in Hawaii for refueling."

"There was an incident."

'An incident? What type of incident?"

"I can explain," Sean said, walking up. "But how about we let the nurse take a look at you first. Kian and I will be in the hall."

"My name is Maria," the nurse said in Spanish.

"I'm Juan."

She smiled. "I know who you are, Agent Hernandez," she replied, switching to English. "I'm glad to see you awake."

"I feel dizzy."

"That's what's left of the sedative, I'm afraid. Dr. Ito was concerned about the amount of pain you were in and Dr. Nara said it wasn't dangerous, just powerful. I think it was too much."

"How long have I been out?"

"For the better part of thirty-six hours."

"Shit."

She began changing the IV bag. "I'm going to keep this in until the dizziness is gone." She took his vital signs and his temperature. "Can I get you anything?"

"A glass of water would be good."

She rolled a table over and poured water into a Styrofoam cup. "When you're not feeling dizzy I will give you a glass."

"I'm not that dizzy," he snapped, then proceeded to spill the water.

"Pride may be a bitter pill, Agent Hernandez, but you would be well served by swallowing it and allowing people to help you once in awhile."

"I'll take that under advisement," he replied in the tone of a petulant boy.

She patted his arm. "If there's nothing else, I'll let your friends in. I know they're eager to bring you up to date."

"No, there's nothing else." He watched her walk to the door. "Maria?"

She turned.

"Thank you for your help."

She smiled. "You're welcome, Agent Hernandez. I hope you're feeling better soon."

"Andrews, get in here."

"He's on the phone, but he'll be in in a minute."

"Kian, what are you two doing here?"

"Tim called us."

"You don't work for Tim."

"In this case, that's a good thing." She looked at the IV bag thoughtfully. "Do you think you could get off that gurney? I ask because there's a bed over there and I think you'd be a lot more comfortable in it. I'll carry the bag and you can lean on me. If you want, you can wait for Sean."

"No, I think I can do it if you help me."

"Of course." She picked up the bag which had been laid on his stomach. "Why don't you try sitting up first and let the wave of dizziness pass. We'll take it from there."

"How far is the bed?"

"That much fun, huh?" She smiled, pointed. "About a six foot walk. Do you think you can do that? Why don't you put your feet on the floor?"

"The damned thing is moving!" he yelped, grasping for her arm.

"No, it's not. The wheels are locked. I'm not going to let you fall but if you want to get this stuff out of your system, you have to get your circulation going."

"Okay" Sean said, walking up. "We're all set."

"We are?"

He stopped in front of the agent. "Can you stand?"

"Swallowing my pride is one thing. Leaning on you is -."

"Don't be silly," Kian said, laughing, "we're both helping you. Wouldn't you do it for him?"

He grabbed Sean's forearm and thrust himself up by sheer willpower. He weaved then stumbled. Sean wisely kept from doing more than standing steady.

After a few minutes the room stopped spinning. "I think I can do it now."

Sean stepped to the side. Kian held his left hand as he took first one step, then two. He stopped at the edge of the bed. "I don't want to lie down again."

"Why don't you sit then? Sean, pull that chair up and let him have it."

Juan grit his teeth and let Sean guide him into a chair.

"I'll take the bed. Kian, you can sit in that other chair."

"Where are we?" Juan asked once everyone had settled down. Kian smiled.

"You don't recognize the place?"

He looked around, frowned. "Should I?"

"The love nest?"

"The cabin with the heart shaped bed?"

Years prior, Juan had been assigned to protect Sean Andrews as he traveled throughout South America. The pretense had been a business trip but in reality they were trying to infiltrate an international crime syndicate. While in Panama, the two men had been taken hostage. Kian and her sister Kaila had inadvertently been caught when they'd flown down from Silicon Valley thinking they were going to install software at a customer site.

The group had been moved to a cabin in the mountains near Talca, Chile. While the syndicate leader was deciding their fate, Sean's best friend Dan Foster, along with an extended team that had included Juan, rescued the three remaining hostages, capturing the leaders in the process.

Sean and Kian now owned the cabin which had once been used as a love nest, complete with a heart shaped bed and a sunken Jacuzzi in the bedroom. He also recalled some interesting bathroom art.   After serious renovation work, they'd turned it into their South American headquarters.

"That bed was the first to go," Sean lamented, "followed by the tile work." He shook his head. "Pity really."

"Spare me," Kian snapped. "Juan, seriously. How are you feeling?"

"A little less dizzy."

"What do you remember?"

"Being on the plane. What incident?"

"One of the men overseeing the refueling of the plane was an operative," she replied, "for the bad guys."

Sean picked up the story. "He came aboard, guns blazing. You launched yourself at him, saving Drs. LeMonde, Nara, and Ito."

"Unfortunately," Kian began but Juan interrupted.

"What happened to Talia? Is she alright?"

"She's fine. The soldiers and the other agent protected her and got the situation under control."

"Where is she? Where are they? The doctors, I mean."

"We don't know," Kian replied. A little too quickly, he thought but he let it go. For now.

"Why am I here?"

"The guy," Sean started, "the operative? He took you down pretty quickly."

Kian sighed. "Sean."

"Sorry. That probably sounded bad. The guy was a master in some sort of Asian fighting. You were already hurt from the poison dart, not to mention recovering from being shot. When you jumped at the guy, you bought critical time for the soldiers to secure the situation, but you paid for it. I understand the operative knew right where to attack, which means he'd had detailed information about your injuries. Including the one you sustained in Hong Kong."

"Someone sold us out," Juan growled.

Sean nodded, his expression grave.

"Which is why we're here," Kian put in. "After Tim's agent in Hong Kong didn't check in, he knew something was wrong."

"He's dead, right?"

She nodded. "I'm afraid so. They found his body in the trunk of a car at the airport, not far from where you were shot with the poison dart."

Ju. The woman must have been responsible for Osiro's death.

"He sent Agent Turner to provide backup while he made arrangements for some equipment to be airlifted by the US military to their base in Japan."

Sean continued. "After finding out that the agent in Hong Kong had been killed, Tim realized that there was a weak link somewhere. Not wanting to risk the mission he called me and -."

"He didn't exactly call you," Kian corrected.

"It's the same thing."

"No, it's not," Kian and Juan answered simultaneously.

"Why do I think getting you clearance was a mistake?" Sean said, sighing.

"You're not in Special Forces anymore," she replied, "so you can throw that need to know shit out." She turned to Juan. "Tim called Kaila who -."

"Well, if you're going to be exact, he called Dan Foster."

"Foster?"

Kian glared at her husband. Her sister's relationship with Dan Foster was a point of contention between Agents Foster and Hernandez. That Sean had brought up that detail was, to say the least, in poor taste in her opinion

"Dan and Kaila were working in Malaysia. He didn't have Sean's private number. Kaila called me and I called Tim back. He wanted the use of the cabin."

"That doesn't explain why you're here."

"It does if you consider that the Chilean government often uses this little cabin," Sean explained. "Because Kian and I own it and come down here for business, we were given levels of clearance. Well," he added, "I still had mine but I suggested Kian get a certain level since she came down here without me sometimes. In case anything happened."

He sighed heavily. "Hey Andrews? Can we swap places?"

Kian rushed over to help him into bed.

"We'll talk more after you've slept."

"I didn't say I wanted sleep," he protested. "I just felt as if I was going to throw up. Damned dizziness."

"I think if you ate something it might help."

"Kian's right. The food will absorb what's left of that stuff in your system."

He nodded and she ran out.

"Tim had a message for you."

"Why didn't he give it to me himself?"

"Because I was on the phone with him and he asked me to pass it along."

"What is it?"

"You're mission is complete. As of now you are on leave."

"For how long?"

"Six months."

Given Juan's expression, Sean decided it was best not to comment. He recognized fury when he saw it. Damned pride. The man had been injured several times in the line of duty. His body needed to heal. But Sean also understood the need to drive oneself forward. He suspected Juan's anger came from the way things had wound down.

"You did your duty," he said finally. "The assignment was completed. Tim said you fulfilled your objective and the case is closed."

"Thanks, man."

Sean had spent enough time around the agent to know that wasn't the end of it, but he kept his thoughts to himself. Not one for small talk, he was grateful when Kian returned with a plate of food.

"Lots of meals have been shared in this room," she said, placing the plate on his lap. "But this is better than the egg dishes, trust me."

"I thought you liked my omelet," Sean complained.

"Your omelet was fine. Fuente's gun aimed at my head? Not so much. Not my idea of a balanced breakfast."

Juan chuckled. She sat across from him.

He pointed a fork at her. "Where's yours?"

"We ate earlier."

"Listen," Sean said, walking toward the door. "I gotta go make a few phone calls."

For several minutes the two friends sat in companionable silence. Juan wolfed down the steak, potatoes, and carrots, then wiped out the blueberry pie. He wiped his mouth, set the plate away and stared at the beautiful blonde.

"Spill it."

"Look," she began, "I took the test and went through the lectures but I don't go for this macho bullshit spy stuff."

"Right."

"I was there, Juan. I was there when the plane landed."

"Where?"

"In Hawaii."

"Maybe you'd better start at the beginning?"

"After the incident in Hong Kong, Tim scrambled to assemble a team off the radar. The plan was that while the military transported Dr. LeMonde to a hospital in Chile, Sean and I would get you and Dr. Blackmoor to Santiago in a private jet."

"Okay."

"I don't know what happened on that plane in Hawaii. I mean I know what I was told, but even I know better than to believe a man with a gun aimed at people I care about."

"Meaning me."

"Yeah, you were under guard. You didn't want to be separated from the research assistant."

"Okay."

She let out a breath. "I tried to talk to them but then the guns were turned on me."

"Go on."

"She and Dr. LeMonde were escorted by armed soldiers. Sean and I were given orders to bring you to Talca and wait to hear from Tim. We were told not to worry about Drs. Blackmoor and LeMonde. Sean called Tim but didn't get much more than a confirmation of the new orders."

"Okay."

"Juan, I understand Spanish."

"I know this."

"Talia didn't."

"What are you saying?"

"She began yelling to you in Spanish. She didn't want to leave you. She didn't understand why you were being separated but when she made a move to get to you, the guns were turned on her. She seemed pretty frightened. Sean doesn't speak Spanish but he tried to reassure her that she was safe. I don't think she agreed."

"What did they do to her?"

"Not her, you."

"What?"

"She started yelling a name and they stuck a needle into your arm. At that point, Sean gave me the signal."

"The signal?"

"One of the first things Sean taught me, after our big adventure here in Talca, was to be able to communicate information in a way other than using speech."

"Smart, given that even coded speech can be picked up."

"Right. So we set up a code. Several, actually. Some were just for us as we rebuilt the company. Then, once we realized we would be working with various governments, in business of course, we decided to have a few signals that might come in handy."

"Sean's a smart man."

'He's Special Forces."

"Not anymore."

She snorted. "Have you ever spent the night in bed with someone who did that kind of work?"

One side of his mouth went up. "Can't say that I have. Sittin' in the mud with nothin' but eyes starin' back at you, yes. In bed with them? No."

"Seeing their eyes?"

"When you're covered in camouflage or buried in swamp water, all you can see are the eyes. Like an alligator."

"Well, as a woman who *has* spent the night next to that kind of someone, I can tell you it never shuts off. Ever."

He pushed the comment aside.

"Sean sent me the signal to stand down."

He laughed. "Stand down?"

"Look, even I could see that we were a hair's breadth from being arrested. I let it go. Sort of."

"Sort of."

"I yelled, in Spanish, that it would all work out. I promised."

"What are you talking about?"

"She wanted you to find someone named Christoff."

He grunted. "Her benefactor."

"I don't know. I just know that I saw more anguish in that woman's eyes than I'll forget anytime soon." She looked at the doorway, back at the man in the bed. "Maybe I'm overstepping my bounds but I think you should know something."

He smiled. "Sounds like you've broken enough rules. What's another?"

"She cares for you. A lot. I could see it in her eyes"

Kian stood, grabbed the plate, walked to the door. She turned and looked directly at him.

"No decepcionaria," she said.

Don't let her down.

CHAPTER 14

Tim put a hand on the research scientist's shoulder and shook it gently. "Ms. Blackmoor?"

The pretty woman lifted her head and looked around in confusion.

"I'm Tim Brightman. We met yesterday. Do you remember?"

"Briefly," she answered, unsuccessfully stifling a yawn. As if suddenly remembering where she was, she jolted. "Kyle?"

He squeezed her shoulder. "He's fine. I promise."

She blinked, looked up at him.

"Who are you?"

"I'm Tim Brightman."

Juan's boss.

"Where is Juan?"

"Home, recovering."

He saw that she wanted to say more but refrained.

Interesting.

"Where's Kyle?"

"He's across the hall. A physician's assistant is with him."

"A physician's assistant?"

"His condition is stable, Ms. Blackmoor. The doctor is sleeping."

"Dr. Nara or Ito?"

"Neither. I had them dismissed."

"I see."

"Would you join me for dinner?"

"What?"

"I thought we might talk over dinner?"

"I'd like to see Kyle."

"Of course. We aren't going anywhere. There's a chef on the premises. Why don't you have a shower and then -?"

"A shower?"

He suspected she wasn't quite awake. "Just a minute." He walked across the room and picked up a phone. After speaking briefly he returned. "I've asked for some coffee to be sent up."

"Where am I?"

"You and Dr. LeMonde are in a safe house in the United States. We have a lot to discuss but I think you'll feel better after a shower and some food. I've got a few phone calls to make but I'll see you at dinner. Say, in about an hour? In the meantime, the bathroom's through there. Dr. LeMonde is across the hall. Dinner is on the veranda but I'll send someone to bring you out."

Tim nodded to the security guard posted outside her room before making his way to an office on the first floor. Shutting the door he sat down, turned on his laptop, and picked up the receiver.

"Mr. Brightman?"

"Yes, Dr. Andris. I wanted you to know that Dr. LeMonde and Dr. Blackmoor are safe."

A sigh of relief came through clearly. "Thank you. How is Talia?"

"As you might expect. I'll be honest with you, Dr., I'd feel a hell of a lot better if I could be more forthcoming."

"I understand, believe me, but I think it's in everyone's best interest at this point if you only share what is absolutely necessary, which in this case is all about Dr. LeMonde's recovery and nothing more."

Tim wasn't quite sure how to respond. It didn't sit well with him but he wasn't exactly on firm footing. He'd been brought into this situation only recently and didn't have enough information to push any sort of agenda. Other than the one already agreed to, that is.

"I understand," he said finally.

"And you know I prefer that my name is kept out of this."

"Yes, I understand that as well."

"Excellent. We have an agreement. I expect it to be kept."

"I gave you my word."

"Very good then. Good night."

Not wanting to think too long on his agreement, Tim checked his email, smiling at the name on the top one. He opened it.

Juan is on the mend. He isn't happy but he isn't complaining. I'd say you'll be hearing from him soon. Sean.

Tim dealt with a handful of emails that couldn't wait, made a few phone calls, and got an update on Kyle's condition. Satisfied, he locked the door and went out to the veranda.

Surrounded by a forest, the oversized deck off the back of the house reminded Tim of home. Closing his eyes, he inhaled deeply, the smell of pine mixing with a hint of ocean air.

The wind must be from the south.

Eyes closed, he mentally reviewed recent events.

The decision to involve Sean Andrews had been an easy one. He wasn't on the payroll. As soon as Tim had realized there was a breach of security he'd been faced with a decision. Abort the mission or find an alternate way to see it carried out. To keep the players involved would likely bring failure and given what was at stake, that just wasn't an option.

Someone was playing both sides, selling information that had already cost the life of one agent. It was suspected Ju was responsible for his death. They were still trying to trace the woman's identity. As far as he could tell, she did not work in government espionage. A private contract, perhaps, since it was rare that corporations employed mercenaries with orders to kill.

He shouldn't have been surprised it had gotten to this point. He'd known what was at stake. But understanding motivation didn't always translate to knowing who the guilty party was. He had no idea where the weak link was and he knew if he snooped around, all the avenues would dry up.

The decision to go outside normal channels was a logical one. He was just grateful he had a qualified professional to tap as a resource. Retired from Air Force Special Forces, Sean Andrews not only had top clearance, he had an impeccable work ethic. The man was intelligent, resourceful, and most of all, trustworthy. He didn't ask too many questions and he didn't speculate. He'd also done government work before. He was perfect.

He'd been more than happy to lend a hand in a difficult situation.

"You have no idea who sold you out?" he'd asked.

"I can't make inquiries without tipping off the wrong people."

"Do you have someone outside who can ask questions?"

'Yes, but it will take time and that is something I just don't have."

"Well, I looked over the paperwork you sent and I'm able to help."

"Thanks, Andrews."

"Can I offer a bit of advice?"

"Sure."

"Find someone who can make those inquiries for you."
"Right."

Fortunately, he had someone in mind. Unfortunately, he'd had to go so far outside normal channels the answers wouldn't be coming anytime soon.

"Mr. Brightman?"

He turned. Talia Blackmoor stood just outside the sliding glass door, a look of uncertainty on her face. There were dark circles beneath her eyes.

He walked to the other side of the table, pulled out a chair. "Please, Dr. Blackmoor, have a seat. What can I get you to drink?"

"I'd really love some iced water please, and don't call me doctor. Talia will do.""

"Okay, Talia." He sat across from her. "Did you see Dr. LeMonde?"

"I did. He's stable but that's not saying much, is it?"

"I'll be honest with you, I'm not sure how to answer that."

"Where's my prototype?"

A man in a white uniform stepped onto the veranda, halting any answer. He set two salads and a basket of bread on the table.

"Can you please bring us some iced water?"

Tim waited until he left before answering.

"It's in a secure location."

"Forgive me if that doesn't leave me feeling particularly overjoyed."

"I think I understand. If it makes you feel any better, it's not in the hands of any government. Not even the US government."

She cocked her head. "You work for them."

"I don't agree with everything they do."

"Meaning?"

"Meaning that I'm not too keen on creating machines to read people's minds."

Ignoring the salad, she leaned back. "So, you know."

"I know that a database of images has been assembled. Images that were gained through scans of thousands of volunteers. These images have been converted into wave form that is then compared against the brain waves of others in an attempt to peg matches."

"I'm being honest when I tell you that the work I was doing had nothing to do with that project. I was trying to find a way to communicate with people who'd suffered brain damage, who couldn't talk but who were aware."

"By hooking them up to a machine? By providing artificial life support that may prolong their suffering? When do you decide the patient is no longer aware?"

"When I was ten years old my mother overdosed. She languished in a coma for three years before dying. At one point, not long before she passed, my uncle took me to see her. I walked up to the bed and spoke softly to her. For the longest time she just lay there. I took her hand in mine and do you know that her eyelids fluttered? For the briefest moment. I saw it. Her hand jerked in mine. The doctor told me it was some sort of reflex and that I shouldn't get my hopes up."

"Is that why you do what you do?"

"To try to save people from the kind of suffering I went through? Hell, yes. I know she never came out of it but for that moment? She was there and she reached out to a teenager who desperately needed to feel her."

She sat back as the waiter set down a glass in front of her. She sipped the cold water, waited until he disappeared back into the house.

"I never forgot that moment or what it meant to me. I returned to my uncle's farm but that moment, that subtle connection, stayed with me. I would think about it while saddling a horse or gathering eggs. I began to see that like my mother, the animals communicated in subtle ways that most people didn't pick up. But I did.

I *had a way with them* people used to say but in reality I just paid attention. I treated them as living beings and not some subservient creature put on earth to do our bidding."

She took a bite of salad.

"I assumed they could pick up on my feelings and my intentions and interacted with them as if that were true."

"Logical."

"I fell into my work with brain waves by accident but at the time it seemed like a noble cause."

"When did it change?"

"When I found out that they wanted to take my work and turn it into a weapon." She closed her eyes and fought against the memories of betrayal. Swallowing the anguish, she continued.

"They wanted to take my brain wave scans and integrate them into their mind reading database. If they could induce states of total cooperation they felt they could still retrieve data." She snorted. "*Total cooperation.* They could use drugs or other methods to render a person unconscious and still get what they wanted in terms of information." She let out a shaky breath.

Cheaper and easier than truth serum or torture, they'd told her.

"It didn't take much to see that they wanted to weaponize my work. They wanted to take something meant to heal and turn it into an implement of pain."

She swiped at her eyes. "I couldn't allow that."

"So, you destroyed the work."

"As much of it as I could."

"Dr. Andris helped you."

"He thought I was mad. He told me what I was doing would only get me killed."

"I'm surprised you weren't."

She laughed. "They'd already stolen everything and built their own prototype. I was shown a picture. They said it would take them a little longer but they could recreate it. They even suggested that in starting over they could do it better." She shook her head. "Fools."

"How does Dr. LeMonde fit in with this?"

"Kyle had worked with me. They figured if they had one of us, they didn't need the other. I had already made the decision to fake my death. Kyle was on his own."

"Did you talk to him about your plans?"

"No."

"Why not?"

Because I didn't trust him.

"Because I didn't have time."

"I take it you read the file on the plane?"

"I refuse to hook that machine up to Kyle. He is not a guinea pig. If that's what you brought me here for Mr. Brightman, you're in for a big disappointment."

"Tim."

She stared in silence. The man in the white uniform had returned to take their salad plates. He refilled her water glass and set down a bowl of soup.

"May I tell you my story?"

"Sure."

"In my line of work -."

"As a spy?"

"Yes, as a spy. We put our agents through a lot of tests. The individuals we hand pick for specific tasks are subjected to every type of scan conceivable. Each test result is evaluated by a team of no less than eight specialists. If any one of them doesn't like something they can order a retest."

Had Juan gone through that testing?

She studied Tim's mannerisms as he spoke. His hands were flat on the table but she could tell by the color differences in his skin that he was pressing the heels of his hands into the table, a definite sign of agitation.

"I noticed that some of the people became ill after being tested. I decided to go through the process myself, so I could understand what was happening."

"Couldn't you just ask?"

"You think a doctor would admit when a test was unnecessary or might cause harm to the person being tested?"

"I see."

"I made some dramatic changes in hiring practices after that. I reduced the number of tests and I eliminated any I considered too invasive."

"I'm surprised you were allowed to make that kind of decision."

"It's my group."

"Who ordered the tests originally?"

"People I trusted to advise me. Let's just say that I made changes in that as well."

"So, you brought me out here to give me a lecture on humane care for the dying? What's next, assisted suicide?"

"I brought you here to tell you that you have many people on your side. I'm one of them."

"I'm not sure what you want me to say."

"I have a proposal."

"I'm listening."

"I made a bargain. I gave the prototype to someone who feels as I do. They have sworn that it will be destroyed if you agree."

If she agreed?

"And what did you get in this bargain?"

"Dr. LeMonde."

'I don't think I understand."

"I don't want him used as a political pawn or a guinea pig. I want him to get the best medical care and have a chance to recover."

"What do you propose?"

"There is a facility in Chile. I would like to move him there. He would be safe and given a chance to recover in a more hospitable environment."

"A more hospitable environment?"

He slid a folder across the table. "Please."

There were photographs of some sort of estate surrounded by lush rain forest. The grounds looked like a nature sanctuary. Photos of the facility itself were varied. Some of them showed rooms better suited to a country cottage than a private hospital. Others, however, left no doubt that it was exactly that. Talia recognized several state of the art machines. She closed the folder and handed it back.

"So, you're showing me the demo. In the age of technology, one better be more discerning than to trust an image. They can be so easily manipulated."

He nodded, blew out a breath. "I know you have no reason to trust me, but I am being honest with you."

"Why can't you keep him here?"

"Because I can't ensure his safety."

That brought her up. For several seconds she studied him. She didn't see any indication he was being less than honest about it. *Hell.*

"But we're here now."

"This is temporary. It's off the radar, if you will."

I see."

"I can't trust people in my organization."

Was that why she'd been separated from the agent? Had Juan sold him out? The thought left her feeling a little queasy.

"In your line of work, I'd say that was a dangerous place to find yourself. Not knowing who you can trust."

A place she unfortunately knew all too well.

"It is but it's a separate issue from the one we're dealing with here."

"Seems one and the same to me."

"I pulled in someone from outside the organization to get you to safety. This house belongs to them."

"The couple at the airport?"

It had been quite a meeting.

"Yes, Sean and Kian Andrews. They were there to get nonessential parties separated from you and Dr. LeMonde."

At first she assumed he meant Agent Hernandez but she recalled his earlier comment.

The two doctors.

"Dr. Nara said you asked him to accompany Kyle."

"I only intended for him to go as far as Hawaii. I have my own physician here. As I told you before, he's asleep. He had a rather long flight."

"From where?"

"The facility in Chile. He's the chief of staff and a world renowned neurosurgeon."

"How do you know about this facility?"

"It's housed more than one of my team members."

"Is it a place they are sent to die? Like a hospice?"

"No. It's a place of recovery."

"So, what about Dr. Ito? He was caring for your agent. Surely, you trusted him."

"He is an organization doctor, true, but since the mission's security has been compromised I felt it best to get him out of the picture."

"I'm assuming you don't suspect the soldiers."

"Of course not.   They did their duty and will be appropriately commended."

"What was their duty?"

"To ensure you and Dr. LeMonde reached a safe location. I'd originally hoped to bring you to Santiago. I could have given you a tour of the facility, introduced you to Dr. Campo."

"Dr. Campo?"

"The chief of staff."

Everything tied up in a neat bow, except for one thing.

Juan.

CHAPTER 15

"So, your agent sold you out?"

"What?"

"You separated Kyle and me from people you suspected. Your agent isn't here. I have to assume he's high on your list of suspects."

"Absolutely not."

"He isn't here."

She worked to dislodge the image of him collapsing after being hit with some sort of injection.

"I was protecting him."

"He just got out of the hospital a few months ago, you know."

"Is he at that facility of yours?"

"No, though he is back in Chile. His injuries did not merit any place other than home for recovery."

"Agent Turner mentioned he'd been in the hospital recently. If that was true, why did you send him to me? Or is endangering the lives of the people who work for you SOP?"

Tim smirked. "I was given to understand that you'd spent a fair amount of time conversing with Agent Hernandez."

"So?"

"Given your background, your expertise if you will, are you going to look me in the eye and tell me that I should have told Juan to sit around and recover longer?"

She couldn't help it. She laughed. The agent was proud, no doubt. She could easily see him pressing his boss for an assignment, insisting he was just fine. The smile faded. She missed him.

"I see by your expression you understand. I was hoping that icing him for awhile would allow him to recuperate."

"I saw how frantic he was at the prospect of being separated from me. I don't know that you kept him as safe as you were hoping. Dr. Ito hit him with something and he went down like a lead balloon."

Tim nodded. "It was necessary. For Juan's own good. Sean and Kian got him back to Chile. They're with him now."

"Making sure he doesn't come up here?"

"He's been told the mission is complete. He's officially on leave."

Something told her that wouldn't matter. The man sitting across from her may think everything was in a neat bow but he failed to realize that the slightest ripple in the wind could untie it.

"How would you get Kyle to Chile? I mean how could you ensure his safety?"

"Military transport. Them I can trust."

The man in uniform handed a piece of paper to Tim.

"Ah, Dr. Campo is awake. I'd like to introduce you."

The neurosurgeon was leaning over Kyle when they walked in. He turned and smiled.

"Dr. Campo, this is Talia Blackmoor."

He extended his hand. "A pleasure to meet you, Dr. Blackmoor. I've read your papers on analyzing low level brain waves. Promising research, to be sure."

"Please, call me Talia. How is Kyle?"

"He is stable. Did you get a chance to read my report?"

"I did. You feel that with the proper care he may come out of the coma?"

"I believe we can help him. At our facility we combine the latest technology with local healing customs. What you might call alternative medicine."

"Such as?"

"Sound therapy, light therapy, prayer healing."

"Do you think I could have some time alone with him?"

"Certainly. We'll be on the veranda."

She waited until the two men were out of earshot before approaching the bed. In her years of research she'd spent plenty of time around intensive care units. She'd just never had to see someone she cared about in one. The hissing of the ventilator made her flinch. She knew the longer he was on it the more difficult it would be when they tried to remove it.

She'd seen all the reports. He was far from brain dead but the EEG had shown considerable slowdown in key areas including communication.

"Kyle? It's Talia. I'm so sorry this happened to you. You know, there's a place in South America. In Chile. It's a beautiful home. You can recover there. You can wake up." She broke. "I need you to wake up Kyle. Please, wake up."

Tear drops fell, splashing on his hand. She squeezed it, wiped them away. Those strong hands had held her. Those slim fingers had brought her to climax again and again. For a brief time they had shared pleasure. Not wanting to think of what happened next, she turned away from the bed.

The PA was across the hall, chatting with the security guard. She walked over. "I'm going out to the veranda."

"I'll go sit with Dr. LeMonde."

"His name is Kyle."

The physician's assistant nodded, but didn't reply. Talia stopped by the bathroom to splash water on her face and went to find the two men.

"Well," Tim asked, "what do you think?"

"I think it's better if Kyle was in your facility." She turned to the doctor. "I don't think a hospital could do more than you could. The grounds are beautiful and the therapies you mentioned can only help."

"We have had excellent results using the alternative healing methods. In fact, we have become known as a center of healing."

"How can you keep him safe?"

"We have gone to great lengths to secure our facility."

"Why?"

The doctor smiled. "We have a variety of patients, from all backgrounds. Privacy is only one concern. More often, it's safety."

"I see."

"Now that we have that settled," Tim spoke up, "we need to talk about you."

"Why?"

"You certainly can't go back to your former life and you are far from secure. It was easy to locate you."

"With your resources, sure."

"The other side has access to those same resources. Surely, you can see that. They almost snatched you in Hong Kong and again in Hawaii."

"I appreciate the need for safety. I already have a plan. You don't need to worry about it."

"If you don't know who the enemy is, how can you protect yourself?"

Dr. Campo cleared his throat. "If you both will excuse me? I would like to get some dinner." The doctor laid a hand on her shoulder. "Come by later and we will discuss a recovery plan for your colleague."

"Thank you, Dr. Campo. I'm honored you think I could offer anything."

"You worked with the man for years. I assume you got to know him, his likes and dislikes."

She'd gotten to know him alright. She coughed and hoped her face wasn't bright red.

"These will all be considered when creating a healing program," Dr. Campo continued, apparently unaware of her distress.

"Okay, I'll come by later."

"Talia, I meant what I said. You are in danger. I can help."

"Coming from a man who doesn't even know who he can trust in his own organization, you'll understand if that doesn't fill me with confidence."

'The issues are separate."

"I don't see that."

"I told you, I went outside the organization to ensure that Dr. LeMonde is safe."

Why did people insist on referring to him in such an impersonal way? His name was Kyle, damn it.

"I can do the same for you."

"As I said, I have my own resources."

"I assume you're referring to Dr. Andris?" Tim asked politely.

"He's the reason I've made it this far. In fact, he is the one who first alerted me to the fact my project was in jeopardy."

He'd also insisted she take all those self-defense classes and he'd hired experts to teach her tools used in espionage. He'd taught her to disappear. More than once.

"So, you think you can trust him?"

"Of course I can trust him," she snapped. "He's the one who helped me get away from -." She stopped. He'd assured her that she was in no danger from either Tim or Juan, yet he'd helped her escape the agent.

"He is a powerful man," Tim acknowledged. "Powerful men often become indebted because of that power."

"What, are you trying to convince me that Christoff wants to hurt me? That he's responsible for this mess?"

"You were attacked in Hong Kong."

"But Juan was there. Christoff arranged it so that I would be protected by your agent. It was a good thing he was there."

"From what I understand, you are the reason Agent Hernandez is alive. Juan was shot with a poison dart. If you hadn't killed Ju, Agent Turner would have been dealing with body bags not relocation."

"Why would Christoff want to hurt me?"

"Because he wants your project?"

"He doesn't want my project. He was the first to point out the potential for its use as a weapon."

"I can see by your hesitation that you are at least considering the possibility."

"I can see why you were put in charge of your elite group, Mr. Brightman. You're a very charismatic man. Intelligent, handsome, you are probably very successful at persuading people to your views, is that right?"

He blew out a sigh. "I can see I have a long way to go in having you trust me. I'm asking you to let me provide protection for you while someone investigates where the security leak is. Can you let me do that? Protect you until we know what we're dealing with?"

"Can I think about it?"

"Of course."

Talia stared up at the bedroom ceiling. She'd never felt so alone.

"When people are in trouble, they need to talk to somebody. If not to their friends, it's usually to their enemies."

The line from *Tequila Sunrise* haunted her. For years, she'd lived in a world where she had to look at every friendly face as a potential enemy, someone she couldn't trust. History had shown how vulnerable she was to those who seemed trustworthy but weren't. Yet living in a constant state of suspicion had taken its toll. The stress was one thing. The loneliness was something else entirely. She wished she could talk with her Uncle Cole.

"Natalia, if I am to protect you, the illusion must be complete. No one must know that you are alive."

"Christoff, I will not do that to my Uncle Cole!"

"The people who want this technology will know about your friends and relatives. They will expect you to be in contact with them."

"Even if they think I'm dead?"

"That is a possibility. I'm sorry."

"No, I'm sorry. I absolutely refuse to have no contact whatsoever with my uncle. I will find a way to explain things to him. I know this much. If I do explain the situation he will keep my secret. He will play his part in protecting me."

The conversation with her dad's brother had been one of the most painful of her life.

"Talia, I know you'd never purposely get involved in anything illegal."

"I appreciate your trust, Uncle Cole. It's well deserved. Now, I'm asking you to trust me to handle this. I wish I could tell you more but I promise that when this is all over, I'll tell you as much as I can."

"How will I get in touch with you?"

"I'll get in touch with you."

"*I don't like this, Talia.*"

"*I don't either, but it's the only way, I'm afraid.*"

"*What do you want me to tell people when they ask about you?*"

"*Whatever you're comfortable with.*"

"*I wish I could help you out of this mess.*"

"*I know you do. I promise that I do have people helping me.*"

"*The government?*"

"*No.*"

"*Do you think you should go to the authorities?*"

"*This is beyond them, unfortunately.*"

"*Talia, how did this happen?*"

"*It happened because I trusted the wrong people.*"

"*Remember this, girl. I love you and you can always trust me. You can always come home. Keep that truth inside you wherever you go. You can count on it.*"

He'd held her tightly as he'd whispered the words in her ear. Then he'd watched her get into a taxi that took her to the airport, and out of his life.

The first missed birthdays, his and her own, had been the hardest. Not going home for Christmas had brought her to a low point. If it wasn't for Chloe and Christoff having come to spend it with her in Australia, she would have drown in despair.

She wouldn't bother calling them now. They'd tell her what they had numerous times before. To be patient and listen to those meant to protect her.

"*Trust, Natlia. Trust.*"

Unfortunately, that was something she was too hesitant to do. Other than her uncle, she'd come to know that people often had ulterior motives. Even Christoff.

"*Why are you helping me?*"

"*I became a doctor to heal, Natalia. I do not believe technology meant to heal should be used to cause harm.*"

He had promised to help her, not just by keeping her safe from those who would take both her and her technology and lock it away in a lab on foreign shores, but to find a way to have a life.

"Be patient. Let me help you. You will live again but you must let enough time pass."

But how much longer could she live in limbo? It wasn't in her nature to distrust people, or to be antisocial.

"I can't do this anymore, Christoff. I'm losing my mind. I am beyond unhappy living in isolation."

"This is why Costa Rica is the perfect solution. You will be with people. Lots of people."

Working alongside others who were as distrustful of outsiders as she was had indeed been a perfect solution. The owner of the coffee plantation had been a friend of Christoff's. He'd done what he could to help her without seeming to give her preferential treatment, a move that might have invited resentment from the other workers. She suspected he'd asked Carlos to keep an eye on her.

The men and women who picked coffee beans alongside her had been cautiously polite. Eventually, they'd come to adopt the American who obviously had a story, but also worked every bit as hard as they did. She'd also done what came naturally to her. She helped them.

The first time she'd seen someone being mistreated, she'd pushed back. The resort owners, also American, had been caught between the property owner and his expectations, and the workers and theirs. Used to talking hesitant sponsors into providing financial support for various projects, she'd helped negotiate a number of improvements for the laborers while managing to avoid wearing out a welcome.

"Natalia, you will bring too much attention to yourself," Christoff warned.

"I can't stand by and do nothing. These are human beings."

He'd sighed. "You are you, of course, and I wouldn't change you if I could. Please, be careful. If word gets around, if you end up in the media for this -."

"I'll be careful."

It hadn't been difficult. No one, especially the owner, wanted word to get around that changes had been made. The small community hadn't wanted attention any more than she had.

"Ms. Blackmoor, we're an exclusive resort. Our guests prize their privacy."

"I understand, Susannah, and I don't want to cause any trouble."

"The people who work in this industry understand how it works. They don't expect to have an outsider come in and make waves."

She'd understood the threat loud and clear.

"I'll be careful."

"See that you do."

Talia hadn't been too concerned by the woman's implied threats. The relationship was between Christoff and the property owner. The resort owners simply leased the plantation land. Although they handed over a sizable portion of their profit to the man, she'd seen that there was no love lost between them. Still, she would be careful. Unfortunately, that proved to be more difficult than she'd expected.

The longer she stayed at the plantation, the more she'd relaxed. The more her true self came out.

"You have a way with animals."

"I used to live on a farm."

She'd overheard one of the coffee pickers talking about sick animals on a nearby farm.

"It sounds as if the animals are being mistreated."

"Si."

The man had gone on to talk about overcrowding and other inhumane conditions.

"That's wrong."

"Would you go look at the ones my cousin cares for? He is not happy by what goes on but he is no veterinarian. He does not have access to what he needs to heal the cows."

"What do they need?"

"Antibiotics."

"Why in the world would the owner withhold medical treatment? Surely, he can't sell sick cows to a slaughterhouse. The beef would never make it to market. He's screwing himself."

In the dark, Talia smiled. The mixed reactions to her colorful language amused her. Mostly shocked, some of the laborers appreciated her way with words.

"Will you come?"

"Yeah, sure."

She'd gone after dark.

"If the owner or his doctor knew you were here -."

"Wait a minute. Are you telling me that there is a vet and he still won't get medicine for the sick cows?"

She'd spent several nights working with the animals. Then she'd contacted Christoff.

"This is not avoiding undue attention, Natalia," he'd said, sighing heavily.

"I know that Christof, but -."

"I know, I know. You cannot stand by and do nothing. I'm beginning to see how you got yourself into this mess to begin with."

His words had stung. They'd also been right. Life would have been much easier if she'd been able to let things go. Unfortunately, she couldn't stand by and do nothing while people or animals were hurt.

"Look, the guy doesn't want the owner or the vet to know he's doing this. He'd be fired. No one here is going to rat me out. Just send me the antibiotics to the address I gave you and that's it."

Carlos had been alternately amused and concerned.

"*I do not know your story, Talia, but I do not think it is wise for you to get involved in matters of controversy. Is dangerous. One of these days you are going to anger the wrong person.*"

What made her confident was that in helping others, she had earned loyalty.

"*They're very protective of me, Christoff. I'd say this situation is working out pretty well.*"

"*Do not get used to it, Natalia. You cannot pick coffee beans for the rest of your life. You must return to the life you were meant for eventually.*"

"*I'm not sure I want that life back.*"

"*What do you mean?*"

"*The farm, the plantation. There's a simplicity about it all. I didn't realize how much I missed that until I got back after being away for so many years.*"

"*You are tired, Natalia. You cannot possibly think to give up everything you have worked so hard for.*"

"*I have a lot of gifts. I could easily do something else, something that would be fulfilling. There's a peacefulness here.*"

"*Just try not to draw attention to yourself.*"

"*I will.*"

She'd never had the chance. Less than a week later, the handsome agent had showed up looking for her.

CHAPTER 16

Juan shoved his security ID into a card reader recessed in the wall and roughly yanked it out again. He stalked down the hall, ignoring a staff member walking in the opposite direction.

Tim Brightman's office was on the first floor toward the rear of the embassy, directly across from that of the Duty Officer. Ignoring the secretary, he kicked Tim's door in, relishing in the feel of the vibrations as it slammed against the wall.

"Where is she?" he snarled. He came to a halt just inside the door. His boss wasn't alone.

The visitor hadn't even flinched let alone turned when he'd kicked the door in. Who had that kind of fortitude? Or was it suicidal stupidity?

"Agent Hernandez."

"Where is she, Brightman?"

"I told you the mission is complete."

"The hell it is. Her life is still in danger. She hasn't been brought to Santiago for your meeting."

"How do you know her life is still in danger?"

"Indeed," the other man said quietly, turning to gaze at him. "It would seem it is your life that is danger, don't you think, Agent Hernandez?"

Juan stared in shock. He quickly shut the door then walked forward.

"You contacted my father?!" he hissed. *"How the hell did you find him?!"*

His boss was one of a handful of people who knew the true identity of his father.

Tim glanced over at the man but remained silent. Upon receiving a cut nod, he replied. "Your father came to me."

There was a knock at the door. Juan opened it to find the Duty Officer standing there, gun in hand. "Everything okay, Tim?"

"Everything's fine, Mateo. You can cancel the lockdown."

The Duty Officer glared at Juan. "You'd better bring her around."

"Who?"

"The woman. I want to meet her."

"What makes you say there's a woman?"

The Duty Officer shook his head. "To make a man lose his mind the way you obviously have? It has to be a woman." Continuing to shake his head, he pulled the door closed.

"Come and sit down," his father said in a way that left no doubt it was not a polite request. Sighing, he went and took a seat facing the two men.

"It's been a long time, Juan. How are you feeling? I understand you've sustained several injuries recently."

He glared at Tim. "Is that why you called him? To try and convince me I need to take a break?"

"Agent Brightman was honest with you. I came to him."

"Why?"

He hadn't seen his father in almost ten years.

"Because I was concerned for your welfare. You were just in the hospital after being shot, you were almost killed in Hong Kong, and again in Hawaii. I felt I needed to step in before you got yourself killed."

Juan gave his standard answer. "It goes with the territory. Surely, you understand that, Benito."

The older man nodded in acknowledgment. "You speak the truth, my son, but it does not sit well with a man that he may lose someone very dear to him."

Juan worked to school his features. He was beyond irritated that his boss was witness to a conversation he considered hypocritical. Who was the man trying to kid?

He had provided for Juan's care, true, but Benito Hernandez had never openly acknowledged him. And he hadn't married his mother.

"You have to understand that a man in my position has other considerations when it comes to marriage. I cannot marry for love. I must marry a woman who can be by my side. I cannot acknowledge you openly, Juan, but believe me when I tell you that I am proud of you and already proud of the man you will become."

He had been ten years old and meeting the man for the first time.

"I will be providing for your future as I have provided for you up until now."

He'd been sending checks to his mother to ensure that they lived a very comfortable lifestyle.

"You have spent enough time among your American peers. It is time for you to prepare for your future. I am sending you to a private school. It will prepare you for the academy," he said, referring to the military academy he himself had attended. *"While you cannot hope to succeed me, it will nonetheless prepare you for a successful life. You will have many doors opened to you. You will be able to choose from any number of opportunities."*

Juan had been too intimidated to argue. Although his father had never raised his voice, it was clear he would accept nothing less than Juan's full acquiescence.

His mother had only had good things to say about the man who had fathered him, going so far as to tell Juan she loved him and always would.

They'd met at a conference in Chile. His mother had been the keynote speaker. According to his mother, Benito Hernandez had fallen in love with her the moment he set eyes on her.

"So, why didn't he marry you?"

"You have to understand, Juan. He's a very powerful man in a very important role. He had to marry a woman who would help him in his life, not just as a wife, but in his position."

"Why couldn't you?"

She'd smiled and kissed his forehead. *"We live in a complicated world, Juan. The customs and cultural differences between our two countries meant I would never be accepted. We wanted you to have the best life possible so we agreed I would raise you in the United States. Benito was determined to do what he could so he always made sure to provide financial support and through a complicated system of communication, I have kept him up to date on your activities. I send him photos and letters."*

"What about you?"

"What about me?"

"Do you tell him how you are doing? Does he even care?"

"Of course, and yes to both."

"Is that why you never married again? Because you still love my father?"

"Juan, you are my priority. I have never met a man I felt was good enough to be my partner in fulfilling one of the most important roles in life, the raising of a child."

"Like I said," Juan told his father, "it goes with the territory."

His father looked at Tim. "May I have a moment alone to speak with him?"

"Take all the time you need, Senor Hernandez."

"Please. Call me Benito."

"Thank you, Benito. Shall I have some more coffee sent in?"

"That would be appreciated."

"Would you care for something stronger?"

"Yes, that would also be appreciated."

The man waited until they were both seated with coffee and Kahlua before speaking.

"You are in more danger than you know, Juan."

"Look, -."

"Do not interrupt."

Juan snapped his mouth shut.

"It is no secret that I keep tabs on you. I told you years ago that I would be proud of the man you would become and I am. I also recognize that you risk your life in the name of justice, but a situation has come to my attention. I could not sit on the sidelines."

Juan knew what he was referring to with that remark. Years earlier, while building a case for racketeering, he'd found himself unexpectedly close to the inner circle of one of his father's political adversaries. Two agents had been killed and he'd come very close to losing his own life. His father sent an emissary to visit him in the hospital.

"You have made some very powerful enemies, Juan Hernandez. I cannot tell you who but I am urging you to remove yourself from this investigation."

"Why the hell should I listen to you?"

"It is not I you must listen to, but Benito."

He'd been groggy from pain medication and thanks to being choked during a fight, his voice raspy, but he'd expressed his dismay.

"He can't expect me to let them go free! Not after what they've done."

"He is asking you to remove yourself from this investigation before you are killed."

"And let someone else die in my place? What sort of a man does he think I am?"

The emissary's words had finally penetrated through the pharmaceutical haze.

"*What do you mean, you can't tell me who? My father knows who is responsible for all of this but he isn't going to help?*"

"*Juan, you must understand, he cannot insert myself into this situation.*"

"*He's going to sit on the sidelines while innocent people die because it may jeopardize his career?*"

"*I cannot explain other than to tell you that he is damned if he does and damned if he does not.*"

Juan sipped the spiked coffee and stared at his father. "Tim already looked into the possibility someone was after me."

"That was before."

"Before what?"

"Before you became involved in this case."

"This case? You mean Talia Blackmoor?"

"That is exactly what I mean. I'm afraid Agent Brightman has no idea what he's become involved in."

"And you do?"

"My spies are still looking into the details but there is more going on than a Chinese company wanting to steal American technology."

He dragged a hand down his face. "Can you share the details?"

"You are right in that Dr. Blackmoor is in danger. It has come to my attention that a kidnapping attempt is imminent. Someone found out where she is."

"Have you told Brightman?"

"I cannot. He is unable to take the necessary steps for fear of tipping off the wrong person. He is still unaware of the identities of those involved in this security breach."

"He said he has someone looking into it but because he had to go outside normal channels, it's taking long. Too long."

"Exactly. But you are not limited to those channels."

"Then tell me where she is and I'll go get her."

"I'm afraid there's no time for that. This attack will be over before you could ever get there."

"Obviously, you have something in mind or you wouldn't be talking to me."

"There is someone quite close by who could get to her in time."

"Who?"

"Agent Dan Foster."

Juan closed his eyes. "You want me to call Dan Foster and ask him to get involved in this?"

"I have already contacted him."

He looked at his father.

"I told you. I could not sit on the sidelines this time."

"How -?" Juan stood and walked over to look out at Tim's garden. He didn't need to see the reflection in the sliding glass window to know that his father had come to stand by him.

"Juan, whether you choose to accept it or not, I do care about you. I love your mother a great deal. I loved her from the moment I saw her. How could I not? She gave me you."

Juan clenched his jaw but remained silent.

That must be a comfort to your wife.

He dismissed the thought as soon as it formed. His father lived and moved in a world Juan would never understand, didn't want to, either.

"I know you do not understand the choices your mother and I made but we did what we felt was best for everyone, and you especially. I have kept appraised of your activities."

"What, has my boss been spying on me for you?"

"I did not need to talk with Tim Brightman to learn about your feelings for Agent Ross."

Juan watched water splash from a fountain into a small koi pond. If it wasn't Tim, then who had told his father about his feelings for Kaila? The answer wasn't difficult for him to discern. In fact, it made sense since that party had been present when the Fat Lady sang.

"The mayor."

The Chilean official had been the one who had Juan assigned to the case. He would have known of his feelings for Kaila since he'd seen them together, not just at the rescue, but in the weeks afterward.

"Agent Foster is, at this very moment, on his way to talk to your Dr. Blackmoor."

Your Dr. Blackmoor. Was she his? Did he want her to be?

"Although I understand he is planning to bring Agent Ross along, I do not imagine Dr. Blackmoor will be happy with the situation."

That was an understatement. After everything that had happened, it was unlikely Talia would trust either one of the agents.

"What do you propose I do, call her, give her a head's up?"

"No. Agent Foster has spoken with his friend, Senor Andrews."

"Sean is involved in this, too?"

"A wise move by your superior. Senor Andrews is not involved with Tim's organization. He was able to get you out of Hawaii without anyone else in your organization aware of where you'd gone. You were able to recover."

He turned to face his father.

"Is someone after me?"

"I believe so and I have an idea who but I am awaiting confirmation."

"Is it someone in my organization?"

"No. That much I know."

"So, Dan's bringing Talia to Chile?"

"No. We cannot risk having her here until we've confirmed where the weak link is."

Confirmed? Did he know?

"Dan knows of a place that is much safer. A place suggested by Senor Andrews."

"Where?"

"I think it would be best if Senor Andrews himself provided the details. He is waiting for you at the airport."

Juan assumed his father meant the military airport in Talca and not the international one in Santiago.

"You will rendezvous with Agents Foster and Ross and your Dr. Blackmoor."

"Why are you doing this?"

The man gave what might be called a smile. "Someone should be with the woman he loves."

A momentary widening of his eyes was the only acknowledgment Juan allowed. He realized his father was holding something out to him.

"What's this?"

"Tickets for you and Senor Andrews."

Another plane. Oh fucking joy.

"Have a safe journey, Juan."

"Thank you, Benito."

He watched his father approach the door, put his hand on the knob, but stop.

"I did not tell any of this to Agent Brightman," he called over his shoulder, then left, closing the door quietly behind him.

Contemplating his father's words, Juan turned to stare at the fountain.

Your Dr. Blackmoor.

"Here."

Juan looked first at the bag of ice, then at Sean.

"For your knee."

He stared for several seconds before finally taking the bag. "Thanks," he mumbled.

"You're a stubborn sonofabitch, aren't you?"

One side of Juan's mouth went up. "Did you read that in my file? About the knee, I mean."

Sean sat across from him. "I have never seen your file, Hernandez, but I have seen knee injuries before."

"Obviously," he replied, referring this Sean's time in the service.

"Closer to home than that," the software executive replied. "Dan has issues resulting from surgery. If he doesn't run or do some type of workout almost daily, the pain and stiffness get pretty bad."

The men sat in companionable silence for awhile. Juan stared out the window.

"What's on your mind?"

He looked at Sean.

"If I were a betting man, I'd say it was more than just the mission."

"What, you a psychic? A mind reader?"

"I could ask you the same thing, couldn't I?"

Juan didn't reply.

"In Special Forces, and in your line of work, a man's ability to glean information through nontraditional methods could mean the difference between life and death. Gut feeling takes on a whole different level of importance. I'll ask again. What's on your mind?"

He blew out a sigh. "A lot of things are going through my mind, including the mission and how it got to the point that I am directly disobeying my superior and following the orders of someone from a rival organization in order to complete it."

"Since I know this isn't the first time you've disobeyed your boss, I'd have to say it's more than that. We've got a long flight to the states. I'm giving you an opportunity to get something off your chest."

"I'm not comfortable with how this went down. Specifically, that you were dragged into this. You're not only not in the organization, you're not in any organization. You work for a software company in Silicon Valley."

"Tim needed help. Security protocol had been compromised, making going outside the organization good sense. Not only do I still have my clearance from my days in the service, I am friends with the agents involved. I can get things done off the radar of prying eyes."

"Are you still in?"

"The service? No. I retired years ago, you know that."

"I mean that other."

"How'd you find out about that?"

Juan opened his mouth but Sean interrupted him.

"More to the point. Why did you find out? Who told you and why?"

"Let's just say I had a hard time with the idea a Silicon Valley executive would be responsible for the lives of several people, including those friends you spoke of. What makes you qualified, given that you retired from the service years ago?"

"So, what, you stole the key to Brightman's files?"

"I didn't get a copy of your file from Brightman."

"Benito."

"He said I needed to trust you. I resisted. He helped me see why I could." He studied Sean. "Why don't you go back in an official capacity?"

"Because my days of government work are behind me."

"And this?"

"This is helping a friend in need."

"And if you find you like helping this friend?"

"My days of government work are behind me," he repeated.

"Right."

Juan suspected he wasn't the only one who didn't fully believe that.

CHAPTER 17

~~~~~~

Talia turned on her side and stared out the window. A sliver of moon played hide and seek with the clouds. If not for the crickets, there would have been total silence.

Kyle had been gone for six hours. Taken by military transport, he was on his way to the private medical facility in Chile. She should be happy or at the very least satisfied since once there, he would have the best chance for a full recovery. Instead, she felt a hollow emptiness.

Maybe it'd been seeing him in a coma. Maybe it was the thought of losing him. Again.

"Why can't you keep him here?"

"Because I can't assure his safety."

"I see."

Or maybe it was the feeling of dread gnawing at her insides.

"Powerful men often become indebted because of that power."

"Are you trying to convince me that Christoff wants to hurt me? That he's responsible for this mess?"

"You were attacked in Hong Kong."

She flipped onto her back and stared up in the dark. Christoff had been adamant that she could trust Agent Hernandez. Why would he have her trust him and then try to kill him?

"I can't trust people in my organization."

Had Christoff discovered Juan wasn't trustworthy? That didn't make sense. He'd looked into the backgrounds of the people involved. Was Tim trying to get her to distrust Christoff for his own purposes? That didn't make sense either. Christoff had sought Agent Brightman's help, so obviously he trusted him.

Talia put her hands over her face and inhaled deeply. Her head was starting to hurt. Second guessing who she could trust had been a part of her life for too long. It left her bone weary.

Because the window was open she knew the moment the crickets stopped chirping. Soundlessly, she rolled to the floor, grateful she was still dressed. Exhausted, she'd laid down after the ambulance left, coming awake long after the sun had set. She crawled over to where she'd tossed her tennis shoes by the door.

Outside, a twig snapped. Under normal circumstances she would assume it was an animal, but she'd said goodbye to *normal circumstances* three years ago.

She debated. She could probably lift the screen out without too much difficulty. Unfortunately, she suspected someone was outside and given the tenacity so far witnessed, it was safe to assume whoever it was had night vision goggles.

She also wasn't too fond of taking her chances with the front door since it was likely whoever was outside was working with someone. Someone who might very well be in the house.

Most of the staff had been dismissed after Tim left for Chile two days earlier. She'd refused his offer of protection, agreeing to stay only as long as Kyle was there. Dr. Campo had remained to personally accompany Kyle to his facility in South America. They'd spent the time discussing a plan of recovery during which she'd shared what insights she felt might help the doctor better understand his patient. What insights she felt her heart could tolerate.

She'd planned on leaving in the morning. She bit her lower lip. That had been Christoff's idea.

Was he behind this mess?

Something bounced off her window. She waited in the darkness, her heart pounding. There it was again. Someone was tossing something at her window.

They were trying to get her attention?

That wasn't how someone acted if they wanted to abduct you unawares. She bit her lip, wincing when she punctured the sensitive skin. Another pebble hit the window as the salty taste of blood mixed with her saliva.

At least, she thought it was a pebble.

It had been years since she'd heard that distinctive *ting* against her bedroom window. In spite of the situation, she smiled.

Billy Truex used to come for her, waiting in the moonlight while she climbed down a rope ladder meant to be used in case of a fire emergency.

"Where are we going?"

"To the barn."

They'd stretched out in the hay and stared up at the stars through a hole in the roof. He'd point out constellations and talk about getting off the farm and traveling the world. The last she'd heard, he'd married a local girl and was about to be a father for the second time.

The sound of another pebble yanked her attention to her dire straits. She crawled over to the window.

"Dr. Blackmoor?" a voice hissed from the darkness.

"What?"

"My name is Agent Kaila Ross. I work with Juan Hernandez and Tim Brightman. I need you to push out that screen. There's a ladder right below your window. I need you to -."

"Shh!" she hissed suddenly as the bedroom door was thrust open. She wasted no time, she went on the attack. Launching herself at the man who'd come in the door, she fought as if her life depended on it. Which, she believed, it did.

Her assailant responded by trying to pin her down. She heard her name but in her panicked state, nothing got through except the primal need to fight. She was holding her own until a second assailant entered the fray, managing to pull her away from her attacker and pinning her to the floor.

"Dan, are you alright?"

Talia looked over to see a man holding his stomach. "Just peachy," he rasped.

"Dr. Blackmoor, I'm Agent Kaila Ross. That man is my partner, Agent Dan Foster. I'm going to get off of you but not until you promise to cooperate. We have to get you out of here."

"Why the hell should I trust you?" she managed to get out. The woman's knee was pressing into her back, compressing her lungs.

"We're taking you to Juan."

All the fight went out of her. "Juan? Is he okay?"

"Mad as hell, more like," the man on the ground said sitting up but holding his stomach.

The woman yanked on her arm. "Will you cooperate?"

"Yes."

She gulped air as the weight was lifted. The woman who called herself Kaila walked over to the man and extended a hand.

"What is it with females and self-defense?" he groused, standing.

Agent Ross just laughed.

"Do you have anything here you can't live without?" Dan asked, "because we want to make it appear as if you've just gone to the store or are still in the area."

"There's nothing I can't leave behind."

"Excellent, let's go." He patted the female agent companionably on the arm. "Good work."

Kaila descended the ladder, followed by Talia. Dan replaced the screen and told them he'd meet them at the rendezvous spot.

"Come on." The agent pulled her up the hill behind the safe house. The going was slow, in part because it was almost pitch dark and in part because of the dense shrubbery.

"Watch out for the roots. Pick your feet up as if you're marching, but put your toes down, not your entire foot."

She followed the woman's instructions and managed to keep from falling on her face twice. After what seemed like an eternity, they stopped.

"What next?"

"We wait for Dan. He'll be along any minute."

The three of them hiked further into the woods, stopping periodically to drink water and rest. She suspected that was more for her benefit as the two agents didn't seem even slightly winded. She also suspected they did more than just work together. To be so in sync in the pitch dark bespoke of something more than spy skills between them, but she kept her suspicions to herself.

"Are you hungry?" Dan asked, suddenly.

"No."

"Because we have chips and soda in the car."

"No, I'm fine, thank you."

Out of nowhere a light flooded the darkness as Kaila opened the door to a black Volvo. Colored dots swam before her eyes. Squinting, she allowed Dan to help her into the vehicle.

"Do you want me to buckle you in or can you take care of that?"

"I'm fine. I can see better now."

"That's a great trick, you know. If you are in a dark area and you want to throw off your attacker? Flip on the lights. It will only buy you a few seconds to a minute but that may be the difference between life and death."

"Thanks, I'll keep that in mind."

Kaila laughed and got behind the wheel.

"Aren't you going to turn on the headlights?"

'No need just now."

She studied the male agent. He didn't seem alarmed by the fact they were driving on a mountain road in the dark, without headlights.

"Where's Juan?"

She felt, rather than saw, the look that went between them. Amusement, and something more.

"He and Sean are waiting for us. It's going to be a long drive, Dr. Blackmoor, I suggest you get what rest you can. We're driving and we'll be driving through the night."

"How long til we get to our destination?"

"Depending on traffic, eight to ten hours. Let me know if you need to stop for the bathroom."

Talia stared out the window. After twenty minutes, they pulled onto a paved road and Kaila turned on the lights.

"Impressive," she murmured.

The agent laughed. "Not really. I've been coming up here every summer since I was ten. That was my parents' place you were at."

"I thought it belonged to Sean and Kian?"

"They bought it from my parents. Kian is my sister."

"I don't understand. Tim said he tapped Sean for help because he's outside the organization. You work for Tim which puts you inside the organization. How do I know you guys aren't the double agents?"

"Sean and I were in Special Forces together," Dan supplied in a tone that said ending the argument was a good idea. But she was no fool.

"So?"

"So, I don't backstab, Dr. Blackmoor. Sean is our safety net. Tim doesn't know Kaila and I are involved."

"How is that?"

"Because," Kaila replied, "we're supposed to be on leave. We just got off an assignment. Tim thinks we're resting up before our next job."

"I still don't understand."

"Tim called Sean," Dan responded, "because Sean is outside the group but he's trustworthy. Tim told Kaila and me to take a break. Sean called me for help when he found out that once again security had been breached and you were in imminent danger."

He didn't mention that he'd also spoken to one Benito Hernandez.

"How'd Sean find out?"

"From Juan," he replied.

"In a roundabout way," Kaila added.

"The point is," Dan continued, "that Sean knows of a place you can be kept safe. He doesn't work for Tim so he can't be involved more than this. We can't be involved more than this because we're supposed to be on leave. But Juan, who was originally tasked with protecting you, can be involved, which is why we're taking you to him."

"If someone is on the inside, won't they know that Juan is back protecting me?"

"They think he's been put on medical leave."

'Because, he has," Kaila put in.

"He has? Is he hurt?"

The silence was brief but uncomfortable. She'd tipped them off that she had feelings, however indescribable, for the handsome agent.

She hated that her feelings had come out in that question. Her feelings for Juan were her own. Hell, she didn't even fully understand them.

"He's fine," Dan said, finally.

"Kaila? That's your name, right?"

'It is. May I call you Talia? I never had any use for fancy titles."

"That would be fine, yes. Is Juan okay?"

"I guess that depends. Physically, he's fine. His pride has been dented and he's probably feeling a bit confused because of recent events, but I'll let him tell you about that."

"What makes you think he will?"

"Because I haven't heard of him losing it before and he lost it when he couldn't find you."

She tried to ignore the thrill of pleasure that coursed through her, however briefly, at that bit of news.

"What do you mean?"

"He kicked Brightman's door in and put the entire embassy on lockdown," Dan replied. "He demanded to be told where you were."

In the dark, she smiled.

"Why are you helping me?"

"We're helping Juan."

Her smile widened.

She fell asleep shortly after they came down out of the mountain pass. She vaguely remembered them stopping for gas but other than that, remembered nothing until waking up as the sun was rising in front of them.

"We're going east."

"Oh, you're awake. We're about to run through Mickey D's. Would you like some coffee? A bathroom break?"

"Yes, to both, but not in that order."

Kaila followed her into the restroom but waited outside the stall. She turned her over to Dan who was in line ordering breakfast before returning to use the facilities herself.

"Want it fancy?"

"I beg your pardon?"

"Want a cappuccino or just coffee?"

A cap would be great. Make it a large one, please. I could use the caffeine."

"Food?"

"Hash browns are good."

By the time the food was ready, Kaila had returned. The three ate in silence and drove toward a sky that was lightening by the minute.

"We're going to New Mexico?"

In the front seat the two agents glanced at each other, amused.

"I calculated based on driving time and the landscape. We're obviously in the desert."

"We're heading for the Four Corners."

"The Navajo Nation?"

That look again.

"Sean's Navajo," Dan explained. "His family is there. They can protect you and Juan while we let this thing play out."

"What does that mean, exactly? Play out."

"As you might suspect, when there's a security breach at this level you have to be delicate when investigating. If you tip off the wrong person or make them nervous, you could lose the thread and your entire investigation unravels."

Something occurred to her.

"If I don't check in with Christoff he's going to wonder what happened."

"I don't think that's a good idea. Not just yet, anyway."

"I think you're making a mistake."

"We're protecting you," Kaila replied.

Intellectually, she understood, but it didn't sit well with her. She owed Christoff. Big time.

"Juan will be there?"

In the front seat, Dan, who was driving, smiled. "Yes, he and Sean flew in yesterday, or maybe today, depending what time the flight arrived."

She was surprised by how forthcoming the agents had been. In her experience, double talk and withholding information was SOP. Their candor definitely put her at ease but at the same time left her a little uneasy. Maybe that was the idea, to gain her trust and then tighten the noose. She chewed on the inside of her lower lip. Maybe she'd get a better idea whether or not there were hidden intentions if she threw them off a bit?

"So, how long have you two been lovers?"

She had to work to keep from laughing at Dan's expression.

"The exact date?" he replied.

"Sorry," she replied, "just trying to make conversation."

"So, when do you plan on becoming Juan's lover?" he shot back.

She was silent the remainder of the trip.

No sooner had they entered the reservation, they found themselves being tailed by a Navajo cop. His expression neutral, Dan pulled over. "Stay in the car." He opened the door and stepped out, hands in the air.

Talia tried to gauge Kaila's mood which was difficult since she was sitting directly in front of her. She was able to pick up on tension but not much else. Outside, Dan was speaking to the officer. After about ten minutes, he got back in.

"We're getting an escort, of sorts."

Kaila cleared her throat. "What does that mean, *of sorts*?"

"He's going to tail us until an unmarked unit meets up with us to take us the rest of the way."

"An unmarked unit? As in the Feds?"

He smiled. "That's the sort of part. It's the guy's little sister. She took the day off school to make sure we get to Sean. For a fee, of course."

"And if something happens? What's his little sister going to do then?"

"You mean bad guys?"

Bad guys? Was he kidding?

Kaila nodded.

"Probably blow their head off with a shotgun, no questions asked."

"Are you serious?"

Dan shrugged. "That's what he said."

As it turned out, his little sister was a cop getting her master's degree in criminal justice.

"I was only too happy to help Sean out," she told them when they stopped for a bathroom break. "It'll be good to see him again. It's been years."

Remaining quiet, Talia worked to keep in the background. The agents and the officer had been very polite, had joked around with her even, but she felt beyond out of place. She felt like a traitor. She hadn't checked in with Christoff. He would be frantic.

"Would you excuse me?" she said suddenly. "I think I will take advantage of the bathroom after all."

Kaila followed her in but waited outside the stall. Texting while doing business proved challenging but she promised to call him later. She turned off the phone and shoved it into her pocket.

They followed the officer's car, a beat up Chevy, as it wound up into the hills of northeast Arizona. After they'd gone up quite a bit in elevation, they pulled over.

"From here," the woman said, "we walk." She went to the trunk and withdrew a rifle.

"Remington 700," she said, smiling. "Machined from a solid block of ordnance-grade steel, then drilled and tapped for scope mounts. 26" barrel crowned at the muzzle for unparalleled accuracy and stability."

Talia wasn't sure how to respond. "Great," she decided.

The officer led them about a quarter of a mile before stopping. "We wait."

CHAPTER 18

~~~~~~

Talia heard it first. A twig snapping. She turned to look at Dan. The police officer noticed and motioned everyone down. Taking a tighter grip on the rifle, she gave the call of a dove.

Incredible.

The officer's lips hadn't moved, yet she had perfectly mimicked the coo of a dove.

After a few seconds, there was an answering call. The officer relaxed, stood, though she kept her hands on the rifle. In another minute, two men approached.

Talia fought the urge to run to Juan. Not wanting to look too closely at the fact he set her system on edge, she decided to chalk her reaction up to relief. After all, he'd promised to keep her safe and so far, he had.

Was he happy to see her? She gave him a brief smile while trying to read his expression. Hating that it mattered to her how he felt, and not really wanting to know at this point, she turned to the other man, the one who didn't work in Tim's organization.

Tall, with hair the color of onyx, his Native American heritage was obvious, though she could tell that somewhere an ancestor had intermarried with a European. His build and his facial features made her suspect French in spite of his Scottish surname.

The tall man shook hands with Dan, hugged Kaila, then swept the police officer off her feet and hugged her so tightly she squeaked.

"Put me down or I'll cuff you!" The threat was lost in laughter, however, making it a shallow parody of the danger the woman faced on a daily basis.

"Look at you, Tina! You're all grown up!"

"That's right, Sean, which means you have to treat me with respect."

He reached out and tugged on her hair. "Yeah, or what?"

"Or I'll toss your ass in jail."

"And I'll be walking out an hour later."

"Because your brother will have let him out," Dan put in.

"Which one," she asked, smiling, "the cop or the judge?"

It surprised her that the officer knew Dan, but then she recalled that the two men had served in Special Forces together. Dan must have met Sean's family at some point. The three of them chatted briefly, while Kaila stood close, offering her own comments now and again.

Like herself, Juan stood back, observing. Hoping she was being unobtrusive, she slowly made her way in his direction.

"It's good to see you, Agent Hernandez."

"Dr. Blackmoor," he replied stiffly.

Talia couldn't help but feel disappointed. She sighed. Sean glanced over but went back to whatever discussion he was having.

"How are you feeling?" she asked.

"Fine."

So much for small talk.

The conversation wound down and along with the silence, Talia found five pairs of eyes all turned on her. It was all she could do not to squirm.

"This is where I get off this merry-go-round," Sean said, stepping forward. "Dr. Blackmoor, you and Juan will be in good hands. Tina Greyhawk is going to take it from here."

She shook his hand. "Thank you for your help."

"I look forward to a time when we can talk at leisure."

She turned to the two agents. "Thank you for coming off your leave to help out."

"Good luck," Kaila said, waiving and heading for the officer's car. Dan walked over.

"Hernandez."

"Foster."

Oh geez.

Were they going to compare whose was bigger?

Dan held out a hand. "Good luck, Dr. Blackmoor."

"Thank you, Dan."

The police officer came over. "We're going to go pick up the vehicle Sean came in. He's going to take mine back down, drop it off at the station." She looked at her. "Have you eaten?"

"Do I look emaciated or something? People keep asking me if I've had food."

She could have sworn a smile flickered across Juan's face.

The officer laughed. "Come on, let's go."

It was a quarter mile hike up in elevation. The switchbacks made it slow going.

"You might want to get comfy back there," the officer called after she'd slid into the back of a Jeep. "It's a bit of a haul from here."

Oh goody.

The terrain was too rough for sleep and she sensed Juan wasn't interested in conversation, so she stared out at the Indian Reservation while the officer chatted about current events.

The Navajo Nation covered over twenty seven thousand miles and encompassed Arizona, Utah, and New Mexico. At once beautiful and intimidating, the landscape was wild, exacerbating her sense of isolation. In spite of everything that had transpired in the last twenty-four hours, Talia found herself relaxing. She closed her eyes and within moments was asleep.

"Dr. Blackmoor?"

Jerking upright, Talia opened her eyes to find Officer Greyhawk looking at her.

"We're here."

"Here?"

Her door was opened. Juan reached in and unbuckled her seatbelt. "Come on."

Groggy, she stepped out of the Jeep and stumbled as her foot slid into a depression. She went sprawling and would have fallen on her face if Juan hadn't grabbed her. Caught off guard, she sent her arms out and for an awkward moment it seemed as if the two of them might embrace.

He uses Ivory soap.

The idle thought passed quickly as she corrected her balance and stepped back. She mumbled an awkward apology before turning to the officer. "What happens now?"

"You'll have to ask your friend. My role is finished. I need to get back to it. Good luck."

'Thank you, officer. Have a safe journey."

The woman gave her a thumb's up before getting behind the wheel and driving off, the tires sending pebbles and a cloud of dust in their direction.

"Come on."

"Do you know where we're going?"

"That way."

Talia held her ground, forcing the agent to turn.

"What?" he snapped.

"What is your problem?"

"What?"

"You have all the personality of a lizard. Where did Mr. Executive go?"

He looked at her as if she'd lost her mind.

"You know, the suit? Costa Rica?" She cocked her head. "Are you sure you're recovered?"

"There's a house a short distance from here. We're on a ranch."

"I see."

"So you do."

She walked behind him, wondering if he was bi-polar. His expression was stony and he looked seriously pissed off. But hadn't Kaila said something like that?

"Physically, he's fine. His pride has been dented and he's probably feeling a bit confused because of recent events, but I'll let him tell you about that."

"Juan?"

He stopped, turned.

"Thank you."

For several moments he said nothing, simply stared at her as if she had two heads.

"Yeah, okay, sure."

He turned and led her toward low adobe walls with a wooden gate in the middle. "The house is through there."

"Have you been here before? Do you know these people?"

He gave her a curious look. "No, I don't know these people. Andrews knows them, though. He's assured me we'll be safe here."

"Do you trust him?"

"We wouldn't be here if I didn't."

A closer inspection of the gate showed it to be padlocked. They walked around the left side and through a narrow break in the wall. The courtyard was mostly dirt with very little landscaping to speak of. A sprawling single-story house connected with the back wall, giving the illusion to whoever stood in the courtyard that they were being embraced.

"Did he grow up here?"

"I don't think so."

Uncertain what to make of Juan's emotional distance, she decided to forgo any more questions.

"I need to go to the bathroom."

"Why don't we knock on the door? I'm sure there's one inside."

She was about to suggest he knock again when the door opened. An older man in jeans and a t-shirt smiled at them.

"Agent Hernandez and Dr. Blackmoor." The man held the screen door open and stepped back. "Welcome."

She followed Juan into the house. "Thank you. Please call me Talia."

"Will do. Why don't we go out back? I have some lemonade."

"Dr. Blackmoor needs a restroom," Juan said.

The man pointed. "Right through there."

Ten minutes later, she stepped onto a porch that ran the entire length of the house. Though in good repair, the wooden floorboards were weathered. In the way of seating, there was a wooden swing and a number of rocking chairs of various sizes and vintages. Several of them were stamped with signs stating they'd been made by veterans. Feeling like Goldie Locks, she looked for the perfect size.

She accepted a glass of lemonade and smiled at the older man who sat down next to her. Juan was behind her in the swing, his feet pushing it into gentle movement.

"Dinner is at six but feel free to help yourself when you're hungry. I'll show you to your rooms in a bit." He looked at the horizon. "You're safe here. My neighbors have been alerted to be on the lookout for strangers."

We're strangers.

As if he read her mind, he added. "I'm going to introduce you so they know you by sight, though they've already seen a photo."

"Do they know why we're here?" she asked.

"Friends of Sean's seeking refuge from the White Man's world."

Well, she thought wryly, that was true enough. They sat in silence. Talia spent equal time studying the older man and her surroundings. Cactus and scrub could be seen for miles. In the distance, buttes in rich red hues provided color in an otherwise muted landscape. She guessed their host to be in his sixties. Beneath a black cowboy hat his long hair, streaked with grey and some white, was tied with a piece of leather. Wearing jeans and boots, he looked every bit the rancher.

"Seen enough?"

She smiled but didn't immediately reply. She wasn't going to apologize for doing the same thing he was.

"Have you?"

He laughed. "I understand you are good with animals."

She nodded. "I grew up on a farm. We also boarded horses."

"My neighbor to the north has beautiful horses. He is having trouble with one of them. Perhaps you can advise him." He chuckled. "I'm not sure he'll listen. He's as stubborn as an old mule."

She found herself relaxing at the man's candid manner. "I love horses." She let out a breath. "I love animals." She glanced over to see Juan staring into the distance, his feet pushing in that same repeated motion yet going nowhere. She turned back to the older man.

"What can I call you?"

"Sani."

"Nice to meet you, Sani. What does it mean?"

"Old one."

What a strange name for a child. Maybe it was given to him more recently.

"When did you get this name?"

"When I was born. My mother looked into my eyes and knew at once I was an *old soul*."

"Old soul?" It was the first time Juan had spoken. "You mean reincarnated?"

"That is one interpretation."

Talia replayed Juan's question, analyzing his tone of voice. Somehow, she suspected the paranormal was not on his list of things to love.

She pursed her lips. Interesting group to be in given the talents of his colleagues. She wondered momentarily if that created internal conflict for the agent and if so, how it affected his decision making. Did he go out of his way to ensure every move was a logical choice?

"What are the rules?" she asked their host.

"Rules? There are no rules."

Behind her, Juan snorted. The old man didn't respond. Either he hadn't heard or he chose to ignore the rude behavior.

"There are choices if that's what you mean."

"What are my choices?"

"You can remain here and be kept safe. I will take you to the neighbors to introduce you so that they may know you. After that, you can choose to work or you can spend your day idly."

"I'm not afraid of work," she replied. "In fact, I prefer it."

That was an understatement. Too much idle time meant too much thinking. Too many opportunities for unwanted thoughts to descend.

"And you can choose to heal."

"What?" It came out like a squeak.

"That was revealing."

"I feel fine," she clarified.

"Your body is fine but your mind and your heart are not."

"Double-talk," Juan muttered.

"You have that choice as well, Agent Hernandez. You can also choose to heal."

A breeze blew across her beck and shoulders as Juan stood and stalked past her. She shivered.

"I'm going to walk around, get familiar with the surroundings."

The older man looked at his retreating back as he stomped across the yard. "Or you can choose to run, as Agent Hernandez does."

"Most of us run at some point in our lives, and it's usually for good reason."

"I'll be right back." He grabbed the now empty lemonade pitcher and disappeared into the house.

The hinges on the back door squeaked badly but she decided that was probably a good thing. No one could sneak into the house from the back without everyone hearing it.

Juan was nowhere to be seen. She assumed he was checking the premises thoroughly, including inside the house. Was that why Sani had gone inside?

She hoped the chip Juan was carrying would smooth itself out or fall off before Sani knocked it off. He might be older but he was incredibly fit and something told her he would have no compunction about doing so. The back door opened again.

"Let me refill your glass."

"Oh, thank you." She sipped, coughed. "You should have warned me."

"Why?"

"Because there's booze in that lemonade!"

"So?"

"So, you should have warned me."

"Why?

"So I was prepared!" she snapped.

"Prepared for what? Does it taste bad?"

She paused, flummoxed. "Well, no, it doesn't."

"The lemonade tasted good before and it tastes good now. What is there to prepare for?"

"Is this what you do?"

"Serve my guests good beverages? Yes."

"I meant -." She stopped, sipped, then laughed. "I don't know what I meant. I'm tired, I think."

"Running will do that to a person."

"I had to."

"No, you didn't. You chose to."

"I chose not to die."

"I do not believe those were your only choices. If you think on it you will know this, too."

"I thought I was going to die, which is the same thing."

"It most certainly is not." He took a long drink of his own spiked beverage. "More than half the time our thoughts are illusions, not truths. If we spent time reflecting on them further, we would find the truth hidden in the illusion. Once we bring the truth to light, the illusion falls away. Then we can make good decisions."

He set his empty glass down on the floorboard next to his chair.

"You cannot make a good decision until you have the truth. You call your decision to run a choice but it was really a decision based on incomplete information."

For several minutes she sat in silence, sipping the spiked lemonade and thinking on his words. She supposed she could see where he was coming from even though she wanted to toss the drink in the old man's lap for passing judgment on her actions.

"Are you going to try to play wise Native American on me then? Is that part of the game here?"

He shook his head. "You never were one to take advice easily."

"And just how in the hell do you know that? Did they ship you my file or something?"

He laughed outright and poured himself another drink from the pitcher, then lifted it in her direction.

She stared at her glass, held it out. God knew, she was beginning to feel good.

"Files? You White People and your files. Your CIA has files. Your FBI has files. Your NSA has files. Every government has files. Hell, the Russians, the Chinese, the North Koreans have files. And what does it mean? Not a damned thing. A bunch of bullshit, is what it is. Black and white bullshit. I didn't need any file to tell me what I can see for myself."

"It -."

He held up a hand, silencing her.

"Your written words are useless. My People have handed stories down for generations, by mouth. From mother to child, from father to child, from grandparents, aunts, uncles, cousins, to child. For thousands of years we have told and retold the stories -."

"Embellishing them when convenient, no doubt."

"The heart of the story, the meaning, that which is sacred, remains. What remains in your files? Black and white type on paper or computer screen. Bits and bytes. Ones and zeroes. Have you looked at a human being lately? They are not made up of ones and zeroes."

She sipped. "Go on."

"The files may identify you by name but they are useless. The file tells nothing of the person behind the name."

CHAPTER 19

~~~~~~

"When the White Man came to My People for the census he was confounded because we did not have last names. We did not see ourselves as the White Man saw us. We have names with meaning."

"White names have meaning."

He smiled. "If you saw your file and saw dates and names and places, would you see you?"

"I bet my picture is in the file."

"What picture? How old were you when it was taken? Did you know your photo was being taken so that you smiled a pained smile at the stranger taking it? Are you your picture at that moment in time, or is there more to you than what anyone looking at the picture could ever know?"

She wasn't sure what to say.

"The file, including the picture, is bullshit. It's someone's made up story about who you are. I'm assuming it isn't your story, since you didn't write it."

Well, that was true. She sipped and as she did so, her original thought came back to the fore.

"So, if you didn't read any file, then how did you know - ?"

"That you're stubborn and independent and don't take advice unless you agree with it?"

Interesting description. Mule-headed, if she didn't miss her guess on his opinion. Then again, maybe the older man thought that of all young people. She shrugged, nodded.

"You are a doctor, yes?"

"I – well, yeah, okay."

She'd earned a PhD. That earned her the right to be called doctor.

"You're a woman, yes?"

"What the hell does that have to do with anything?"

"You just proved my point."

"What are you talking about?"

"You couldn't have gotten to where you are unless you knew when to ignore advice and make your own way. You have to think. You have to be independent. I didn't need any file to tell me that."

"Is that an apology?"

He laughed. "There is never a cause to apologize for the truth. I do not apologize for enlightenment, for bringing the truth to the light."

"So that good choices can be made?"

"Exactly. Now, let us go find Agent Hernandez, show you to your rooms, and prepare for dinner."

"That had to be one of the strangest conversations I've ever had," she muttered, shaking her head and rising to follow him into the house.

※ ♪ ♫

Talia sighed in frustration and flipped onto her back. How much longer was she going to lay there, knowing sleep was an impossibility? A full moon peeked through dozens of pinholes in worn curtains, illuminating the room, but that wasn't what kept her from being able to sleep. It was knowing she was being held captive.

Oh, Juan and Sani had made a big production at dinner of telling her she could sleep easy, that she was safe. What they didn't seem to understand was that regardless of who had her, captivity was captivity, and she was being held in it. That she was in the country she was born in was immaterial. She wasn't free. She couldn't leave. How was that anything other than being a captive?

She sat up and leaned back, ignoring the uneven texture of peeling wallpaper poking through her t-shirt. She plucked absently at the pills of an old Navajo blanket and considered the irony of landing exactly where she'd worked to avoid. Captivity.

"Until I can assure your safety," Tim told her on the phone after dinner, *"I want you to stay where you are."*

That he hadn't known where that was had been both baffling and terrifying. How could he protect her if he was so out of the know?

"I trust Sean Andrews," he'd explained, before bidding her good night.

She'd tried talking to Juan about it but he'd brushed her concerns aside and, claiming jet lag, had gone to bed early.

Sani had done his best to make her feel at home. He'd offered to play backgammon and had given her the remote, adding that it was a rare man who would turn it over.

"You saw the satellite dish on the roof? I have plenty of choices."

In the end she'd excused herself early, intending to go to sleep. That had been hours ago and she was no closer to meeting the sandman.

Most of the holes in the curtains were tiny and caused moonlight to scatter like tiny dots and rays on pieces of mismatched furniture. The effect was chaotic and yet soothing. Her eyes followed the light from piece to piece, coming to rest on her backpack. Her cell phone was in it.

Christoff would be frantic.

"I don't think you should contact anyone at this point," Tim had advised. *"I'll assure him you're safe."*

Her fingers twisted in the blanket. Why should she trust a man who was keeping her captive because he had problems in his organization? She'd been safer with Christoff. She hadn't felt like a prisoner while staying with him and his sister. She pursed her lips. She certainly trusted the Andrises more than Tim Brightman.

Juan.

She tossed the thought aside and threw back the covers. Pulling her cellphone from the pack, she powered it up. Several messages scrolled across the screen.

All but two were from Christoff and those two were from Chloe. She smiled. They worried over her to no end. It gave her a warm feeling. She read through the messages before texting. She was surprised how quickly a reply came back.

Can you talk?

No.

Not without possibly being overheard, at any rate.

Where are you?

On the Navajo Nation somewhere.

What?!

She briefly explained.

Tim Brightman told me Agent Hernandez was on medical leave.

She bit her lip. Was he upset that the man he assured her could protect her was with her?

The next sentence was long in coming.

This isn't how it was supposed to be.

What did he mean by that? Did he know something about Brightman or Juan? Was she in danger just by being where she was?

I will get you out of this situation. I will contact you shortly with a plan.

Okay.

She turned off the phone and stowed it.

"This isn't how it was supposed to be."

Feeling more unsettled than ever, she stared through curtain holes at the night sky. A glance at her wrist showed it was well after midnight. She could suffer in silence, tossing and turning 'til the sun came up or she could go outside.

Walking around probably wasn't the best idea given the wildlife she'd encounter, but that didn't mean she couldn't sit on the porch and see what else might be seen in the night sky.

The door outside was off the kitchen. A bottle of tequila was on the counter next to the refrigerator. She knew for a fact there was another pitcher of lemonade inside because she'd seen Sani put it in there before going to bed. She debated only moments.

Arms full, Talia used her elbow to push down on the screen door handle, wincing as it screeched open. She'd forgotten about that. Hell, she hoped she hadn't woken the whole house up. Letting out a breath she stepped onto the porch in her stocking feet.

She was surprised to find Juan sitting in the swing.

"Do you mind if I join you?"

"No." He took the pitcher and set it on a small round table.

"Thanks."

"Sure."

She sat in a rocking chair next to the table and began to pour. "Want one? I can get another glass."

"No, thank you."

She splashed tequila into the glass, then moved the glass in a circle, but finally stuck her finger in to stir. "No drinking on duty?"

"Right."

She turned the chair so that it half faced the swing. Unfortunately, between a cloud that had passed in front of the moon and the fact the swing was recessed beneath the porch overhang, she wasn't able to make out Juan's expression. Did he mind that she had disturbed his space?

"Listen, I can go back to my room -."

"Why?"

She took a drink, coughed. Her eyes watered.

"I take it you don't drink much tequila?"

She shook her head, coughed some more. She took another drink, being sure to sip.

"A lot of people prefer to drink it straight."

She didn't comment.

"Why are you up?"

She took another sip, frowned at the glass. Sani was the better bar tender.

"Well?" he asked.

"What?"

"It's past midnight. Why aren't you sleeping?"

"Why aren't you?"

"Jet lag."

"Bullshit. Something's eating at you. You've been a real bastard all day. I'm surprised Sani didn't burn your dinner as repayment for how rude you've been."

"Were you always like this?"

A thrill surged within her. A passionate Juan Hernandez ready to snap at her was much better than the distant Juan who'd all but ignored her.

"What do you mean?"

"You know what I mean, Talia."

She stood, sipped, stared in his direction, cursing the fact his face was hidden in shadow. "Are you asking if I ever cowered before a man?"

He didn't respond.

"Yes. There was a time I cowered."

She'd cowered. She'd given in. She'd been betrayed. Then she'd conquered.

"But no more."

"Is that right?" he said, his voice barely above a whisper.

She took a step closer to the swing. "What happened in Chile?"

Instead of replying, he pushed himself out of the swing and stomped toward a wall positioned about seventy yards behind the house. Sani's property went out further but the wall, and the locked gate that was in its center, kept out unwanted wildlife. She ran after him, wincing when jagged rocks poked into the tender soles of her feet.

"Juan, where are you going?" she bit out.

He kept stomping away from her. Ignoring the pain in her foot, she picked up the pace until a nasty stone took her down.

"Oof." Pushing herself up, she wiped her hands against her jeans and sat down in order to massage the bottom of her right foot. Damn, but that rock had been sharp. Served her right for not wearing her shoes.

"Let me look." She sucked air between her teeth as he ran his thumb over the bottom of first one, then both feet. "Where are your shoes?" he asked, looking down at her stocking'd foot.

"In the bedroom."

"And you didn't think to put them on before coming out because -?"

"I thought I'd be sitting on the porch looking at the stars, not chasing you across the yard."

She fought not to shiver as he slid his thumb into her sock and slowly pulled it off. He began massaging the bottom of her right foot.

"Why did you?" he asked quietly.

"Chase you across the yard?" she replied, equally as quietly. He nodded and slid the other sock off.

God, his fingers felt good as they applied both light and hard pressure and moved in circles around the soles of her feet.

"A couple of reasons, I guess."

"Such as?"

"I was mad that you walked away from me."

"I can understand that since you split on me in the airport in Costa Rica."

"Given everything that's happened, can you blame me?"

"What was the other reason?"

In the dark she smiled. He obviously wasn't ready to concede that she'd done the right thing. At least in her mind she had.

"I wanted an answer."

"Why?"

His fingers slid between her toes and she shivered, swallowed, took a deep breath. "I know something happened in Chile. Something that hurt you. I – I wanted to help."

"She cares for you. A lot. I could see it in her eyes"

Kian's words in Talca came back to Juan. Not knowing how to respond, he focused on her ankles, gently rotating them. He began massaging the backs of her calves, the rhythmic motions as soothing to him as they would be to her.

"Why are you doing this?"

"Someone should be with the woman he loves."

He hadn't allowed himself to think on his father's words. Instead, like he'd done countless times before, he'd shoved the words, and the feelings they inspired, away. Especially when the feeling was hope.

"Your Dr. Blackmoor."

He drew a shaky breath. This time, for some reason, the feelings wouldn't stay buried.

"Let's say something did happen. What makes you think you could help?"

"Because I'm a good listener and most people feel better after getting painful events off their chests."

When any field agent came off an assignment they were given the opportunity to talk to a specialist about any events considered painful. Since Juan typically filed such events under the *goes with the territory* category, he generally skipped such sessions. In effect, he wasn't a person to get things off his chest. He just stuffed them down into some place deep inside where they were shut away. After all these years, he doubted he could do it any other way.

"One of the first rules of field engagement is emotional distance."

"I understand the need to shut off emotions when it means survival."

"Is that what you had to do?"

"I shut off emotions long before I -."

"Faked your death?"

"Right."

"Why?"

"I want to know what happened in Chile."

"And I want to know why you shut off your emotions."

"I asked you first."

"My father put in a rather unexpected appearance."

She remained silent.

"At my place of employment, no less."

"The embassy?"

"He was sitting in my boss' office when I -."

'When you?"

"When I stormed in there."

"You mean when you kicked in the door and demanded to know where I was?"

"Who told you that?"

"A number of people, actually. Your dedication to your mission is admirable."

"Yeah, well, I wasn't -."

"You don't have to explain."

Had he been about to admit that she wasn't just a mission, that he had feelings for her? While she would have loved to hear that, what mattered now were his feelings.

So, your dad was sitting -."

"My father."

"Okay. Your father was in Tim's office. I take it he was there to see you, though?"

"Yeah."

"What did he want?"

"He claimed to be concerned because I'd been injured."

"But you have a different idea?"

"I hadn't seen the guy in some ten years. He shows up out of the blue and I'm supposed to think he gives a shit whether I'm alive or dead?"

Talia considered the situation. She was a good listener but she wondered if maybe talking might be a better way to move forward. After all, being abandoned by a parent was something she could relate to all too well.

"I'm an orphan."

"Yeah, I saw that in your file. You were raised by your uncle on a farm in Kansas. Your parents died. They didn't walk out on you."

Sani's words about files came back to her. *"The files may identify you by name but they are useless. The file tells nothing of the person behind the name."*

"Actually, they did. At least, my mother did."

"To be an orphan," he said slowly, "your parents have to have died."

"She did, but she walked out first." She went on to explain.

"Is that what led you to your work with coma patients?"

"Yep."

"Is that why you shut your emotions down?" Before she could reply, he continued. "No, that can't be it. Your work with the machine was a manifestation of those emotions. If anything, you allowed your emotions to drive your actions."

"Right."

"What changed?"

Kyle.

Talia ruthlessly shoved the images away. "I want to talk about you. How old were you when your father walked out?"

"He never walked in," he answered, then went on to elaborate.

"Do you get along with your mom?"

"Sure, I suppose."

"How often do you see her?"

"I try to get home for either Christmas or her birthday, which is in June."

"Being the dutiful son?"

"What's that supposed to mean?"

"I wonder if you're doing it for you or for her?"

"A little of both, I suppose. Maybe more one year and less another."

"Do you want a relationship with your father? Would you accept one if he offered?"

CHAPTER 20

~~~~~~

Juan snorted. "Trust me, Benito Hernandez wouldn't offer."

"I didn't ask if he would offer. I asked if you would accept it if he did."

"No, I doubt it."

"I think your solution is in that answer. Part of you thinks you want the father who wasn't there for you but you wouldn't accept him if he wanted to become a part of your life now."

"He wasn't there when I was younger, when I needed him."

"But you don't and won't know the difference. You only know the life you grew up with. You can't resent something you cannot compare your circumstances to. Not really. Neither can I."

"Yeah, I see where you're coming from."

They were quiet. He'd stopped massaging her legs but they still rested in his lap.

"What about you?" he asked. "You had it and then it was gone. Do you resent that?"

"I went through a period in my life when I did."

"How old were you?"

"Eighteen. I'd just graduated from high school."

"What did you do?"

"I went off to college and poured all my frustrations into my work so I didn't have to think about it."

That wasn't all she'd done but she didn't feel comfortable talking about it to the agent. To anyone, really. It sat inside her like a shard of glass she was afraid to remove for fear the bleeding would never stop if she did.

"So, you never really worked through it?"

"I don't resent her anymore. I guess I must have."

"What do you think I should do?"

"Honestly? I think you should ask yourself what you want in your life and go for it."

"Huh? I meant about my father."

"I know what you meant, Juan. You can't do anything about the situation with him. Don't waste your energy. You can do something about the things in life that make you happy though. Do you like your job?"

"Yeah, sure. I catch bad guys. I serve the greater good."

"I didn't ask what you do, I asked if you liked it."

"Yeah, I must because I've been doing it for years."

"Do you think maybe you aren't mad about your father so much as mad that his presence made you think about what you are doing and whether or not you want to keep doing it?"

"What are you talking about?"

"Do you want children of your own? I don't know how many spies have kids, but -."

"A lot of them do."

"What kind of a life is it? Do they move around from place to place? Do they really know their fathers? Or their mothers, for that matter since there are obviously women spies. And what about the spouses? Do you have to marry another spy or are you allowed to marry a civilian? And what kind of a relationship would it be given the number of lies that exist within it? Is that what you want for yourself?"

"I hadn't thought about it."

"Maybe seeing your father brought it into your subconscious. Maybe you looked at the man and wondered, on some level, if that was your future. Would you not know your own son?"

"I would never walk out on a child."

"Okay, but what kind of life would you have with him or her if you are a spy who is routinely wounded in the line of duty."

"Cops and firemen have kids."

"But those kids understand why their parents get hurt. You wouldn't be telling your son that you are a spy and therefore sometimes get shot with poison darts."

"You know, I'm tired. Thanks for listening."

Talia blinked. The sudden shift in conversation wasn't entirely unexpected but it hurt just the same. She sighed.

"Any time."

"I'll carry you back."

"Thanks. And thanks for the massage. It was very relaxing. I think I'll be able to sleep now."

She let him carry her as far as the porch. "I can take it from here."

Juan stared up in the dark, Talia's words replaying in his head.

"What kind of a relationship would it be given the number of lies that exist within it?"

Kaila.

He fought to push away the image of wavy blonde hair, smiling green eyes.

Lies.

The woman had been a lot more than she'd seemed and it was better if he remembered how easy it was to lose perspective. Especially if he let the little head do the thinking for him.

Years ago, he'd been on a mission to bring down a fairly small international crime ring working out of Talca, Chile. In the course of trying to find the ring leader, he'd been captured at gunpoint and hauled into a cargo shipping container, along with three other individuals, one of them Kaila Ross.

The woman had proved to be a tremendous asset and was greatly responsible for their being able to not only free themselves, but to bring the leader, along with his number two and number three associates, to justice. It was only after the debriefing that he'd discovered the real reason behind her ability to not only effectively improvise, but to anticipate the enemy's next move.

She was a psychic. Not just a psychic, but a psychic who had been trained as an operative for a sister organization. It was bad enough she hadn't been completely honest with him, telling him she was an archeologist. To find out she was part of a group he held in suspicion, if not derision, had quickly put out the fire. Beautiful or not, she was *one of them*.

Growing up in the Latino culture, he had seen more than his share of individuals claiming to be gifted with supernatural powers. From psychic surgeons to shamanism to self-proclaimed healers, he had listened to ridiculous claims of miracles to be gained. For a price. And therein lay the rub.

More often than not, these *supernatural wonders* had preyed on vulnerable souls who, in their moments of suffering, were willing to do almost anything, including going broke, and all for whatever miracle they decided they couldn't live without.

Discovering that the beautiful intelligent woman he'd been passionately attracted to was one of them had royally pissed him off. He'd never seen any evidence that she used her abilities to harm anyone but the potential was there. And that wasn't the only thing that angered him.

He'd missed it. He'd been taken in by green eyes that laughed even in the midst of danger. Her calm, her ability to laugh in the face of death had made him blind to the truth, that there might be more to Kaila Ross than was on the surface. In the end, that killed the relationship. The lies that were between them, would always be between them.

It was beyond ironic, really. In his heart he knew honesty in a romantic relationship was paramount yet an impossibility as long as he was a spy. He lied for a living.

"Do you think maybe you aren't mad about your father so much as mad that his presence made you think about what you are doing and whether or not you want to keep doing it?"

On the nightstand, his phone lit up. He snatched it and focused on the text message. It was from Foster.

Call me.

He replied. *Five minutes.*

Not wanting to wake anyone, he walked out the front door and moved as close to the edge of the property as he could. The satellite phone ensured he got critical updates from Andrews, and the occasional report from Foster. He dialed.

"You need to know something."

"What?"

"She contacted Andris."

"When?"

"Earlier. She sent him a text. She's setting up to run and he's promised to help her. She told him she's on the Rez but she doesn't know where. Given the man's reach, not to mention the resources he can call on, I'd say it's only a matter of time before someone shows up to help her run."

"Have you updated Andrews?"

"He's standing next to me."

"What does he suggest?"

"He's spoken to his uncle already and you're both being moved as soon as possible. Sani's making the arrangements."

"I don't think I should snatch her phone."

"Definitely not. We're able to keep tabs on the communications at this point which means we can stay one step ahead of them for now."

Juan stared at Talia's bedroom window. Was she the victim she claimed to be? She certainly didn't come across as frightened. If anything, she seemed determined. Determined, but to do what?

"Is Kaila there?"

A pause.

"Yeah."

"Put her on."

Another pause.

"Okay."

He continued staring at Talia's window, imagining her beneath the sheets.

"Juan?"

He blinked, mentally shook himself. "Listen, I need you to do something for me and I don't want you to discuss it with anyone else. Not yet anyway."

A long pause.

"Okay."

His eyes on the bedroom window, he relayed his request.

A heavy sigh came over the line. "Yeah, okay. I get it."

"I mean it. No one else."

"Yeah, I get it."

The line went dead.

Juan stood beneath the stars staring at Talia's window. She hadn't been honest with him. She acted like she cared about his feelings but she intended to run the first chance she got. He wondered briefly what she'd planned to tell him before she did so. Maybe she hadn't planned on telling him anything.

Had the whole talk in the backyard been one big lie? Not wanting to consider the answer, he returned to his room and hoped sleep would come soon.

🌶 🌶 🌶

Juan stared at the empty place at the kitchen table, then at the wall clock. She'd gotten to bed late, no doubt, but he still expected to see Talia up by now. The kitchen door screeched as Sani walked inside, carrying an empty bottle.

"She drank *the whole thing*?"

Sani shook his head. "Not exactly. The bottle wasn't full to begin with."

He stared at the hallway leading to the bedrooms. When he put her down on the porch he'd assumed she was going to go to bed. He sighed, made his way to her door.

A tequila hangover? Not good.

He knocked.

"What?"

It was a piteous sound. He couldn't help it. He smiled. He cleared his throat and tried to wipe the smile from his face. He turned the knob.

"It's like a cave in here."

"Don't you dare open those curtains!" she snapped. "Ohh."

His smile widened as he sat on the edge of the bed.

"You enjoy seeing people suffer, do you?" she asked.

"No."

"You're smiling and there's nothing funny about how I feel, I assure you."

"I'm sure there's not. What were you thinking to drink -?"

She held up a hand. "Do – not – lecture me."

"Fair enough. Be right back."

He went to the kitchen. "Oh, hair of the dog." He accepted a Bloody Mary from Sani. "I'm sure she'll appreciate that. Got any aspirin to go with it?"

"And breakfast too."

"I am not serving her in bed."

"Of course not. She's got two good legs. She has to come to the table."

Juan was surprised to see her sitting up. He handed her the drink.

"Thanks." She sipped, winced. "Vodka."

"When your head quits pounding you'll be grateful."

"Would you believe that's the first time I drank tequila?"

"What, no margaritas?"

"No. I don't drink foo foo drinks. Wine or beer."

He shook his head, held up his cell phone.

"Hangover symptoms occur typically after the intoxicating effect of the alcohol begins to wear off, generally the morning after a night of heavy drinking." He looked at her. "Too much tequila can make for a mean hangover."

"So I see."

He tried to smother a laugh.

"The least you could do is suggest a remedy."

He looked back at the phone. "There is no compelling evidence to suggest that any remedies are effective for preventing or treating alcohol hangover. Avoiding alcohol or drinking in moderation are the most effective ways to avoid a hangover."

He looked at her. "You shouldn't have had so much tequila."

She glared at him.

"Hey, I brought you the Bloody Mary."

"Well, you can see I'm still alive. Now get out."

"You need to come to breakfast. Sani made pancakes."

"No. I'm going to finish this and go back to sleep."

"You need food and then a shower. You can walk to the kitchen or I can drag you."

She glared at him.

He sighed, shoved the phone into his front pocket, and then moved to stand next to where she sat.

"You wouldn't."

He slid one arm beneath her knees, another behind her back, and lifted her from the bed.

"Put me down," she hissed.

"I will. In the kitchen."

"What happened to those two good legs?" Sani asked, adding two sausage links to a plate.

"She hurt her foot last night."

"There's nothing wrong with my foot," she snapped. "It's my head that's killing me."

Sani put two aspirin in front of her, along with a plate of food.

"Thanks."

"Eat."

"Then a shower," Juan added.

She opened her mouth to suggest he stop ordering her about but shut it when he began shaking his head. "I will dump you under cold water myself. If you don't think I will I suggest you remember how you got in here."

Symptoms occur typically after the intoxicating effect begins to wear off.

She was beginning to think she didn't have a tequila hangover, but a Juan hangover. She shoved a bite of pancake in her mouth.

Sani and Juan sat at the table.

"Where's yours?"

"We ate already."

While she finished her breakfast, Sani shared the plan.

"When do we leave?"

He slid another pancake onto her plate. "Tomorrow morning. Do you have anything other than tennis shoes?"

"No, why?"

"We'll be hiking over some rough terrain. I'll find a pair for loan."

"I'm not wearing anyone else's boots."

Juan stood. "I'll take care of it. What's your shoe size?"

"You mean my boot size since it's a half a size bigger."

"Write down both."

The old man slid a piece of paper across the table. "Write it on that. It's a list of what we need. If we aren't here when you get back, we'll be visiting the horses."

"Wait a minute." Talia carried her plate to the sink. "I don't understand why we're leaving in the first place."

She began washing dishes. "I thought you said I could choose to heal yet you're dragging me to this healing place you talk about. That doesn't sound like a choice."

She continued washing and rinsing, but no one said anything. She turned. "Is something wrong? Are we not safe here?"

"We are being proactive," Juan answered.

"Being proactive? Why? What aren't you telling me?"

He cleared his throat. *What aren't you telling me, Talia?* "I'll see you later."

She stared at Juan's retreating back, then looked at Sani.

"When did you decide this and why?"

"It was always part of the plan. I was hoping you would want to go to the healing place. It is a sacred space and a place of peace. A good place to recover."

"I already told you, I feel fine."

"Would you keep Juan from having the opportunity to heal?"

She thought of the previous night's conversation.

"Am I in danger? Is that what you mean by proactive? Or are you just using that as an excuse so you can get us to go to the healing place?"

"Perhaps a little of both in this case."

She handed him a plate and a dish towel to dry it with. "Are you staying with us or are we being shuffled off to someone else?"

"You would be denied access without me."

"Are you a shaman?"

"Let's just say I can set people on the path to healing."

They finished the dishes.

"I'd better go pack."

"Pack later. I told Ketsoh we'd be over by noon."

"Ketsoh?"

"My neighbor."

"What does his name mean?"

"Big feet."

"Does he have big feet?"

"Yes, and one of them is usually firmly planted in his mouth."

She smirked. "Let me go get my shoes on and I'll meet you out front."

Her backpack was sitting in the corner next to her tennis shoes. She slid her phone out but didn't immediately power it on.

Juan.

Guilt tugged at her conscience. Should she tell him she was in touch with Christoff? Her benefactor seemed upset that the agent was with her which didn't make any sense since he'd not only told her she could trust him to keep her safe, he'd arranged to have him meet her in Hong Kong. To keep her safe.

While she waited for the phone to power up she pulled on her shoes. Before she could change her mind, she sent a text.

We're being moved tomorrow morning.

Where?

Some place called the healing Place.

Acknowledged.

She switched it off and shoved it to the bottom of her pack.

CHAPTER 21

~~~~~~

Talia ran her hand down a velvety equine nose. "How long have you had him?"

"Three months."

"Where did you get him?"

"I bought him from a man who said he captured him on the range."

She leaned around the beautiful mustang's head to gaze at Sani's neighbor. "Do you know the guy who captured this horse? Have you purchased from him before?"

"He comes through every other year," Sani answered.

"How long had the trader had him before he sold him to you?"

All the while she spoke she ran her hand over the horse. He shuddered more than once which told her he'd been badly mistreated.

"Do you care for him or do you have help?"

"My sons help me."

She rubbed his nose, smiled when his ears flicked toward her. "Do they know what they're doing?"

"Of course they know what they're doing."

"I ask because this horse isn't recovering from whatever trauma he's been put through and if he's been well cared for, three months should bring him further along, given how young he is."

She looked at the owner. "What are your plans for him? Are you going to sell him?"

"Of course."

She slid a hand down the horse's neck. "How soon?"

"That depends."

She gazed into its beautiful eyes. "On what?"

"On whether or not he gets caught."

Talia turned to see Juan standing at the entrance to the stables. He walked over and ran a hand down the horse's neck.

"Isn't that right?"

"Gets caught at what?"

"Illegal horse trading," Juan answered. "Trading without a license."

"You mean there's a chance this horse could be confiscated and let free again only to be recaptured later?" She looked at the beautiful chestnut horse. "No wonder he's so traumatized."

She continued smoothing her hand slowly down the horse's body. "How much do you want for him?"

"Two hundred," Sani answered.

Ketsoh sputtered. "I will decide -."

"He's green broke, right?" she interrupted, meaning he was not ready to accept a rider though he might be willing to accept a saddle and bridle.

"Yes."

"Then two hundred is fair. I have someone who'll take him."

"Who?"

"Me. I'll buy him from you."

"You're in no position to buy a horse," Juan snapped.

She turned to him. "Excuse me, are you part of this conversation? I think not." She turned back to Ketsoh. "How much to get him where I need him to go? In Idaho."

She could feel Juan's eyes boring into her as she haggled over the cost of transport. Thanks to Sani's interference, she got the price dropped in half.

"Who do you know in Idaho?" Juan asked, following her toward Sani's Jeep.

"Someone who knows about horses. He'll be happy to have that mustang. He's a beauty and young enough that with the proper care he can be turned into a decent trail horse. The man I have in mind has patience for the work it will take and he has the right people around him. Ketsoh's sons aren't the best qualified from what I've seen."

"They're in it for a buck."

"That's clear enough. Still," she said, turning and looking at the stable, "I don't think they're abusive." She sighed, got in the vehicle. "At least that one will go to a good home."

🌶 🌶 🌶

Talia sat on the back porch and drummed her fingers against the floorboards. Another sleepless night only this time, no company.

When they'd returned from Ketsoh's that afternoon, Juan had disappeared into his room after informing her he had a lot of work to do. He'd made a brief appearance at dinner where he barely spoke two words, then returned to his room.

She'd used Sani's computer to send a message about the mustang. As she'd suspected, her friend was more than happy to take him.

How much do I owe?

Nothing. Consider it payment for working with him.

When are we going to see you up here? It's been too long.

Her eyes had burned with unshed tears as she'd stared at the screen. It had been years since she'd been to Idaho.

Perhaps more than any one place, that ranch symbolized the life she'd left behind. The life she'd lost.

She swiped at her tears and typed the truth.

Soon, I hope.

Blowing out a sigh, she studied the horizon. Away from city lights, with the moon intermittently hidden behind clouds, it was pretty dark. There were plenty of stars and she was fairly certain she could see Mars, Mercury, and Jupiter, depending on which direction she looked.

"Cole, can Talia stay at our house tonight? I got that telescope I got for my birthday working and it's supposed to be clear tonight."

"If she wants to go."

"Of course I want to!"

She'd loved staying at the Truex house. It was a wonderful way to escape the quiet of home. With three boys, there was never a dull moment and Mrs. Truex was a wonderful cook. Talia got her own room and because the Truexes only had boys, she was treated like a princess.

The telescope had been set up in the loft of their barn. There was a large hole in the roof from when heavy snow had caused boards infected with dry rot to collapse.

"Thank you for having me over."

"You're doing me a favor. My brothers leave me alone when you're around. My mom makes them. When you aren't here, she just looks the other way."

"I can't see it. Where am I supposed to be looking?"

He moved behind her and gently guided her head. *"Do you see it now? It should be in the upper and middle left. It's kind of fuzzy but -."*

"I got it. That's Venus? Wow."

"Here, let me adjust it and you can see Elnath."

"Elnath?"

"It's a star."

He slid his arms to her shoulders and guided her away from the telescope. Instead of adjusting the telescope, however, he turned her toward him. For several seconds he just looked at her.

"Billy?"

"You're growing up."

She reached out, touched the soft whiskers along his jawline. "So are you."

The fifteen year old boy had been shaving for years and the whiskers were prickly. She closed her eyes as he leaned forward and pressed his lips against hers. When his tongue touched hers it was as if she'd touched the cord to the barn light. It was worn in several places and if you weren't careful you usually got a shock.

"Did I scare you?" he whispered.

"No, just surprised me, that's all. Well, maybe. A little."

"It's called French kissing."

"It makes my tummy feel weird."

"Bad weird or good weird?"

"Good weird. Definitely good."

"Well then…"

A sound to her right snapped her out of her daydreaming. She cocked her head and replayed the sound, trying to make out if it was one of the guys or an animal.

"Must have been an animal," she murmured after minutes of silence.

She knew why she couldn't sleep. Her mind was restless. Not enough to do and way too much think time. She hated being held captive, and what else could she call it? Other than the trip to Ketsoh's, she hadn't been allowed to go anywhere, not even the local market.

"Tell me what you need," Juan had replied when she mentioned it. "Or Sani."

She studied the boots Juan had bought for her. They were a perfect fit and quite comfortable. She was also wearing a soft flannel shirt he'd picked up.

"I don't know why I couldn't have gone with him."

"It's for your own safety," Sani replied, looking at her with sympathy.

Even Christoff had advised her to remain at the house when she told him she was going stir crazy.

"Be patient," he'd advised in a text message earlier that evening.

"Be patient," she grumbled. "For how much longer?"

She stood and stretched. A glance back at the house showed all was dark and quiet. A steady wind blew clouds across the moon. The eerie appearance made her think of Lon Chaney's *The Wolfman.*

Far from tired, she stood and walked toward the rear wall. She had no intention of wandering the high desert after dark though Sani had assured the adobe barrier kept most of the dangers away from his house and immediate yard. Apart from scorpions or the occasional snake.

"That's another reason I wanted you to wear boots. Be sure to tuck your jeans into them if you decide to go out at night again."

It had been all she could do not to look at Juan.

A sudden gust lifted the hair off her shoulders. She pulled the pale blue flannel blouse tighter around the orange t-shirt Juan had grabbed off the sale rack. They were high up enough that it didn't get as hot as it did in the Phoenix Valley, but once the sun set it cooled significantly.

She walked to the gate, wrapped her fingers around the bars, and stared into the darkness. It amazed her to think of all the life sitting or slithering in the dark, perhaps eyeing her at that very moment. She shivered. Maybe she should head back to the house.

To what purpose, stare at the bedroom ceiling for a few more hours? Count the pills on the Navajo blanket spread across the double bed?

She wasn't just restless, she was lonely. In the nightmare that had become her life since she learned of the company's plans for her dream, she'd had to cut herself off from so many people. Too many people. People she trusted. People she loved.

Love.

She'd cut herself off from love. She'd had to. When the images had flashed across the screen in the conference room she'd known that those who wanted her machine would stop at nothing to have it. She didn't worry for herself. They'd already told her they could do it with her or without her. She had to think of those they would hurt, those she loved.

Christoff had helped her fake her pedestrian death which, in New York City, was both easy and difficult. With so many bodies and cars in the same small space, the idea of a woman being hit by a car was far from unheard of. Having all the right people in place to bring it off at a moment's notice was nothing short of a Broadway production. All arranged and paid for by one Christoff Andris, MD.

He'd assigned a personal guard who was never more than three blocks' away from her location. He'd had an ambulance sitting in an old garage halfway between her office and her apartment. Men in uniform were a dime a dozen so the players had been the easy part.

When he'd first floated the idea, she'd worried that something would go horribly wrong and she would truly wind up dead. He'd assured her that this body guard had been through the ultimate test in driving.

"He was with the Israeli army before he came to work for me. He is the best. You will be tapped but the rest is up to you. You need to make it look as if you've been hit with enough force to kill you."

Therein lay the second concern. She wasn't that good of an actress. Little did she know, her boss, a man she decided was evil, would save the day.

She'd left the conference room that cold November morning completely numb. She'd walked like a zombie away from the office, visions of previous rehearsals playing like a movie in her mind. In her state of shock, it had taken little more than the sight of her bodyguard behind the wheel of the car that tapped her with its bumper to bring her down.

The man had jumped out of the car and, before a crowd had begun to gather, liberally dispersed the fake blood. He held her hand and promised her everything would be alright.

"Somebody, call an ambulance!"

The decoy had arrived first and she was driven away even as sirens hailed the approach of the real one.

A cool wind wound beneath Talia's hair, brushed against her neck, and slithered down her back. Wanting to avoid a shiver, she shrugged, tilted her head first one way then the next.

She may have faked her death but there was no doubt. That was the day her life had ended.

She'd been flown by private jet to Sydney, Australia, where another hired guard met her at the airport. He'd taken her to the Australian outback, to live away from prying eyes.

The locals had been eager and anxious to befriend a new face and God knew, she'd wanted to. But, she also knew that if The Company found out she was still alive, the ones she loved the most would suffer.

So, she'd lived in isolation. In fact, once she'd gotten her bearings, she'd moved to the outer edges, close to the Aboriginals who were only too happy to keep their distance.

"It's time for you to move."

"Why? Am I in danger? Have they found me?"

"No, dearest, they have not found you. I simply believe that it is best for you to move. Eighteen months is a long time in one place. The chances of discovery go up with every day that passes."

"Okay, where to?"

"Costa Rica."

She'd been skeptical.

"The US military is close by, in Panama."

"The US military is not looking for you. Costa Rica is not far from my home. I can better protect you -."

"Fine. When should I start packing?"

Talia stared at Sani's house. The only visible light was from the stovetop range hood. Was Juan sleeping? She hoped so. Unlike Sani, he seemed so on edge. Maybe the old Native American was right and he needed the healing place.

Last night she'd heard his story but in her heart she knew there was more. Something was eating at Agent Juan Hernandez and it had nothing to do with his father. Or his mother. If she was reading him right, and it was a skill she prided herself in having, she would bet he was as lonely as she was. So was the Native American, though he wouldn't admit it.

The old man had acted aloof but she'd seen beneath his ploy the moment he'd showed her his medals.

"I was in the Air Force Special Services," he'd explained.

"With Sean?"

He laughed. *"No, before Sean. Who do you think suggested he serve?"*

"Why would you care?"

"Because he is my nephew."

"Brother or sister's child?"

"Sister."

He'd gone on to tell her several stories of valor by various members of their family, including Sean. By the time she was setting the table for dinner, there was no doubt that, for as long as she was his guest, she would be kept safe.

As if Fate was showing her hand, the sound of a twig snapping carried over the wall. Was someone out there or was it just an animal poking about for food? She'd seen yellow eyes peering at her through the rear iron gate the night before.

"It is a good omen," Sani had told her that morning at breakfast.

"How do you figure?"

"Yeah," Juan had seconded, "how do you figure? I don't know that that omen wouldn't find her a tasty meal if given the chance."

"He is a totem," he'd asserted. "The wolf won't hurt her. He wouldn't have shown himself if that had been his intention. He was letting her know he is protecting her."

Instead of replying, the agent had ordered her not to go close to the gate.

"What do you think he's going to do?" she'd taunted, *"jump over it and eat me?"*

"The better to taste you with, my dear."

Her musings were cut short by a hand going around her mouth. Even as she tried to pry the fingers away, she was grabbed and dragged backward. She struggled violently until she realized she recognized the voice hissing in her ear.

"Dmb?" she mumbled against fingers holding her jaw in a vice grip.

"Will you promise to keep silent if I take my hand away?"

She nodded, the movement jerky since he was holding her so tightly. He loosened his fingers but didn't remove his hand.

"Dan?" she hissed.

He pulled his hand away and ordered her to drop down.

"I have to admit," he said a little breathlessly, "your being out here at this late hour is damned convenient. I didn't relish the idea of going in to get you."

"Why not?"

"Look."

Orange light danced behind ragged curtains.

"Fire?" she gasped, scrambling to get up. Dan yanked her back.

"Exactly. Your location has been compromised."

"I have to get back there!"

"Whoa! Wait!" He worked to keep her from running back to the house and when that proved difficult, he pushed her down and used his weight and size to keep her there.

Talia thrashed and twisted, struggling to get free.

"Let me go," she snapped.

"Are you nuts? The place is burning to the ground!"

"I have to go back!" she yelped, tears spilling down her cheeks.

Dan stared in disbelief. "Don't tell me. A necklace?"

She stopped struggling for a moment and looked at him in confusion. "What?"

"You need something from the house? Something you can't live without?"

"Juan's in there!" she yelled. "I have to get him out!"

"Oh, geez. Is that all?"

She struggled with renewed vigor. "Is -?"

"He and Sani are safe. I was going back for you but you saved me the trouble by being outside."

"Juan's safe? Where is he?"

In spite of the clouds covering the waning moon, she could tell he was smiling. She could see his teeth. "Care for him do you? Good. He needs that. Stubborn ass. Yes, he's safe and I'll be taking you to him but not just yet. For right now we have to sit tight."

"Why?"

"Because we don't -."

His words were cut off when the house suddenly exploded.

"Gas?"

"Propane," Dan answered. "I told Sani two years ago that he had the tank too close to the house. Stubborn fool. Then again, the bastards won't look too closely to see if -."

Fireballs rained down on the yard. The wind carried one of them to their location where it proceeded to set Dan's jacket on fire.

CHAPTER 22

~~~~~~

Talia wasted no time. Using the element of surprise, she shoved him off and pushed him onto his back. She kept pushing as she rolled him until the flames went out.

"You okay?" she panted.

"Yeah, I don't think it got to the skin. Thanks to your quick reaction."

"Glad to help."

Talia could read the agent's expression in the fire's reflection.

"What? This? Listen, when you work in a lab full of highly flammable chemicals -." She panted. "You learn to put out fires as quickly as you can."

"Ah."

"What's that supposed to mean? Ah?"

"It means that working in a lab doesn't teach you the calm you need to do what you just did."

"Running for your life does."

He intended to ask her about that later. He nodded briskly. "I think we can go now. That show ought to keep them occupied for a bit."

"Them?"

"The bastards who set the fire. I doubt they want to hang around to answer questions. They're likely high tailing it down the mountain. Follow me."

"Wait, there's a wolf -."

"If you mean that pup that hangs out by the gate, I saw him earlier. He's not going to cause any trouble for us."

"A totem?"

He laughed. "I see you've been talking to Sani. No, he ran off. We're safe enough. Follow me."

After Dan locked the back gate, he grabbed her wrist and led her toward Ketsoh's.

"Where's Juan?"

"Waiting for you. If he saw that fireball, and I can't see how he'd miss it, he will be pretty frantic right about now."

She stopped so suddenly she nearly yanked him off his feet.

"You're stronger than you look. You about ripped my arm out of joint. What's the matter?"

"Juan won't be frantic. He's all but turned my safety over to Sani."

Dan seemed to debate something for several seconds. Letting out a breath, he shook his head. "Men who are used to hiding their feelings for a living don't have an easy time expressing them."

"What are you saying?" she asked quietly.

"I know you don't have anything to make a comparison to but trust me when I tell you that he hasn't been himself since he took your case."

She waited, said nothing.

"Juan was known for his even temperament. The man just never lost it. All that shit about hot blooded Latinos? I don't know where the man stuffed it, but he was as cool as they come. Made him the best at his job."

She nodded slowly, digesting the information.

"When he kicked Brightman's door in? He brought the entire Embassy to a standstill. Total lockdown. The Duty Officer told me he thought he was going to have kill him. He thought Juan had snapped."

"Everyone has a breaking point, Agent Foster."

"And his was you. He wanted to know where you were."

"And Tim ordered him on medical leave."

"Which he obeyed, right?"

She smiled down at the hiking boots. "I hope you're right," she said, finally.

"Do you want me to be?"

She looked up. "Yeah, I do."

"Good. Now come on. I'm sure he's going crazy thinking I didn't get to you in time."

"Actually, he isn't."

At Dan's sudden stop, Talia slammed face first into his back. Damn if her face didn't feel like it was on fire, and that wasn't because of the recent run in with a fireball. How long had Juan been standing there?

"Bout time you showed up, Hernandez."

"Sani was worried."

"Sani was, huh?"

She smiled into Dan's back.

"Actually, it was Agent Ross. She was worried about you. I was just trying to save your delicate ego."

For Talia, it was as if the sun had come out from behind a cloud. If Juan was insulting his colleague then there was a good chance Mr. Robot had taken a vacation. For how long she didn't know, but even an hour or two would be welcome. Taking a deep breath, she stepped around Dan.

"He caught on fire, you know."

"What?"

She told him about the fireballs raining down.

"You need to check your back."

Dan shrugged. "Then I guess we'd better get a move on."

Talia was surprised to find Sean Andrews at the stables.

"Are you okay?" he asked her.

"We both are." She told him about the explosion and rolling Dan around on the ground.

"That was quick thinking. Let me take a look." He examined his friend's back in silence before slapping him on the shoulder. "Kaila won't be pissed."

"What?" Talia asked, confused.

"She doesn't have to be on the bottom because his back hurts too much."

She rolled her eyes, shook her head, then laughed outright.

Pop! Pop! Pop!

Before she could react, Juan yanked her over to a corner of the stable and shoved her behind him. In fact, he was practically sitting on top of her, firing a weapon.

"Can you ride?"

"Of course!"

"Get on a horse. I'll cover you!"

"What about you?"

"Don't fucking argue with me! Get up there!"

"Not until you tell me -."

"I'm going with you! Damn it, but you're stubborn!"

"The only kind to have if you ask me!" Dan shouted from where he stood at the entrance to the stable, shooting out into the night.

Working frantically, she began saddling the mustang.

"Are you nuts?" Juan shouted. "You can't ride him!"

"I'm not leaving him!" she yelled back, continuing to secure the saddle. She leaned close, pressed her lips to the horse's head near the ear. After speaking words she hoped would reassure the young horse, she pulled herself into the saddle.

The horse shifted, threw his head, and tried to throw her. Because she'd been expecting as much, she compensated.

"You are nuts!" Juan shouted, coming up behind her.

"Like I said," Dan shouted over the gunfire, "the only type of woman worth having. Get out of here! We'll cover you!"

At that moment she saw that Sean Andrews was also firing into the darkness. She heard the sound of gunfire overhead and assumed Kaila Ross was up in the loft.

"Go!" Juan shouted and she kicked her heels, sending the horse sprinting through the stable door and into the line of fire.

"That way!" Juan yelled, pointing.

"How do you know?" she shouted back. Still, she obeyed.

"I'll tell you later!"

"Riding out into the darkness is not a good idea!"

"And sticking around to get shot at is?"

His voice, deep and soft in her ear, sent chills down her spine. In response to her shiver he leaned close, pressing into her back. The heat from his body seeped through her shirt. God, he felt good.

"Where are we going?"

He reached around her and took the reins out of her hands. "Where we'll be safe."

Having his arms around her felt better than reassuring. It felt wonderful.

"I was supposed to be safe there."

"Trust me."

"I do."

And she did. In fact, she was coming to realize he was the only one she felt truly safe with. She didn't want to think what that said about Christoff so she concentrated on keeping the horse from throwing them.

They rode for over forty-five minutes, almost straight up into the dark. The higher they climbed the colder it got.

"I didn't know you could ride," she observed.

"I had lessons."

"When?"

"At the academy."

"You were in the military?"

"Naturally."

"Whose?

"What do you mean, whose? The US military!"

"Which group?"

"I went to an elite academy, okay?"

"Marine, then."

He didn't respond. The academy his father had sent him to, that he himself had attended, was known for turning out some of the world's finest military leaders. It was in a class all its own.

"There should be a blanket in that saddle bag Dan handed me. I'll wrap you in it once we get where we're going."

After another fifteen minutes he guided the horse sharply to the left, toward a butte. What looked to be a crevice was actually an entrance into a small canyon. They began riding down into it.

"Is that a tipi?"

"It's a sweat lodge."

"Then they'll know about this place."

"It's been abandoned for decades. Besides, we aren't staying long. If they're using satellite they may pick this up but by the time they can send anyone up here, we'll be gone."

"You're assuming we weren't followed."

"Trust me. We weren't followed."

"Do you guys just have some sort of trust thing?"

"No. But I do trust Andrews and Foster. They saw combat."

"Afghanistan?"

"How'd you know? You a psychic?"

"No, just guessing."

"Good guess."

"Deductive reasoning. How many places could they have seen combat? Given their age, I mean."

"You're assuming the US government is forthcoming about every place they send soldiers to kill."

"Um, no, actually, I don't assume anything."

Not anymore.

"I just put together the fact they are retired and they were in Special Forces. Then I combed through my meager memory resources -."

Juan snorted. "I concede."

"No -."

"No, really. I give up. I give up." He kissed the space behind her ear. "I don't want to argue with you."

She smiled. "Do you think they will send drones?"

"On the Navajo Nation? I think not. A more powerful country within a country -."

"The Vatican."

"Ah, but corruption can only continue for so long before being brought into the light."

"Juan!"

"Hey, I don't like the way religion has been a front for -."

'Let's not argue, okay?"

He kissed the back of her neck and when she shivered, he held her tighter. "Okay. Let's park this guy." He guided the horse next to the Native American sweat lodge and swung down.

"I have to admit, I'm impressed. You handled him beautifully." He rubbed a hand affectionately down the horse's nose. "You, too, young fella. You performed beautifully."

The horse nickered and Talia smiled. "You do know horses."

He held his arms out for her and helped her off the horse, quickly grabbing the reins when the mustang made as if to bolt.

"Him, we'll have to hide."

"What do you mean?"

"I don't think we want him in the sweat lodge with us."

"Why not?" She worked not to laugh at Juan's expression. His mouth moved but nothing came out.

He let out a breath. "Well, it'll stink."

"Never slept in a barn?"

"Have you?"

Uh -.

Hmm, she'd put her foot in that one, hadn't she?

"I want to hear all about it."

"No!"

"Natalia Blackmoor? In exchange for bringing this beautiful young horse into our erstwhile abode, you are going to tell me the story of spending the night in a barn."

She lifted the saddle off of the horse, considered.

"Maybe."

"Not maybe."

She jumped, surprised to find him suddenly so close. How had he snuck up on her?

As if he could read her mind, he replied. "One of my many talents as chief bottle washer."

She snorted and the horse shied away. She quickly calmed him. "Chief bottle washer? Is that spy speak?"

"It's Andrews speak."

"Sean?"

"Remind me to tell you about the time we were kidnapped and Dan saved our butts."

"Really?"

"Yes, really." He opened the door to the abandoned sweat lodge and led them inside.

"Um, I don't think this place is as abandoned as you think. Look."

The remains of a campfire in the center of the lodge showed that indeed, someone had been there not long before. He leaned down, sifted through the ashes.

"Within the past week."

"Do you think they'll come back tonight?"

"Once they see that someone's in here? No way."

"What makes you so sure?"

He lifted his hand. "Look. Teens. Or, early twenties."

Frowning she tried to see what he was talking about. She laughed. Part of a distinctive foil packet hadn't burned.

"Okay, so they'll think we're doing the same."

He looked up but said nothing. She rubbed her arms. "Didn't you say something about a blanket?"

He walked over to the mustang. "You don't mind sharing, do you?" He pulled a rough blanket out of the saddle bag and wrapped it around her shoulders. "Better?"

Instead of replying, she placed her hands on his shoulders, leaned forward, and pressed her lips against his. She pulled back. "*That* was better."

"Mm," he replied, pulling her against him and bringing his mouth to hers.

Talia sighed then opened her mouth, and the door to her soul, to Agent Juan Hernandez. His soft lips moved against hers even as his tongue slid across them. She slid her hands from his shoulders, down his arms, to his hands where her fingers intertwined with his. He pulled back.

"Do you have a name for him?"

She blinked, confused. "Wh- what?"

"The mustang. Do you have a name for him?"

She shook her head. "Not yet." She rested her forehead on his chest. "Juan? You taste like water."

"What?"

"Crisp and clear and delicious."

"Are you hungry?"

"No."

"There are some protein bars in the saddle bag."

"You were prepared."

"Dan was. It's one of the things that makes him so good at his job. He plans for contingencies within contingencies."

"Sounds like you have a lot of respect for him."

"I do. He's a professional."

"Ah."

"What's that mean? Ah?"

"Just ah. Nothing more."

After making sure the mustang was settled, he sat in the opposite corner and patted the ground in front of him. She went and sat cross-legged, facing him.

"So, why did you sleep in a barn?"

Talia considered telling him about the time her Girl Scout troop had spent the night at her farm as a step toward getting their Farming badges. Something told her, however, he'd never be satisfied with that.

"I'm waiting."

"I'm gathering my thoughts."

"Must be a good story."

"It is," she replied, sighing. "I was in Iowa, on my grandmother's farm. She'd died and we were back at the house after the funeral. All the neighbors and farm hands had brought food."

"I thought you said this was a good story?"

"I haven't even finished and you're critiquing it."

"Sorry. Go on."

"I hadn't been back to the farm in over a year and I was feeling pretty out of sorts."

"How old were you?"

"Don't interrupt."

"Sorry."

"Sixteen."

"Seems pretty normal reaction for a funeral."

"That wasn't it. I'd grown several inches since my previous visit. Everything that used to seem so huge suddenly seemed small. I felt a bit like *Alice in Wonderland*, I suppose."

She let out a breath. "I couldn't stomach the idea of sleeping in my old room. It felt too claustrophobic. Billy suggested I sleep out in the living room but we already had a house full of guests so that was out."

"Who's Billy?"

"A friend. He was a neighbor back in Kansas. He'd come with us. He and I were close and he knew I'd be out of place."

"How'd he know that?"

"I told him."

"Why was that?"

"Aside from the obvious?"

"The obvious?"

"I don't know many people who feel at ease at a funeral."

"Okay. Why else?"

"What makes you think -?"

"If your friend -." He stopped suddenly. "How old was he?"

"Eighteen. He'd just graduated from high school and was going off to college in the fall. I think that's another reason he came with me. He knew how much I'd miss him, so he wanted to spend as much time with me before going away as possible."

"Was he your boyfriend?"

CHAPTER 23

~~~~~~

Talia smiled. "More like love buddies."

"Love buddies? What's that?"

"I thought you said you weren't going to interrupt?"

"Sorry. Please, continue."

"I told him I wouldn't be comfortable because it was my mom's side of the family. I visited my grandmother a couple of times but otherwise had nothing to do with that side of the family. Especially, after my mom died."

He took her hands in his, rubbed his thumbs over the backs.

"Billy suggested I go sleep in the barn. It was early summer but it was pretty warm. Back in Kansas I'd spent lots of time in barns -."

"With Billy?"

"Yeah, he helped with the horses and we used to look at the stars through a hole in the roof of his barn. He had a telescope set up in there. Most of what I know about constellations I learned from him. He was pretty smart."

"So, you decided to sleep in the barn with Billy?"

"He stayed in my old room. He offered to take the living room floor and let one of the cousins who had come in for the funeral have the bed but she said no."

"And that's it? That's the story of you sleeping in a barn?"

"You said you weren't going to interrupt!"

"I just don't want to be cheated."

"Juan -."

"Sorry. Go on."

"Well, you know a bit about my childhood. My grandmother, and then Billy had been stabilizing points. I was losing both, if for different reasons. Needless to say, I spent most of the time up in the loft tossing and turning."

"I can imagine."

Hadn't he done plenty of that the night before?

"A little after midnight I heard arguing. It was my uncle Cole and Billy. Before I could go see what was the matter, Billy had climbed up into the loft with me."

"I take it your uncle caught him sneaking out of the house?"

"Billy didn't sneak. He told my uncle he was coming to spend the night with me because it would make me feel better."

"Oh, to be a fly on the wall during that conversation."

She smiled. "When my uncle started yelling, Billy insisted they take it outside."

"For all the good it likely did," Juan commented.

"Right. Anyway, he pointed out to my uncle that with a barn full of students, it was ridiculous to think there'd be anything inappropriate going on and besides, he wouldn't do that to me in my fragile emotional state."

"He said that?"

"He did. When my uncle continued to argue, he said he was going to put the question to me since I was old enough to make that decision for myself."

"He could have gotten in a lot of trouble, his being eighteen and you being a minor."

"As if anyone would have pressed charges. Besides, we didn't have sex."

"You didn't?"

"No. He simply lay down beside me and wrapped his arms around me. It worked. After awhile, I was able to relax and then sleep, which I desperately needed."

"How long of awhile?"

"That's the part of the story that's so nice. Before I fell asleep."

"So something did happen?"

"Not like what you mean. What happened happened inside of me."

He turned her hands over, lightly traced circles in the palms with a finger.

"Billy was a good listener but he also knew when to be quiet. We just lay side by side, my head on his shoulder. In his arms I felt safe. I began to relax. As you can imagine, I was emotionally and physically exhausted and in that semi-dream state I had a wondrous experience."

"Can you describe it?" Juan asked softly.

"My senses were incredibly heightened. The smell of the barn, normally familiar, was suddenly so sharp it was strange. The light in the library was on so -."

"The library?"

She explained about the students who lived in part of the barn. "There was always someone studying for something. Anyway, it meant I could see every notch in the wood where the light reached. I could examine every nuance of color in the straw. It was as if for that one night I was part of the barn or it was part of me."

"And the love buddy? Were you part of him too?"

"No. In fact, in that moment I realized that while I would miss him, I was going to be okay. I don't know how to explain it but laying in his arms? I went through some sort of inner transformation. I suddenly grew up. I don't know, maybe it was my grandmother's passing. Maybe it was just time marching forward. Anyway, it was a magical moment. One I might not have experienced if not for Billy."

"How is it you guys became love buddies?"

"Well, we were friends and we were neighbors."

"Yeah. And?"

"We lived in a small rural community where everyone pretty much knew everyone else. Neither of us was too interested in any of the kids at school. Still, we were normal teenagers. We trusted each other so we made an agreement to explore the mysteries of life with someone we trusted."

"An agreement?"

"We were friends and we cared about each other but neither of us was in love with the other one. We never talked about getting married or anything like that."

"Did you lose your virginity to him?"

"Yeah, but not for years. After I'd graduated from high school."

"Interesting arrangement."

"It was a good one, actually. There were no strings attached to it. When he'd come home for visits, if neither of us was seeing anyone, we might fool around. Like I said, we trusted each other. That's a big deal when it comes to sex."

"Definitely." He pursed his lips, considered. "How long did you two continue your relationship?"

"Until I graduated college. I was living out east and applying to grad schools. He'd moved back home."

"And?"

"His father had had a heart attack and Billy went to help them settle things on the farm. It was too much for his parents but his older brothers weren't interested in taking it over. One was living in Hawaii and one was studying in Europe."

"Did he feel obligated?"

"I think so. He knew selling the farm would break his parents' hearts. He ended up opening an insurance agency in town and hiring a manager to oversee day to day operations on the farm. He'd majored in business and I think that helped him keep the farm profitable while still managing to run his own small business."

"When was the last time you were home?"

"Years."

"You said there were no strings attached. What did you mean by that?"

"Billy and I cared for each other but like I said, there was never any talk about marriage. Much to my uncle's chagrin I think. In fact I think after that night in the barn he expected that I'd lose my virginity to Billy, and then I'd marry him. He's sort of old-fashioned that way."

"Why aren't you?"

"Because I live in the modern world."

He stood suddenly. "I'm going to go take a walk around." He looked down at her. "Thank you for sharing that story with me."

She nodded but didn't reply. His sudden departure left her feeling a bit confused, if not empty. He couldn't have been jealous, could he? That made no sense. Still, he'd seemed a bit distant all of a sudden. Because she wasn't old-fashioned? Too tired to think about it, she lay down on the blanket and closed her eyes.

✤ ✦ ✦

"Thanks for the update, Sean." Tim Brightman disconnected the call that he'd played on speaker and looked across at Benito Hernandez. "What do you think?"

"I think it's time to put this to bed. Before someone gets killed."

"I'm in agreement with you but I'm afraid we're far from done. We may know who is behind this mess but we don't know why."

"I have given this situation a great deal of thought and have come up with a hypothesis."

"I'm listening."

"Before I share the details I would like to test it."

"What do you need?"

"I am honored by your trust."

"You honored me with yours. We work for organizations that do not always see eye to eye. I know you took a risk coming forward with what you suspected. I appreciate you bringing the situation to me personally."

Tim was still in awe of the fact that Benito Hernandez had been responsible for the yellow tagged file finding its way into the cold cases stack the day that Tim was to sort through it.

"You have earned the respect of many."

"Meaning you asked around."

"Actually, you were my first choice."

"Because of Juan?"

"But of course. Doing so kept things simple."

"He's not going to be happy when he finds out he's been played."

"I believe the ends will justify the means."

Tim nodded, understanding. And there were worse things than a ticked off field agent. In the end, if Juan survived, he'd deal with it.

"Okay, what do you need?"

"First, a moment of privacy. I have a phone call to make."

Tim stood. "Feel free to use my office."

"I won't be long. Then you can sit and listen as I set the trap."

"I'll be across the hall, talking to the Duty Officer. Open the door when you're ready."

Juan's father pulled out his cell phone and dialed.

"Senora Ross? Benito Hernandez."

"Tim told me to expect your call."

"Excellent. I looked into the situation he asked you about. You were correct about Dr. LeMonde and Senora Blackmoor."

"Juan was."

"I beg your pardon?"

"Juan is the one who asked me to look into it. I didn't have the means to do so without involving others and he asked me not to."

"It was fortuitous that you reached out to your superior. He brought the matter to me and I was able to confirm Juan's suspicions. Is he there with you now?"

"No. He and Talia are at another location. We're discussing a plan of retrieval right now."

"Is Sean Andrews there with you?"

"Standing about ten feet away, why?"

"I need to talk to him before you go any further."

"Okay. Let me get him."

"No, wait. I need Senor Brightman to listen to what I have to say. We will call Senor Andrews in a few moments from Tim's phone."

"Alright."

Benito hung up the phone and opened Tim's door.

"Do you mind if Irena sits in? She's been my right hand in this delicate situation."

"If you wish."

"She's pretty resourceful and she's discreet."

"You are a lucky man to be surrounded by people you can trust."

"I hand pick those very few. Juan is one of them."

"Speaking of which. I believe it is time to put the trap in motion. Please call Senor Andrews on your speaker line."

Dan stared at his friend. "Run that by me again?"

"We have to lead Andris' men to their location and let them get close enough to think they've killed Juan."

"Sean," Kaila spoke up. "If they're that close, what's to prevent them from actually killing him?"

"That's where you come in."

"Me?"

"You need to move out immediately and prepare him. You won't have much time since Dan and I need to lead the men to their quarry."

"Their quarry. You mean Talia."

"She'll be expecting Andris to get her out. He's already told her he would."

"And she'll be expecting Juan to protect her. Andris told her that, too."

"But he'll be killed in the process of doing so," Sean supplied. "At least, that's how it has to look to her."

"What's to stop them from following me?" Kaila asked, saddling a horse.

"Sani's got them in his sights. We won't let them follow you."

She swung up into the saddle. "Is there any way to get word to Juan? In case something goes wrong?"

Dan stepped forward, handed her a weapon. "Already done. I just texted him, told him we are pulling the trigger and you're the carrier pigeon."

She used her knees to move the horse out of the stable. "Just what is it I'm bringing?"

"Here." Sean handed her a backpack which she quickly put on.

"But go," Dan said, slapping the horse, "there's no more time. This thing is going down."

The two men watched Kaila ride into the distance. The clouds covered the moon, making it difficult to see her.

Dan turned to Sean. "Now what?"

"Let's go talk to Sani. How'd Juan react when you gave him the news?"

"About how you'd expect."

"Yeah, well, it's the right thing to do. He'll come to see that eventually."

Dan snorted. "If he survives." He stopped, looked at his friend. "Would you leave Kian?"

Sean opened his mouth, then closed it again. "There was a time when I did. Now? No. I would have come up with another plan."

The two men met up with Sean's uncle in the courtyard.

"There are two of them," Sani said quietly. "They saw Agent Ross ride off but haven't moved yet. I think they're waiting to see what you two do."

"Hey Sani?" Dan spoke up. "Can you throw some food and water in a backpack? I want to take the stuff to Juan and Talia."

"Sure. Let me go get it for you."

"I'll go saddle a horse," Sean said and disappeared into the barn where he saddled two.

"Here. There's enough food and drinking water for three days. I also put a first aid kit in there, along with an anti-venom kit."

"Good thinking, Sani."

Sean led a horse to where they stood. "You'll be able to find them, right?"

He swung into the saddle. "Sure. The old sweat lodge down in the canyon past the butte."

"Right. You know your phone won't work there," Sean lied.

"Right."

Sean slapped the rump of the horse and watched as it trotted into the night.

"Where'd he learn to ride?" Sani asked quietly.

"In the service. There were plenty of times in Afghanistan we rode horses and mules up steep mountain passes. Sometimes, in the dead of night with a lot less light than he'll have tonight. Plus, he's been to that canyon."

"Yes, I was the one who sent him there."

He clapped his uncle on the shoulder. "You saved his life, you know. You and the Old Man."

Sean's grandfather had passed away two years earlier. He and Dan had stayed with Sani for a month after the funeral. In part to comfort his grandfather's two widows and in part to comfort his uncle. Sani put a hand over his nephew's. "I miss him too."

"I'll give them about fifteen minutes then -."

"No need."

"What?"

"They're gone. They took off right after Dan left."

"I'd better get on it then. I'll give you an update when I can."

"Be safe."

Sean gave his uncle a salute before going into the barn and climbing up on a beautiful black horse. Knowing he was backup to the backup, he paced himself. He didn't want to ride into the line of fire but he needed to be available should things go south. As he kicked the horse into a trot he heard the sounds of a helicopter in the distance.

"Bingo!"

Talia woke to the sound of a helicopter. She rubbed her eyes then looked around in confusion. Except for the mustang, the sweat lodge was empty. She jumped up.

"Juan?"

The helicopter sounded closer. Panic snaked its way up her spine. She ran outside.

"Juan!"

The area around the sweat lodge was suddenly illuminated.

A helicopter? Where was Juan?

She watched in consternation as a helicopter set down on the canyon floor. The sound of chopper blades was replaced by that of gunfire.

"Talia, get into the sweat lodge!"

More bullets only this time, there was return fire from the men in the helicopter.

"Juan!"

"For once in your life listen to me, woman! Get in the damned sweat lodge!"

Talia found she wasn't able to move. She could hear gunfire and could hear her name but she couldn't move. Until she heard the horse.

"Oh my god, the mustang!" She ran into the sweat lodge. The horse was frantic.

"It's okay. I'm here. I'm not going to let anything happen to you."

She debated. If she untied the horse he would likely yank the reins from her hands and flee into the night. However, if she left him tied up, in his state of panic he would most likely injure himself. She untied his reins and watched him bolt through the entrance. Thankfully, he ran away from the line of fire.

"What do I do?" she whispered to herself. Juan had told her to come into the sweat lodge but she couldn't just leave him. She cocked her head.

Silence. Talia found that far more terrifying than the sound of bullets.

CHAPTER 24

~~~~~~

"Dr. Blackmoor?"

She didn't recognize the voice.

"I have a message from Christoff."

She sighed. "What is it?"

"We're here to take you home."

She snorted. *Home?* She had no home.

"To Christoff. We're taking you to Dr. Andris."

She didn't respond.

"I have him on the phone, ready to speak to you."

She walked to the entrance.

"Here you are, Dr. Blackmoor."

She took the phone.

"Talia? Are you alright, my dear?"

"I don't know how to answer that, Christoff. Someone blew up the house I was staying in and I was almost shot by the guys you sent to rescue me."

"You were not in danger, I assure you," he replied. "The men are very good at their jobs. They would never have allowed you to come to harm."

"And Juan?"

"I'm afraid I misjudged him."

Her throat went dry. "I don't understand. How?"

"It seems he was the bad apple in Tim Brightman's organization."

"*Juan?*"

"I'm afraid so, my dear. I'm sorry. I understand you have come to have feelings for him."

How the hell had he learned about that?

"I don't understand. He didn't seem like someone who would betray -."

"And that wouldn't be the first time you misjudged someone you had romantic feelings for."

His words stung. All the more so because they were true.

"What happened? Who did he betray them to?"

"How much do you know about his father?"

"Um, only what he told me. That he's a very powerful man in -."

"Exactly. A powerful man in a rival organization."

"Juan defected to his father's organization?"

"In this case it would seem that blood is thicker than water."

"Wh – what if you're wrong? What if he only planned on being a – a – what do you call it? A double agent? What if he only wanted to be a double agent?"

"I'm afraid I have undeniable proof that this was not the case. "

"Proof?"

"Which I will be happy to show you when I see you next."

Tears streamed down her cheeks. How could she have so mis - ? Clamping down the thought before it formed, she swiped at her cheeks. She'd misjudged him because she couldn't see past her damned hormones.

She wanted to shout at Christoff. She wanted to blame him.

"You said I could trust him."

"I'm sorry, Talia."

She let out a shuddering breath. "What now?"

"The men who are there are going to get you home."

"Home?"

"To me. To me and Chloe. You can stay with us for as long as you like. We will be your family. We will keep you safe."

"So, you want me to go with these men?"

"Yes. I will be waiting for you."

"Where?"

"In Chile."

"Chile?"

"I am with Kyle. I thought you'd want to see him at the clinic. He is doing much better. They were able to remove his respirator this morning. I believe he will make a good recovery."

"You're at the clinic?"

"Chloe and I are here with Dr. Campo, yes. After a visit with Kyle, we will take you home with us."

"To Nicaragua?"

"Why don't we discuss it when we are altogether?"

She looked around the empty sweat lodge. There was no sign of the horse. No sign of Juan which probably meant he was dead. A man in a suit stood patiently outside the entrance.

"I guess I'll be seeing you then."

❦ 🌶 ♪

"Hold still, Juan," Kaila snapped, "so I can get this thing off."

"Damn, that hurts like hell. Why did the bastard have to hit me in the same spot?"

"Hey, at least you had the vest on and thank God those weren't armor piercing rounds. "

He let her help him stand.

"I'm taking an awful chance."

"I know but trust the plan, okay? A lot of thought went into it."

"What did you find out?"

"You were right. Kyle and Talia were lovers. For quite awhile, as a matter of fact."

Well, Juan thought, it would make it that much easier when it came time to walk away from the beautiful research scientist.

He nodded.

"Who's going down?"

"Just you."

He looked at her. "You and Foster aren't going?"

"We're on leave. Officially, now. We're going to see our families."

That caught him up. His eyes slid to her left hand. "Congratulations."

"Thanks."

Time fell away as he looked into her eyes and saw sympathy there. Sympathy, and something more. Something of a memory perhaps.

"Hernandez!"

The spell was broken. He stepped around her and walked toward the cave entrance.

"Up here!" he yelled, then gasped. "Fuck."

Kaila came up next to him and shined a light down, letting it rest in front of Dan to light the way as he and Sean made their way up.

"I take it Kaila got here in time?"

"Barely."

"I hustled him up to the cave and got him into the vest seconds before the helicopter landed," she explained.

"To help things along," Juan put in, "I opened fire. That tipped them off where to aim."

"He stayed in the shadows but he was hit. Once."

"Are you bleeding?" Sean asked.

"No."

"But he's hurt," she countered.

"It'll pass," he snapped.

"I imagine it will," Dan replied meaningfully.

Sean cleared his throat. "We leave tomorrow."

"We?"

"I'm flying you and Kian down to Santiago."

"You're going with me?"

"It's convenient. I can tie it into a business trip, debrief with Tim, get paid, then return to Silicon Valley."

"That explains why you're going, but not Kian."

"She insisted. She wanted to see for herself that you are okay. And, she said she wanted to talk to you."

"We'd better head out," Dan spoke up. "Sani's waiting."

"Dan, I need to talk to Juan a moment."

He looked first at Kaila, then Juan. He hesitated only the briefest of moments but it was enough.

"We'll be with the horses."

"Hey, Foster?" Juan called.

The agent turned.

"Did you by chance see the mustang? I saw it bolt out of the sweat lodge."

"I got it," Sean answered. "He's waiting with the others. You can ride him back."

Oh joy.

The two men hiked back down into the valley. Kaila turned to him. "Juan, I spoke with Kian this afternoon. There's something you should know."

Talia blinked at the light, forgetting for a moment where she was.

"Oh, good, you're awake. How are you feeling?"

"Chloe?"

"Yes, love, I'm here. Is your head any better?"

"My head?"

"You had a terrible headache last night. I think you just needed sleep but Christoff insisted we give you something for the pain. To help you sleep."

"What time is it? What day is it?"

"You poor dear. It's two o'clock."

"In the afternoon?"

"Yes. And it's Monday."

"Could you please get me a glass of water?"

"Of course. And food. You need to eat."

Promising to return as soon as she could, the woman went off to get her something to eat. Talia assumed it would be accompanied by a glass of water.

She swung her legs out of bed and stared out the window. She recognized the view from Tim's photographs. She was at the private hospital in Chile.

Kyle.

Juan.

She closed her eyes. Both would have to wait.

"Chloe said you were awake."

She stood. "Dr. Campo."

"How's your head?"

"Better. How's Kyle?"

"Settling in."

"Settling in?"

"Forgive me. I was using familiar terminology. You can imagine the importance of giving hope, so we tend to use phrases associated with everyday normal behavior."

"But it's a code?"

"Exactly. In this case it simply means that he has suffered no ill effects from the transfer. His condition is stable."

"Thank you for explaining."

"To use such words when talking to loved ones. It brings them great comfort."

Loved ones. Was that what he thought?

"Christoff said you'd removed the respirator."

"He is doing quite well, as you shall soon see."

She nodded. "That's great. Thank you."

"Ah, here is your meal. I would be happy to take you on a tour of our facility when you're ready. I will take you to Dr. LeMonde's room and show you how we are implementing the plan of recovery we spoke of."

"I look forward to it."

She felt like a wrung out dish towel.

"Here you are, love, coffee, water, food, and a glass of wine. The coffee will keep as it's in a hot pot. Shall I leave this all with you then?"

She stared at her friend as if seeing her for the first time. The neurological overlay was disturbing. She shook herself. 'Yes, Chloe, thank you." She paused. "Where's Christoff?"

"With Kyle, my dear. He's barely left his side."

For some reason that was not as comforting a thought as it might have been.

"I'm sure he will be up to see you soon. He'll be thrilled to know your head is better."

My head, but not my heart. That's broken.

Juan.

In the end, she barely ate. She ignored the wine, gulped the coffee, her eyes watering when it scalded her tongue. Chasing it down with water did little to put out the fire.

Juan.

She walked to the window, leaned her forehead against the glass. Captivity. For some horrible reason she couldn't explain, she suspected she'd traded one form of imprisonment for another. Only this time, there was no handsome agent to ride into the picture, to keep her safe.

To listen to her stories.

Stuffing the feelings deep inside where she planned to lock them away forever, she went in search of Dr. Campo. She had a tour to take after all.

Talia was amazed at Kyle's transformation.

"It's incredible."

She listened as Dr. Campo extolled the virtues of the alternative therapies they had utilized.

"Prayer therapy, sound therapy, light therapy. Each has its place alongside modern medicine."

"That may be all good and well, Luis, but I will credit Natalia with Kyle's recovery."

What on earth was Christoff talking about? She shot him a puzzled look.

"You mean to tell me you haven't noticed?"

"Noticed what?"

"You must still be tired."

Talia looked around the hospital room. She gasped.

"You hooked him up to the machine?"

She stared in horror at the prototype. "Christoff, how could you?"

"I do not understand," Dr. Campo spoke. "I was told you'd given your approval."

"I did no such thing. In fact, I said the opposite. I would never make Kyle into a guinea pig."

She gaped at Christoff.

"We were months, a year away from trials. I can't believe you didn't follow proper protocol -."

"Proper protocol be damned!" he roared. 'We're talking about a human life, Natalia! How could you deny this man comfort at such a time?!"

"Comfort? Christoff, if something had gone wrong, he could have been irreparably harmed."

"First, do no harm, isn't that right?"

She whirled, gaped. *Juan?*

Christoff sputtered. "How -?"

Yes, how? She was told he'd been killed. Judging by Christoff's reaction, she wasn't the only one.

Juan kept his gaze on Christoff. "Awfully convenient that you had a test subject close at hand."

What?

Talia looked at the bed. The man who lay hooked up to her prototype, to *their* prototype, had been coworker, friend, lover, and ultimately betrayer.

Christoff sneered. "Just what are you implying, Agent Hernandez?"

Talia couldn't bring herself to look at Juan. Feeling as if she'd been kicked in the gut, she stared at a man she'd called friend. A man she'd trusted.

"Did you -?" She paused, glanced at Dr. Campo, pointed at the bed. "Did you do this to him?"

Her voice was barely above a whisper. She cleared her throat. "Are you somehow responsible for his stroke?"

"That's absurd," he scoffed.

"Is it?" Juan asked.

"How could I be? I was in Nicaragua." He pointed at her. "With you."

"But you were only a phone call away from the men who held him," Juan countered.

"*Held him?*" She wondered if she'd throw up. "You had him captured? Why?"

"Yes, Agent Hernandez, why? What possible reason could I have for wanting to harm a man I have called friend for years?" He looked at her. "Are you going to believe a man who is a traitor to his own organization?"

She was stopped from answering by the sudden appearance of a man she didn't recognize. Tall and broad, he was very fit. Charisma rolled off of him as he walked forward, coming to stop just behind the agent. Although there was no grey in his hair, she guessed him to be in his sixties. Oozing confidence, he was stunning in a tailored suit.

"The only traitor is you, Andris."

His voice was deep, cultured. There was no doubt. This was a powerful man. Whoever he was.

"Well, isn't this convenient? Father and son." He looked at her, pointed a finger at Juan . "I told you he was a traitor."

"Do not believe him, Senora Blackmoor. My son is no traitor."

Other than a muscle in his jaw spasming furiously, Juan didn't react. His gaze remained fixed on Christoff. It was as if she wasn't even there.

Talia found it hard to breathe. There were too many people crowded into the small space and the room was stifling. Fighting dizziness, she took a shaky breath.

"Would someone please tell me what's going on?" she managed.

"Answer her, Andris," Juan sneered. "If you have the balls to, that is."

Talia stumbled and would have fallen if Dr. Campo hadn't steadied her. He slid a chair over. "Here, sit. And keep silent."

She looked at him in confusion. Was he friend or foe?

"Please," he whispered.

She sat.

"Well?" Juan prodded.

"Dr. Andris?" It was Tim Brightman. He was holding a gun on Christoff. "For a man who is never short of a convenient answer, I find your sudden silence interesting. Or should I say, damning."

Her ears began to ring and time seemed to grind to a standstill. She knew the image of that moment would be forever burned into her brain. Until the day she died she would be able to describe who was present, where they stood, what they were wearing.

Christoff's glare morphed into a mocking sneer. "Dr. Campo. When did Dr. LeMonde begin to respond to treatment? To truly respond?"

"After we hooked up the machine and began communicating with him."

"Who hooked it up?" Talia asked, her voice barely above a whisper. Juan still hadn't looked in her direction.

"Dr. Andris," Dr. Campo replied.

"I did indeed and he began to respond immediately. And do you know why?" He'd directed the question at Juan. "Because I told him that his beloved Talia was on her way to his side."

Talia closed her eyes as despair. "Oh, Christoff," she whispered, "no."

~~~~~~

CHAPTER 25

Christoff turned to her. On her. "You," he spat, "were all that mattered to him. The mere mention of your name set him on the path to recovery! That is true love!" He pointed at Juan. "What could that – that – that spy ever offer you? Could he offer you love? No! Could he offer you a home? A future? Would he provide a way for you to continue your research? No, I say! And no again!"

With each word her heart broke a little further. She couldn't bring herself to look at Juan or Tim or even Dr. Campo. Was this what it had come down to? Her dream stolen, twisted, destroyed at her feet?

"All I wanted -."

"I suggest you keep quiet, Talia," Juan snapped.

She closed her eyes. Tears streamed down her face. In those tears, her future dripped to the floor. Gone. Like so much rubbish.

"It wasn't supposed to be this way," she whispered.

"I said to be quiet!" Juan thundered.

"Don't you scream at her," Christoff roared. *"You bastard!"*

"Please."

It wasn't the soft voice that got Talia's attention. It was the soft beep.

My machine.

She'd programmed the sounds herself. Not wanting the harsh tones normally associated with hospital equipment, she'd taken sounds made by the animals on her farm and run them through a converter. The result had been soft tones that were soothing, not startling.

As if in a daze, she approached the bed. His eyes were open.

"Kyle?"

"Ta – Ta -."

She squeezed his hand. "I'm here, Kyle." Tears streamed down her face. "I'm here."

Across the room, Christoff shouted. "See? I was right! He loves her! Talia's love is what brought him back!"

Dr. Campo drew himself up. "This man's health is more important than anything here. Everyone, out."

"No." It was Kyle. He was looking at her.

"He wants me to stay."

"You, but none other," the neurosurgeon snapped.

"I want Juan to stay."

Tim waved his gun toward the door. "Dr. Andris? After you."

Juan took two steps in her direction to let Christoff get to the door. His father was already gone.

Dr. Campo smiled at his patient. "It is so good to hear your voice, Dr. LeMonde." He looked at her. "Watch yourself. Don't think for one minute I won't have you thrown out."

"No," Kyle croaked. "Please. Love."

She squeezed his hand. "Oh, Kyle."

"Tim can stay," Juan said suddenly. "I've got other business."

Kyle squeezed her hand. "Need to tell you -."

"Dr. LeMonde, you need your rest."

"I agree, Kyle. It can wait."

"No," he rasped. "It can't. Story. Long – long story."
And it was.

🌶️ 🌶️ 🌶️

"Dr. Blackmoor, are you sure I can't get you anything to drink?"

"No, Agent Brightman, I'm fine."

"You understand that you are not under arrest?"

Yet.

She gave a weak laugh, turned away from where she'd been staring out the window. "But I'm far from free, isn't that right?"

"We've kept you under guard for -."

"My own safety," she finished. "A rose by any other name is still imprisonment."

"The sooner we get through this," Benito Hernandez said, "the sooner we can work to rectify that situation."

She turned to look at Juan's father. "I don't understand why you're here."

"I will be happy to provide what answers I am able. After I hear your story."

Across the room Juan snorted. "Honesty from you would be a refreshing change, Benito. You have no intention of telling her the truth and you know it." He sent her a look of impatience. "Can you please answer our questions? We're all prisoners until you do."

"Juan," Tim warned.

"No, he's right, Agent Brightman. I suppose I've had enough time to collect my thoughts."

She'd been a *guest* of the US Embassy for three days. She'd been put up in a suite at a high-end hotel in Santiago and waited while the wheels of bureaucracy turned. As they turned exceedingly slowly, the wait had been long with very little communication with the outside world. In fact, other than a daily trip to the fitness facility, where she worked out alongside an almost completely silent Juan Hernandez, she hadn't been allowed to leave. Every meal had been brought to her room. Other than dinner the previous evening, those meals had been eaten alone.

The previous evening, Tim's secretary, Irena, had come to explain the day's events.

"*Agents Brightman and Hernandez will be conducting your interviews. Senor Benito Hernandez will also be in attendance. He may ask you questions as well.*"

"*Okay.*"

"*I will be there, too. I will make both video and audio recordings of the proceedings. I understand you've waived the presence of an attorney?*"

"*I haven't done anything wrong so yes, I said no thank you.*"

"*Did Agents Brightman and Hernandez explain that, based on your testimony, you could be charged with espionage?*"

"*I feel confident that they will understand, based on the testimony I'll give, that I was not working with Christoff Andris as a spy against the US government.*"

"*But you did work with Dr. LeMonde.*"

"*In a legitimate capacity at what I thought was a legitimate corporation. I had no idea -.*"

She'd held up a hand.

"*I'm not at liberty to receive any information. I'm here to go over the details of tomorrow's debrief. I wanted to offer representation.*"

"*No. Thank you, but I am declining.*"

She looked at the people gathered to hear her words and wondered, briefly, if she'd been hasty in declining an attorney.

"Would you please sit down?" Tim asked.

She rubbed her arms. "I'd prefer to stand if it's all the same."

He nodded at his secretary. She turned on the recording equipment.

"Where do you want me to start?" Talia asked.

"How do you know Dr. LeMonde?"

Her eyes flicked over at Juan, away again. She swallowed. "I met Kyle at work. He was assigned to me. As my assistant."

"Why?" Juan asked.

"He was a technologist. The man who took my instructions and made them work. I was the why and he was the how."

"Would you characterize the relationship as that they were your ideas but his implementation?"

"Sort of. If I didn't like his implementation, I ordered a change."

"When did you first meet Dr. Andris?" Benito asked.

"He approached me at a conference. I introduced him to Kyle." She cleared her throat. "It was all an act. They already knew each other."

"How is that, Dr. Blackmoor?" Tim asked.

"Um." She shifted. "Kyle worked for Christoff. He was a plant. The Chinese and South Koreans were both very interested in biotech and in my work. They'd already approached me to work for them but I declined. Christoff told them he would get my project. He intended to sell it to the highest bidder."

"If you'd already refused," Juan put in, "how was he going to get your agreement?"

She let out a breath. This is where Kyle came in.

"He sent Kyle to work with me, the intent being that he would persuade me to go to work for Christoff."

"Can you be a bit more specific?" Benito asked.

"The plan was that I would come to trust Kyle. As my work partner. Which, I did. Then, Christoff would approach, tell us the company had sold us out. Several scenarios were put forth by both Christoff and Kyle. None of them were very appealing."

"And then what happened, Dr. Blackmoor?"

She looked at Tim. "While I was wallowing in shock, Kyle began suggesting that if I didn't make some dramatic move, either I would die or someone I loved would. He told me that the people involved were willing to kill for the project."

"Which was true," Juan replied.

"I was manipulated."

"How?" Juan again.

"I was ready to walk away. No project was worth dying for. Hell, I could go back to farming or ranching. "

"If they had the project and Dr. LeMonde, why did they need you?"

"Kyle had a doctorate in technology. He was a brilliant programmer, but he didn't have the medical background. They needed me to move forward because it was my formula that enabled the communication."

"But couldn't they have just used your notes?" Juan asked.

Old wounds ripped open. She shook her head and blinked rapidly.

"Do you need a break, Dr. Blackmoor?" Tim asked.

His tone had been polite, bordering on cool even, but his expression told her he was sympathetic.

She glared at Juan. "No, I don't need a break. They needed more than my notes. The machine was a prototype. It needed constant adjustments. I had to try a number of frequencies and since a lot of it was audio, it was a matter of knowing when I had the right sounds. By hearing them."

"Couldn't someone else have learned those sounds?"

"I programmed the frequencies, Agent Hernandez. It's like knowing your own heartbeat. I am able to detect subtleties no one else was able to. At least, at the start."

"What changed?" Juan asked.

How in the world would she be able to answer without dislodging the glass shard? She couldn't, and she highly doubted Juan would lift a finger to stop the bleeding.

"Dr. Blackmoor?" Juan pushed. "How was it that Dr. Andris was able to correctly hook up the prototype if you weren't there to perform the appropriate audio adjustments?"

"Kyle must told him how I did it."

"Must have?"

"Yes, Agent Hernandez, must have. I never told Christoff about the frequencies. He knew the overview based on my research proposal but he had no idea of the specifics behind the frequencies."

"But Kyle did?" Juan asked.

"What research proposal?" Benito asked.

She decided to answer Juan's father. "Everyone who needs funds has to put forth a business case. I needed to develop a proposal to get my project funded. I outlined the basics. Only a fool reveals details. After all, I wanted them to fund me for the project, not a competitor."

"Were there competitors?" he asked.

"Several, though each had a difference of one sort or another."

"Such as?"

"Such as wanting to focus on the mind reading part of it. I focused on the healing part. The recovery."

"I thought you said that you were the only one who understood the frequencies?" Juan asked.

"That's right."

"Then how did Kyle learn about them in order to pass that information on to Dr. Andris?"

If Juan was trying to cause her pain, he was succeeding. Her head began to pound in a way no tequila hangover could ever manage.

"Before you answer," he continued, "you might want to remember that how we view your testimony will influence whether or not you are placed under arrest."

Tim opened his mouth but she held up a hand. "I understand."

She considered. She'd held the truth in for so long. While there was pain in its revelation, perhaps there would be healing, too. Hell, the shard holding her emotions in place was halfway out anyway. What the hell did the rest of it matter?

"Kyle became my lover -."

""Was that typical?"

"That was uncalled for, Hernandez."

"Why don't you tell me? Or, should I ask Agent Ross?"

Tim stood. "Let's take a break."

Irena shut off the equipment. "I'll have a meal brought up."

"I need to make a phone call," Benito said. "I will return as soon as I am able." He left the suite.

Tim pointed to a conference room. "In there, Hernandez. Irena, I want you there, too."

"Why Irena?" Juan asked, disappearing through the door.

"To keep me from strangling you," he shot back.

The secretary sent her a look of sympathy before quietly pulling the door closed.

Talia stared down at the busy street. People crowded the sidewalks, some at cafes, some shopping, most probably workers moving from one place to another as part of some

daily ritual.   She imagined some of them were tourists.
Behind her, a door closed.

"May I speak with you?"

She turned to look at Juan's father.

"Sure."

"Perhaps, in there?"

She followed him into the guest bedroom.

"Please, sit."

She sat in one of two chairs near the window.

"How are you holding up?" he asked politely.

"I'm alright."

Other than an aching head. And heart.

"Juan was right when he told you I will not tell you
everything. I cannot. I am not at liberty to divulge the
official reason for my presence. However, I wanted to tell
you that not everyone is happy with humanity's dabbling in
biotechnology. There are many who do not consider the
human body to be flawed. We do not consider the need to
improve on Mother Nature. Perhaps that sounds like
something that would come from a spiritualist, but it is
truth."

"You have to admit, thanks to progress in robotics, men
and women who have lost limbs or mobility have a chance
for a more fulfilling life."

"You are young and perhaps naïve to believe that such
technological wonders will only be used in healing."

"I'm not," she snapped. She let out a breath. "I'm sorry. I
am far from naïve, Senor Hernandez. Yes, there was a time
when I was, when I trusted people I shouldn't have."

"There are many who do not enjoy watching men play
God."

"So, you're here on official business, but you have a
personal stake, too. Is that it?"

"Yes."

"Well, I have nothing to hide so I don't have a problem answering any of your questions. I've figured out that you don't work for the US government, nor are their interests necessarily yours. I'm assuming that if you asked something inappropriate, either Juan or Tim would stop it."

"I'm certain."

The bedroom door opened. Juan poked his head in.

"We're ready to continue."

"We'll be there in a moment," Benito answered, coolly.

Juan ducked back out.

"Agent Hernandez?"

He poked his head in again.

"May I suggest that you try to avoid contention so that we may get through questioning as quickly as possible? There is no need or call for disrespectful behavior."

His gaze raked her. "Understood." He shut the bedroom door. She stood.

"Wait."

She sat down.

"About Juan. He cares a great deal for you. In spite of how it may appear."

"I know."

"You do?"

"He wouldn't be hitting out at me unless he was hurt. He wouldn't be hurt unless he cared. What I'm hoping he'll come to understand is that I was manipulated. Kyle and Christoff used a sexual relationship -."

"I know about that."

"You do?"

He glanced at the door, sighed, looked into her eyes. "I know a great deal about who has done what and when. I had been keeping an eye on unfolding events, and when I felt I had enough evidence to bring Drs. Andris and LeMonde to justice? I sought the assistance of Tim Brightman."

"How did you find out about it?"

"It was brought to the attention of someone in my organization."

She wondered just what organization that was. Chilean government? The Chilean version of the CIA? Or something else entirely?

"Why?"

"It would be putting it mildly to say that if China was suspected of stealing US technology and using it for mind reading, if not mind control, diplomatic relations would be strained beyond repair."

"And South Korea?"

"The Chinese were using them to bring Andris in."

"So, neither government was interested in my technology?"

"Beyond making sure it wasn't brought to full potential? No."

She doubted that.

"Perhaps I am being too naïve," he conceded.

"So, you knew that Christoff had Kyle -."

"Used you? Yes. I do not think he anticipated you developing feelings for someone else."

Juan.

"It most certainly interfered with his plans." He cleared his throat. "Perhaps you should wait so that you only need to share such painful details once."

She nodded.

"I admire your courage. To have such personal information bared has to be difficult."

She stood. "I'm not going to just sit there and let him snap at me. I can give as good as I get."

"Your remark about Agent Ross should alert him to this truth."

"Men can be notoriously blind to what's inside a woman. Especially when they only see what they want to."

"Another truth. You are a wise woman, Senora Blackmoor."

She shook her head. "Experienced. If I was wise I wouldn't be in this situation."

"One does not become wise without living down their mistakes, Senora."

"I guess."

"And you are wise. While it is true that wisdom can come with experience, not all who live become wise."

"Ready to go back?"

"After you."

CHAPTER 26

〰〰〰〰〰〰〰〰〰〰〰〰〰〰〰〰〰〰〰〰〰〰〰

Lunch was mercifully silent and mercifully short. Talia was more than anxious to finish the interrogation.

"So, you and Dr. LeMonde were lovers," Juan began.

She mentally sighed and reminded herself that after pain came the chance to heal.

"That's right."

"How does this explain Dr. Andris' ability to utilize your machine?"

"In becoming sexually involved with Kyle, my trust of him deepened. I began sharing details about the frequencies."

"Specifically?"

"We've all been to health class, Agent Hernandez," Tim snapped.

"I think he wants to know how Kyle learned about the frequencies," she offered. She looked at Juan. "Am I right? Was that the intent of your question?"

"Yes."

"I told him the stories behind how I selected the frequencies. I told him how I developed them and how they sounded, to me. He had to have passed that information along to Christoff at some point because they were able to tune the machine."

"Did you know that Kyle had passed that information along to someone else?"

"No."

"How long were you two involved?"

"Until I found out it was all a lie."

"Can you please explain?"

"Yes, Agent Hernandez, I can provide all the sordid details you want. Are you going to submit them to the *National Enquirer?*"

He opened his mouth but she held up her hand.

"I ask because if you intend to, I want part of the royalty check."

She ignored the chuckle coming from Juan's father.

"Can we please move along?" Juan snapped. "Share what you feel is relevant, Dr. Blackmoor."

"I had to return to the lab one night. I'd wanted to work on something and had left my notes behind. Kyle was on a video conference with someone. I overheard him say that my agreement was all but a done deal. He felt confident that when he told me he was going to work for a competitor, I would go with him."

"Did he see you?" Tim asked.

"No. I hid out of sight."

"Did you ever confront him?" Juan asked.

"No. The next day my boss brought me into the office and told me that I was being transferred to China."

"What happened then?" Tim asked.

"I refused."

"Why the need to fake your death?" Juan asked.

"Because when I refused my boss showed me doctored photographs."

"Of what?" Juan again.

"People that I loved being hurt."

"How?"

"A lot of different ways!"

"That's enough, Hernandez."

"Some were financial, some were physical. Some of the photographs were pretty morbid."

"What happened then?" Juan asked.

"Christoff had told me that my boss would come to me, that he would try to force my hand."

"How did he know this?"

"Well, gee, Agent Hernandez, I guess since, unbeknownst to me he was behind the whole thing to begin with, he probably knew a hell of a lot. Why don't you ask him?"

For several seconds they glared at each other. She looked at Tim.

"He said we had to plan for it. He had a plan. All I had to do was text a code to a certain number and it would be executed. So, I did."

"Why the charade afterward?" Juan continued. "Why not just offer you a safer place to work? That way he'd have the project and you, and he could oversee its completion and then sell it to the highest bidder."

"I'll be honest with you, Agent Hernandez, I only learned the answer a short while ago. From Kyle, no less."

"What?"

"He told me from his hospital bed. Up until that point, I had no idea that Christoff was behind this."

"You had no idea? None?"

She shook her head. She hadn't begun to suspect anything was wrong until she'd read his text message. *This wasn't how it was supposed to be.* Then Juan was killed. Well, she'd been told he was. At that point, she knew there was more to Christoff's motivation than the kindness of his heart. She had no idea what, but she knew there was something.

She recalled the ugly scene in Kyle's room. She certainly hadn't had to wait long to find out.

"Would you please share the details of what Dr. LeMonde told you?" Benito asked. He pointed at the video camera. "For the record?"

"Kyle said he thought they should wait, not to push me. He told Christoff that if they put that proposal before me so soon I would suspect something. He was right, but he didn't know why. I'd already found out he'd used me."

Betrayed me. She pushed the memories aside.

"If Christoff had approached me right away, I would have realized he was behind it all. Kyle told him to wait, to earn my trust. In fact, he told him that waiting would let me see how much I missed my work. He suggested icing me would make me quite eager to finish my project."

"Why did he think that?" Juan asked.

She knew in that moment why Juan had been assigned to her. The agent could see inside a person. He knew what made them tick.

"Kyle knew how important people were to me."

"Because of your childhood?"

Damn him. He was using what she'd told him in the sweat lodge -.

"You don't have to answer. I'll assume he used knowledge gained through your intimate relationship to come up with a strategy."

She swallowed. "Well, like most people, he had jumped to the wrong conclusions."

"How's that?"

"Because he misunderstood what was important to me. He thought it was important to me to trust people." She shook her head. "That had nothing to do with it."

"What did it have to do with?"

"In the interest of moving along, "Benito said, "can we assume he misjudged you? What happened after that?"

"Isolated like I was, I had a lot of time to think. I was isolated from people, but I had access to the media. I read the papers, watched the news. I realized that my work, whether I did it for the US or anyone else, could be turned into a weapon.

'If only I had known, I should have become a watchmaker.'

One side of her mouth went up. "Maybe that's arrogance, to put myself in the same league as Einstein, but I understood the sentiment."

"What else did Dr. LeMonde tell you?" Tim asked.

"You were there, Agent Brightman, as was Dr. Campo. I know you've gotten a sworn statement from him already."

Tim looked at the video equipment. "I want to hear Dr. Blackmoor explain, as part of her testimony."

"Kyle told me that Christoff wanted both Kyle and me, not just the project, but the both of us. He said he came to realize -."

"Who came to realize?" Juan asked.

"Kyle said he came to realize that Christoff was using him to get to me. He is the one who suggested Kyle become intimately involved with me. The idea was that if Kyle and I were together, where he went, I went, and vice versa. The project became immaterial at that point. Christoff felt that it was only the beginning. With Kyle and I, there would be dozens of projects."

"When did Dr. LeMonde realize that he too was being manipulated?"

"Right before Christoff -."

"Before what?" Juan asked.

"Christoff ordered him incapacitated. Kyle told him he was out. He wasn't going to continue the charade. He wasn't going to try to draw me back."

"So, in retaliation, Christoff had his captors induce a stroke?"

She nodded.   "He had been working at the Beijing location."

She stared at Benito.   "That location.   If the Chinese government didn't want the project to be successful, why did they allow Kyle to work with another medical team to finish it?"

"I said they did not want to see it weaponized."

She nodded, looked back at Tim. "Kyle told Christoff he was through.   Christoff was furious.   He threatened to destroy Kyle's reputation but Kyle only laughed and threatened to tell me the truth.   A few days later Christoff ordered them to induce a stroke."

"Why?" Tim asked.

"Because he thought that once I found out Kyle was hurt I would be anxious to use my machine to help him heal. He thought that once Kyle and I were together, I would be eager to work with him again.   Especially, once I saw how successful my machine was."

"That was quite a gamble," Benito said. "Your machine was a prototype and had not gone through any trials, correct?"

"Not to mention, controlling the severity of a stroke is almost impossible.   He could never have determined the extent of the damage."

Or the recovery.

"Shows what a ruthless man he was," she continued, her gaze on the carpet.

"Why did Kyle change his mind?"

She stared at Juan. "What?"

"You said Kyle decided not to work with Christoff to bring you back. Why?"

"Because I loved you. I couldn't hurt you."

Kyle's words at the clinic came back to her. She let out a shuddering breath.

"Because he loved me."

"If that was true," Juan countered, "it would seem that he'd be eager to have you back again."

She looked at him, held his gaze. "If you think that then you don't understand love, Agent Hernandez."

For several seconds, no one spoke. Talia worked to breathe. *In. Out. In. Out.*

"Did you ever suspect the company you were working for was anything other than it appeared?" Benito asked, breaking the uncomfortable silence.

"No. I had no idea they were a shell corporation."

"How could you not have known you were working for a Chinese company?"

"Because, Agent Hernandez, I'm not a spy," she snapped. "I saw the name on my badge, the name on my Direct Deposit wires. It matched the name on the front of the building. It seemed like a legitimate US company. They funded my research. They had all the right connections to the universities. They paid for my trips to conferences. I had absolutely no idea that they were anything other than what they appeared to be."

"Dr. Blackmoor?" Tim asked, "do you think you have anything else to offer at this point?"

"No."

"Senor Hernandez, do you have anything else for Dr. Blackmoor?"

"I do not."

She managed to smile at Juan's father.

"Hernandez?"

"No."

The smile disappeared.

Tim nodded at his secretary. She turned off the recording equipment. He stood, walked over and put his hands on her shoulders.

"I know this has been hell and I'm sorry to have had to put you through it. I'm afraid you aren't free to leave Chile just yet, but I am having you relocated somewhere more comfortable."

"When?"

"A car is downstairs waiting."

"I would be happy to escort Dr. Blackmoor to the limousine," Benito offered.

"Give me a moment to get my things," she replied.

"Where's she being moved to, Brightman?"

She heard the question because her bedroom door was open.

'That's classified. As of this moment, as far as you are concerned, this case is closed. You are on leave. I'll be preparing your next assignment."

Tim's sigh easily carried to where she was shoving clothes into a suitcase. She couldn't help it. She smiled.

"I mean it, Hernandez. You're on leave. If I find out you've been snooping around and have involved yourself in this situation? You will find yourself in hot water. Do I make myself clear, Agent Hernandez?"

"Sure."

She shook her head. Stubborn man.

"Juan!"

"I said okay!" he snapped.

Talia came out of the larger bedroom.

"Good luck, Dr. Blackmoor."

She gave a wave and followed Benito Hernandez onto the elevator.

Juan snatched a white towel from the handrail and stepped off the treadmill. Wiping the sweat from his forehead, he looked around the gym, tried to decide which machine to hit next. Maybe the rowing machine. His injuries had kept him from working his upper body as much as he wanted.

"Haven't you had enough, Hernandez?"

Working to keep his expression neutral, he looked over at Dan Foster. "I thought you preferred the rock climbing gym?"

The agent laughed. "You must be tired, Hernandez. Do I look dressed for a workout?"

"I figured you hadn't changed yet. Brightman send you?"

"More or less. Go shower and get dressed. Meet me out front."

Fifteen minutes later they were pulling into the parking lot of what looked to be an abandoned building.

Dan opened his door, looked at Juan. "Get out."

"Where are we going?"

"Inside."

Juan opened his door and stepped out. "I've heard of clandestine meetings before, but this is ridiculous. Are we here to do a bust or something? Meet some sleazy underworld contact?"

Dan smirked. "We're not here in an official capacity. At least, not once we step through those doors."

It took several minutes for Juan's eyes to adjust to the sudden darkness. "What the hell is this place?"

"Follow me."

They stepped through a construction obstacle course.

"Watch your step," Dan warned. "Stay on the sheets of plywood. There's holes beneath most of them. Also, turn sideways when walking past those sawhorses. I got my side scraped up pretty badly because I wasn't paying attention."

A man stood behind a small bar set up in a far corner. When he saw Dan, he smiled.

"Good afternoon, Senor Foster. Always a pleasure to see you."

"Have a seat, Hernandez."

"What can I get you to drink?"

Juan looked around. 'You're open during construction? Is that legal?"

Dan snorted. "Stop being an ass and order a drink. God knows, you need it."

Don Julio 1942."

"Excellent choice."

The high-end tequila was produced in small batches and aged for a minimum of two and a half years. It was a tribute to the year that Don Julio González began making tequila.

"Make that two," Dan added.

"I thought you preferred beer."

"I do but I've seen that stash at your apartment. I figure you know the good stuff."

"I do."

"Cheers."

The two men clicked shot glasses with the bartender who'd decided to join them. Dan introduced Juan.

"He's getting back on his feet after a bit of trouble," Dan explained. "Tim's rotated a few of us through to make sure Miguel here doesn't suffer any repercussions for helping us out a few months ago."

"Ah."

"I saw Talia yesterday. She's not doing too good."

Juan snorted. "Waiting to hear if you're going to be charged with espionage might stress a person out."

"That isn't it." He set his shot glass down. "Again, Miguel."

"She sick?"

"Heartsick. From you, you stubborn ass. I saw the transcript. She isn't guilty of anything other than trusting the wrong people and falling in love with a guy too stupid to set aside his pride and accept it."

"She's better off without me."

Behind the bar, Miguel shook his head. "Stubborn, hell. The man is stupid."

"I'll drink to that." Dan tossed back the tequila. "Another."

"Better watch it, Foster. You might wind up with one hell of a hangover from that stuff."

CHAPTER 27

~~~~~~

"I'm not so sure this is a good idea," Talia said to the pretty blonde standing in front of the stove.

"I am," Kian replied, and continued stirring a mix of peppers and onions.

Sean came up behind her and gave her shoulders a reassuring squeeze. "I know it's hard, Talia, but trust in the process."

"And before you answer," Kian added, "consider how often that process has worked."

"I don't know. This whole setup just seems like a mockery."

"Parody would be a better description," Dan said, opening the refrigerator and pulling out two bottles of wine. He handed them to her. "I know you aren't free but you're a lot freer than you were."

That was true.

"Just don't tell me it's for my own safety. That's where it becomes a mockery."

"I won't. Hey, Kian? We're hungry. Snap to it. Talia, would you take the wine outside?"

Kian turned. "Go ahead. I've got things under control. And Sean can help. He's a great cook."

"I make a mean omelet," he said before kissing his wife's cheek. He turned. "Go on. Go sit at the table. We'll be along in a few minutes."

"Come on, Dr. Blackmoor," Kaila said, stepping into the kitchen and reaching for the wine.

She shook her head. "I can carry these. And I thought we agreed you'd call me Talia? No use for letters and all that."

"Sorry. I've spent the last two weeks around my betters."

"Betters, my ass," Dan snapped, walking in from where he'd been barbequing. He handed a covered platter to Kaila. "Here, make yourself useful."

Talia followed the agent through the main room and out to a large patio where several tables had been set up.

"What did he mean by that? The remark about your betters?"

"We were visiting his family. When they found out we were engaged they invited people over for parties. A kind of coming out. It was more formal than I'm comfortable with. Dan likes to tell people he's blue collar because of his family's fishing background but in reality they are every bit the elite New England aristocracy. Education and how many letters you have after your name are very important. Still, I will admit, they are a very loving family."

"Ah." She looked around. "How can I help?"

"Sit. Drink."

"I beg your pardon?"

"I mean it. Sit. Have a glass of wine. Red or white?"

"Red please."

"Good. This is from Tim's vineyard."

"Tim? Brightman?"

"Well, we call it his vineyard but in reality it belongs to the family of a little girl he dated."

"Little girl?" Talia asked, confused.

Kaila laughed. "That was my way of teasing Brightman. She was a lot younger than him."

"I wouldn't call her a little girl," Dan said, walking up. "She was a D cup."

Talia took a long drink of wine. "And just how in the hell would you know that?"

"Well, Juan and I had a bet -."

"Juan? Juan Hernandez?"

"That'd be him."

She mentally sighed. She hadn't seen or heard from him since the interrogation.

"Juan's a runner. So is Tim. Apparently, she was so taken with Brightman's charms, she told him she'd like to run too. With him."

Kaila shook her head. "Dan, quit teasing."

"I'm not," he replied, setting a salad on the table. "I have no sense of humor whatsoever."

"I want the story," Talia urged.

Another voice kept Dan from answering.

"I told Brightman there was no way a woman with knockers like hers could ever run. Sports bra or no. Too painful."

Talia leapt up and ran into the darkness, toward the sound of the sweetest voice. "Juan!" She threw herself into his arms, her body wrapping around him like a wire.

The agent held her tightly and buried his face in her hair. Before he could say a word, she burst into tears.

"Oh, Talia. Talia, -." He kissed her wet cheek. "Foster?" he shouted.

"Yeah?"

"Carry on, aye?" he shot back.

"Will do!"

"But the meal?" Talia whispered, wiping her tears on his shirt. God, he smelled good.

"Later. We've got a date." He slid an arm beneath her knees.

"Where are you carrying me?"

"Not far. Don't worry."

❦ ✿ ✿

Talia stared out the sliding glass door. The blinds had been pulled to enable them to look out but keep people from seeing in. People, who at that very moment, were eating and drinking on the deck behind the cabin.

"Are you sure they can't see in here?"

"Positive," he murmured, sliding his hands beneath her shirt. He removed her shirt and bra and reached around to undo her jeans. She allowed him to strip her down and then closed her eyes as his fingers glided first down her back, then up again, over her shoulders, coming to rest on her breasts.

She frowned, touched her fingers to her collar bone. "What's this?"

"A gift."

"Can I see it?"

He guided her over to the mirrored closet doors.

A beautiful silver chain hung below her collar bone. At the bottom dangled a silver charm.

"Is that a wolf?"

"Your protector."

And it had been. The wolf had alerted Sani and Juan that someone was sneaking around outside. They'd chased the men off the property, confident Dan Foster would get Talia out of the house.

She met Juan's eyes in the mirror.

"If the wolf hadn't led Foster to you in the yard, he probably would have been killed because he likely would have been in the house when it exploded. He saved you both."

She fingered the charm. A gift with meaning was a gift from the heart. She smiled at his reflection. "Thank you."

He lightly bit the back of her neck while his hands rubbed her nipples til they stood completely erect. His polo shirt rubbed against her back, reminding her of rolling around in a loft. Fresh hay was soft yet scratchy, just like his shirt.

He turned her around and pulled her into an embrace. He tasted warm and sweet and she leaned into him while his hands roamed up and down her back. She pulled back.

"Enough. You have to take that shirt off. It's too scratchy."

He leaned down and took her nipples into his mouth. "That's because your skin is so tender," he replied. "Tender and delicious."

She smiled down at his head as he slid his tongue along the front of her body. "Seems unfair that only one of us is naked. Or do you plan on making love to me with your jeans on?"

He stood. "You think I'm making love to you?"

Her smile widened and she slid her hand beneath his shirt, pulling it off.

"Don't try to tell me you aren't considering it. I won't believe you."

"You might. After all, I lie for a living."

She stared into his eyes. "Don't lie to me."

"Deal," he said finally.

"You hesitated."

"I'm a spy, Talia. There are some things I'm not going to be able to be honest about."

"Then tell me you can't tell me the whole truth, but don't lie."

"Deal."

"That's better." She drew a finger to his left nipple. "The dart?"

He shivered. "A bullet, actually."

"You like that, eh? Good." She sucked his hardened nipple into her mouth, flicked her tongue over it. Again, he shivered.

Once she had him naked, she drew him against her body, sliding her thigh between his. "Mm, that feels nice. Want to try out the bed now?"

"I was thinking we might want to sit in the hot tub."

"Water isn't a very good lubricant."

"The voice of experience?"

She nodded.

"The love buddy?"

"Are you jealous?"

"If I was?"

"I'd tell you that he's married and has kids. Besides, I told you. Marriage was never a consideration."

"But did you love him?"

"As a friend."

"A good friend."

"What about you, Juan? Don't tell me there isn't someone in your past that you have fond memories of."

"Of course."

"Did you want to marry her?"

"I thought I did."

"But -?"

"I came to realize it would never work."

"Did you continue to have sex with her after that?"

"No."

"No?"

"Look, maybe we're different in that regard."

She moved against his naked body. "Yes, we are different."

He pulled her hand to his chest. His heart pounded against his ribs.

"I meant here, Talia."

"Maybe not so different."

"Oh?"

"I'm done with casual sex. It isn't what it's cracked up to be."

"When did you come to this conclusion?"

She put her hands on his shoulders, stared into his eyes. "When I saw you."

"What, in the coffee field?"

"That very moment. I took one look at you and I knew my life had changed."

He stroked her hardened nipple, fingered the wolf charm. "I'm glad we got that straight."

"Make love to me?"

He kissed her deeply, then guided her to the bed.

EPILOGUE

~~~~~~

"Why can't I open my eyes?" Talia asked.

"Because, it's a surprise."

Sighing, she kept them closed and allowed Juan to guide her.

"Is that water?"

"Okay, open 'em."

She blinked. Several familiar faces grinned up at her.

"That's quite a hot tub."

"Get in," Dan suggested.

"The warm waters are very healing," Sani added.

Smiling, she allowed Juan to help her over the edge into the hot tub. He climbed in after her.

"Want one?" Kaila asked, holding out a glass of wine.

"Yes, thank you."

"Hey, Sani." Juan handed over a bottle. "I get this from the factory at El Arenal Jalisco."

He studied the label. "Tequila Cascahuin. Thank you, Agent Hernandez."

"It's better than the cheap stuff you have."

Talia leaned forward. "Oh?"

Sean passed a beer to Juan.

"Thanks."

"How's the new arrangement working out?" Dan asked.

"I -," she replied.

"Well," Juan started.

Kian laughed. "Don't fall all over yourselves."

"There's still a lot of fallout in the system, and Tim's still plenty pissed Juan disobeyed his order to stay away from me, but the new arrangement is turning out to be a pretty sweet deal."

After the testimony, she'd been taken by limo to a nearby park where she was picked up by Sean Andrews. From there, she was driven to their office in Talca where Agents Ross and Foster were to keep her safe. Or imprisoned, if you considered it in such a light. Which she had.

Her testimony was analyzed and it was deemed that no charges against her were necessary. In exchange for additional information about the Andrises, and Dr. Kyle LeMonde, who would face charges of espionage, she was allowed to pick her next relocation.

"It would be dangerous to assume that Andris won't retaliate against you," Tim had explained. *"We can keep Kyle safe at the clinic, but we believe you would be better served by leaving the country."*

She hadn't wanted to leave Juan but she'd been under the impression there was no choice.

"He's on leave."

"I told you," Dan said, opening a second beer, "trust in the process." He nodded toward the Native American. "Sani taught me that."

Kian clicked her wine glass against Dan's beer bottle. "Thank you for helping Tim see the wisdom of Benito's plan."

Juan's feelings for Talia had been obvious to everyone but Tim. Well, maybe that wasn't true. He knew Juan had feelings for her. He just didn't understand the nature of them. He'd worried that Juan wanted some sort of retaliation for being humiliated.

In the end, it was Benito who'd come up with the ideal solution.

"*Juan needs an assignment and Talia needs to be kept safe. It is a perfect solution,*" he'd argued.

"*I –.*"

"*I thought you were concerned for my son's welfare? You wanted him to take time off, to heal.* "

"*Protecting her from Andris' goons may not keep him all that safe, Benito.*"

"*Now that he knows where to look?*"

"*Besides,*" Dan had added. "*He won't be alone. Many eyes in various agencies will be looking out for signs of trouble.*"

"*You just want him away from Kaila,*" Tim groused.

"*I don't need to worry about where Juan's heart is,*" he'd countered.

"*Indeed,*" Benito agreed.

"*I don't think I understand.*"

"*My son is in love with Talia Blackmoor.*"

Tim was silent for many moments as he digested that news. He smiled. "*It explains a hell of a lot. I thought the guy had lost his mind.*"

"*Only a woman can do that to a man,*" Foster said, shaking his head.

Tim had drummed his fingers on his chair, then nodded. "*When you add that detail, it does make it a win-win situation. Will he go for it?*"

"*I've spoken to him already,*" Benito said, "*and he is more than willing to have this assignment.*"

"*I'll have to speak to Talia. I need to see where she's considering for her relocation.*"

"*I've taken the liberty of speaking to Dr. Blackmoor,*" Benito said. "*She has agreed to spend the next several months living on the Navajo Nation.*"

"That will give us time to wind this situation down," Dan explained. *"Sani said he would be more than happy to have them as his guests. Especially, as he is rebuilding. They can help him."*

"I did have to agree to one concession," Benito explained.

"What's that?"

"She wanted to go to Idaho. To see her uncle and the mustang."

He nodded. *"That was inevitable, though I'd rather she waited a few months. We've had people watching her uncle and there's been no sign of trouble but I'm not going to chance it."*

"She will understand. As long as it is in her future, I believe she will be satisfied."

"Talia," Kian started quietly, "I know you've been through a lot. I know you've lost a lot of people over the years, a lot of family."

She nodded, sipped.

"Family is what you make it." She swept a hand around the tub. "If you'll allow it, you can have a family. A close family."

"In the service," Dan said, "if you're lucky, you find a family." He thrust his beer toward Sean. "And if you're especially blessed, it's a family for life."

"People like us," Kaila added, "who do what we do -." She nodded toward Juan. "Too often we have to give up our families. We have to leave them behind because of the life we choose. But, if we're blessed, we can find a new one."

She wondered, briefly, if trust among spies was like honor among thieves. As she could understand it, she could accept it. She looked at Juan. "What do you think, Hernandez? Can you forge a family of your own choosing?"

He tilted his head in Foster's direction. "With him?"

"Would it be incest then?" she asked, pointing at Kaila.

"Oh," Kian replied, "that's sick."

"I had to add some levity," she defended. "All that mushy stuff was giving me a stomach ache. Too sweet."

Talia looked at the man sitting next to her. Her hot blooded Latin lover. She smiled.

Sweet indeed.

ABOUT THE AUTHOR

~~~~~~

Elizabeth spent twenty years working as a consultant in the Information Technology industry. Her customer base included global Fortune 500 companies and she is a repeat speaker at industry conferences.

Elizabeth learned that Mother Nature is the best doctor and laughter the best medicine. She studied alternative medicine with an MD for several years and eventually earned a Doctor of Philosophy in this field. She also holds a bachelor's in holistic childcare. After a successful career at a Fortune 500 IT Company, she returned to her first passion, writing.

Elizabeth Maxim is the author of multiple books, both fiction and nonfiction, and multiple blog sites.

Visit her website at elizabethmaxim.com.